FROM
ROCKET
WITH LOVE
Book Two The Rocket Series

Chris Dyer

This is a work of fiction. Names, characters, businesses, places, events and incidents are either the products of the author's imagination or used in a fictitious manner. Any resemblance to actual persons, living or dead, or actual events is purely coincidental.

ISBN-13: 978-0692927311
ISBN-10: 069292731X

Monday Creek Publishing
Ohio USA

DEDICATION

A thank you to all those people who have been a part of my life in one way or another, in friendship or love even dislike. Each of you gave me something, which helped me in putting the words together for this book.

A special thank you to my old friend Roger who regardless of how many phone calls he receives and how miserable I am, always kicks me in the proverbial and makes me try again. Bloody tiring, though he never lets me give up!

No words to write from empty hearts,
No soul when souls are torn apart,
The millions that mattered not,
Yet no life thrives from empty pot,
To feel the void of pure despair,
To look not touch a fuse so fair,
From fiction life itself be born,
A curse, a talent, what was sworn?
Remember, words, remember me,
In years I may be then set free,
Why this ache so sharp so gay,
And yet alone so cold so grey,
The holding back, to test restraint,
My walls of black so bright you paint,
The lone wolf in his cloak of worldly sneers,
Pacing slowly through the years,
Pray don't look on him with such disdain,
Behind his eyes are tears of pain,
Yet look though through wooded hills he slinks,
Inside his heart like lamb he thinks.

CHAPTER ONE

Mike Willett didn't feel much like a man whose achievements would go down in racing history and he certainly didn't look like one. The sleepless nights and over indulgence in the whisky bottle were taking their toll. Always fairly conscious of his appearance he now had no care at all, his face was unshaven and his clothes dishevelled.

Yet Mike's recent world rolled him along from one success to another. He could literally buy anything he wanted. Yet just a few short months ago he was struggling to support his yard. If it hadn't have been for Ann, he would not have been able to have carried on. She went to work to pay the bills. Now he wouldn't, or rather couldn't, even bring himself to speak to her. Pride comes before a fall, they say, and Mike's pride had brought him crashing down from a great height. He sipped his mug of tea hoping the pounding in his head caused by another night of heavy drinking would relent. But we all know it never does. The inner misery that is numbed by the alcohol comes rushing back with more vengeance. Seeming to have the ability to store itself up, waiting for that moment when reality zooms back into focus before once again releasing its full force.

It's a strange thing self-esteem, when you have it, you

haven't a clue it's there, but when you lose it, boy do you ever know it. And so does everyone else.

John Cullen sat chewing absently on a piece of toast. He was thinking of his friend Mike, and how their friendship had blossomed. Mike had become his closest friend as The Rockets career had taken off. Mike had gone from being broke to having so much money that Lloyds were seriously considering building another branch, so much money was entering Mike and John's racing account. Rocket had not only made history on the racecourse but was also making history as a stallion. The demand for his services were unbelievable, he had become leading sire through earnings in his first month of standing at stud. His services were so sought after, that potential clients were attempting to outbid each other to bring their mares to visit him. Mike however showed no interest, either in the finances that poured in, or the horses themselves. The bottle seems to be a good place to hide, but at some stage you have to realise that glass is clear, and the world can see you anyway. There is never an answer in the bottom of a bottle... no matter how hard you look!

The ringing of the telephone interrupted Mike as he retched in the downstairs loo. Tea and whiskey seldom mix well in the early hours of the morning. He tried to collect himself, and picked up the receiver, looking at the clock as he did so. He didn't even wait to find out who was on the other end of the phone. "Who the fuck is it? Do you know what the time is? Four fucking thirty."

John Cullen's voice drifted down the line. It was friendly, but held a sarcastic edge.

"You've obviously had another successful evening out!" There was no reply, and John's voice took on a tone of annoyance. "If you can shake what little brain you have left into focus, I have some rather important news. Rocket's first foal is a colt!"

Mike spat his reply down the phone. "I hope you'll be very happy together... Personally I don't give a toss if it's a piglet. I'm retired. In fact I think I may well piss off somewhere where I don't get phone calls at all, let alone at four fucking thirty in the morning." And he slammed the phone down.

John Cullen stared in complete disbelief at the buzzing telephone. He couldn't even place the phone back on its cradle for a full minute in the misplaced belief that at any second Mike's voice would come ringing back down the line with an apology, and all would be well.

It didn't and John regretfully put the phone back. The feeling of sadness for the loss of his friend's character and love of horses very nearly overwhelmed him.

Mike stamped his way round the kitchen throwing curses at any inanimate object that would stay in one piece long enough to listen to the curses he issued. He cursed himself for being so stupid, he cursed himself for having such a short fuse, and he cursed himself for not having the self-control to stop it being lit in the first place.

Most of all he cursed himself for having too much pride to pick the phone up and apologise to John. Mike slipped further into despair.

John spent the rest of the day admiring Rocket's son, along with the rest of the staff, who were ragging Seamus wickedly after listening to him explain to the foal just what races he was going to win. But for all the camaraderie there was an air that bordered between expectancy and gloom over the non-arrival of Mike. Every time a car was heard in the distance everyone craned their necks to see if it was Mike's. John tried to re-contact Mike on the telephone but failed to get a reply. It took the edge off what should have been a very special day.

Mike stood with a small holdall in the lounge of Bournemouth airport, his gaze towards the floor. Mike didn't notice the activity that surrounded him, the children laughing and playing excited by the thought of a ride on an aeroplane and a holiday in sunnier climes. He didn't really know what he was doing there other than the ticket he held said *Single to Spain*. All he really could remember was leaving a note on the kitchen table asking Seamus to look after the yard and Jody his dog, he would see them all when he saw them. Other than that, the whiskey had taken over, telling him the best course of action was to make a run for it. There is no logic to whiskey, but when it tells you to do something, nine times out of ten it makes sense regardless of how ludicrous it appears to those with sober minds. The tannoy system made its final mumbled call for the departure of Mike's flight, and he slowly made his way towards the aircraft. Soon he would be settled into what had become his normal routine, in a seat, glass of scotch in hand, and flying, but this time he was flying for real.

Rocket suddenly struck out at thin air, screaming it appeared at some unseen foe. Everybody turned from his foal to see what had upset him so, Rocket whickered, moved to the corner of his box head held low. And was silent.

The plane droned on relentlessly, and Mike matched its relentless progress glass for glass. By the time the plane touched down at Malaga, Mike had lost any semblance of reason that he may have retained before boarding the aircraft. He staggered through the arrivals lounge, unaware of the disgusted stares he received from the other passengers. He was just another drunken British tourist, something popular holiday destinations are well used too. Mike wandered aimlessly around the back streets looking for a hotel, convinced that there would be one just around the corner. There wasn't, just more backstreets, eventually he found refuge in a bar, placed a large amount of money in the barman's safekeeping, took a bottle to a table, and drunk himself into oblivion.

He awoke, sore and dishevelled somewhere on a beach. He still had his bag, and surprisingly some of his money, but no idea of where he was or what he had done. Another goal to whiskey, the score line was looking pretty disastrous for Mike.

CHAPTER TWO

It had been several weeks since Seamus had discovered Mikes note, and though they had tried hard to discover his whereabouts, they could find no trace of him whatsoever. In his normal state Mike would have been so concerned to have given his friends such worry, and that fact just made them worry all the more.

John Cullen had even taken the trouble to employ the services of a private investigator, but he came forward with no more information than they had received from the note. Mike may just as well have gone to Mars so effective was his disappearance.

"What do we do Seamus?" John asked. "Do we put the mare back in foal, do we cover Silver Dollar? Oh shit Mike, I could quite easily shoot you. You're not only self-destructive, but you're also destroying what we've all worked to build. I never thought I'd say this, but you are such an asshole!" John held his head in his hands as he spoke, when he finished there was a silence before Seamus spoke. His Irish accent seemed more pronounced for some unknown reason, as he rose to defend his friend and 'guvnor'. "Too be sure he's a funny bugger is our Mike, and I know what he's done is not the answer, but I've been there. I did two years for it, lost everything I'd worked for, and didn't care. The one thing I did care about was the loss of my self-esteem." John looked up surprised at how profound Seamus sounded. "Now that's a funny old thing to lose, you don't even know you have, and don't really care. Mike's a strong character, it'll take time, but he'll pull through, and when he does he'll come out the other side a far better man. I'd say he'll just appear back one day as though he's never been away, and expect everything to be right." John Cullen was unconvinced, and he had a sneaky suspicion that Seamus was as well. Time would tell.

If they had been standing by Rocket's box at that moment they would not perhaps have been so unsure, Rocket was sure.

Mike's sojourn to Spain became one long blur, every night becoming a heavier drinking session. The headaches he suffered would have downed a Rhino but Mike was stalwart, and stuck to the whiskey bottle like a fly to honey. Some nights he became so drunk he failed to make the trip back to the villa he had rented. The turning point came when he carelessly stumbled in the path of an oncoming Spanish taxi driver. His left leg proved to be much less solid than the bumper of the white Mercedes. Mike woke up with a screaming headache, and a pain in his leg that was almost unbearable. The Spanish doctor was obviously trying to give him a real ear bashing for being such an idiot, but his words were totally wasted on Mike as the only thing in Spanish he knew was to say *no entiendo...* I did not understand. The doctor turned and spoke to the nurse that stood in close attendance, Mike simply held his hands up, and shrugged his shoulders.

"You look as though you're having problems?" The voice came from a stunningly beautiful woman Mike immediately guessed was in her mid to late twenties. The small girl that held the woman's hand broke free, and without any embarrassment whatsoever started to inspect the plaster cast on Mike's leg. "Would you like me to sign it? My friend Millicent had a plaster on her arm, and everybody in the school signed it, even Miss

Cowpole, that's a very funny name isn't it, but actually she's a very nice person, mummy says she's an awfully good teacher. I've not been very well myself, that's why I'm here, but I'm all right now." The little girl had hardly drawn breath, Mike was so amused at her verbal onslaught that he completely forgot the searing pain in his leg. "That's quite enough Becky." The young women interrupted. "Where ever are your manner's? We came over here to try and help, not to tell this poor man our life history." The woman turned to Mike. "I'm so sorry…" Mike stopped laughing and smiled at her, and as he did so felt something he had only once felt before, and that was for Ann, total loss of control of his feelings. Everything else went out of his mind, all he wanted to do was to find out more about this woman. He suddenly felt that all the pain he had endured through the past few months had been for a reason. Mike fell in love. The young woman repeated herself. "I'm so sorry, Becky has a tendency to go on a bit…" She continued. "You seem to be experiencing some difficulty understanding the doctor. I speak a little Spanish. Perhaps I can help?" Mike stared at her and nodded his ascent. He was looking deep into her beautiful blue eyes. *No they're not blue*, thought Mike, *but blue green, well maybe blue grey!* They seemed to change colour the deeper into them he looked. The woman flushed slightly and looked embarrassed. Mike spoke," I'm sorry I'm staring, that's very rude of me. My name is Mike, and yes I am experiencing difficulty, and could definitely do with some help." The only thing that Mike could not decide is what help he needed first.

"Like I say, I speak a little Spanish, perhaps I can find out exactly what the doctors are trying to explain too you? From what I overheard I'm afraid they don't seem to have a very high opinion of you," she smiled and all the worries of the past months flooded down the river and into the sea, Mike felt his heart for the first time since his problems with Ann, "something about you being a typical drunken English holidaymaker, they're also extremely worried about the bill to put your leg right." The knowing smile remained, it was as though she was enjoying some private joke at Mike's expense.

It was all he could do to speak, he found himself totally lost in those unusual blue eyes, after stammering incoherently for several seconds his vocal cords managed to untangle themselves.

"Please tell them not to worry. I can pay the bill. If they would like clarification, ask them to contact their local branch of Lloyds bank. I'm sure they'll confirm what I say." The woman turned and walked over to where the doctor now stood inspecting the chart of another patient, and spoke in Spanish. She returned briefly to establish that Mike was who the ID they had found in his pocket was correct then walked back to the doctor to continue her conversation. Mike's eyes never left her lithe form, his mind worked overtime as he took in her splendid figure. A small voice interrupted. "Mummy's very pretty isn't she?" It enquired then without further ado went off on a complete tangent, "We came on holiday here. We've been here three weeks, and I've already fallen over twice. I didn't cry the first time, and I only cried a little bit the second time, but it was a very bad cut!" She lifted her leg onto the bed, and pointed to a vivid red scar of about half an inch long on her knee. "It bled an awful lot. There was blood everywhere, the swimming pool went completely red, and mummy had to use ten towels to mop up the blood at the pool side." The little girl was in full flow, her face screwed up tight as she relived the momentous battle with the bleeding knee. She was still going her eyes never leaving Mike to ensure he did not miss one second of her tale when her mother returned. "Becky I think that's quite enough of your nonsense, it was just a scratch. If you hadn't have made so much fuss we would have put a plaster on it ourselves instead of wasting the nice doctors time." Once again, she spoke to Mike. "Sorry! She gets a little carried away sometimes." She waited for a reply, but Mike just stared at her. She laughed again. "You're going to make me nervous if you keep staring!" Mike spluttered and she continued. "The doctor says you were very lucky, your leg had a clean break, and you should be up and about in a few days. Look we're here for a couple more weeks if you'd like me to pop in every now and then, I'll try to translate for you. Where are you staying? I'll let them know what's happened so they don't clear your room or something silly." Mike didn't know what to say The Beach Hotel just didn't sound right somehow. Though he had spent most of his time lying on its gritty bed. Although he hadn't seen the inside of his apartment for several days and certainly didn't possess a housekeeper Mike lied.

"It's okay I have a rented villa, the cleaner will look after things until I'm up and about, but I would appreciate you coming in to translate." Then before he realised he had said the words

"Perhaps I could buy you dinner when I'm out of here." She tipped her head to one side in a coy gesture that melted what little self-control Mike had retained, he fell hook line and sinker. "I don't think my husband would be very happy about that!" Mike was lost, there was no way he was backing off, and decided to go for gold. He smiled. "Who said anything about your husband coming?" She laughed at his cheek, and it sounded in Mike's head like the ringing of tiny silver bells as she turned to walk away. "Now you be good, and we'll come and see you tomorrow." The little girl ordered as she turned to run after her mother, Mike called after them.

"What's your name? I forgot to ask." But all he received was a turn of the head, and that stunning smile.

Night crept suddenly up on John Cullen's stud and in the stygian gloom something moved. Rocket moved restlessly in his box, a soft wicker sounding in the still air. Storm, his new foal, lifted his head to listen to his father. Storms mother rose and pawed the box floor in concern as the stable bolt was drawn back.

The Spanish doctor went berserk the following morning when he found Mike wandering around the ward on the pair of crutches he had borrowed from his neighbour. As far as Mike could make out from the broken translation he received from another patient, he was a typically stupid English madman whose parentage was without a doubt in question. It also seemed that the doctor had an urge to repair the other leg, which he hoped would also soon be broken. Mike laughed at the doctor's remonstration. It was not the Mike with a broken leg, not the Mike with his soul in the bottom of a whisky bottle, but the old Mike. Eyes alive with life, his face cheerful, the step of his one good leg had that old vitality to give it spring. Mike was on the mend.

CHAPTER THREE

Rocket screamed a challenge as the strange man pointed what looked like a stick at JC. It was obvious to him that the man intended to hurt his beloved mare and foal. There was a quiet sound, PHUT, and after staggering around the box JC sunk slowly to the ground. Rocket was confused why was she sleeping when these men were approaching their foal? He furiously kicked the stable partition in an attempt to break through and protect his son. His hooves thudded against the wood with deafening effect. "For fuck sake give that bastard one next door, and shut him up, or he'll have every fucker awake and on us!" The shorter of the two men said, passing the long-barrelled pistol to his accomplice. The shorter of the two grinned maliciously as the huge man standing beside him winced and hesitated. His weasley face took on a look of derision. "Get a grip you oversized pratt… knock him down!" then on seeing that his accomplice still hesitated, took the pistol himself and pointed it between the bars on the front of Rockets stable. *PHUT!* Rocket stood silently for several seconds his legs starting to shake, then fell to the ground motionless.

The colt panicked, frantically fighting as the two men tried to pull him from the stable where his mother now lay still. His confusion was exacerbated by the rough handling of the two men, as they unceremoniously dragged him further from his mother, the humans he had known to date had always treated him with great affection. In fact, attention had been lavished on him, and he could not understand why these men were hurting him. A knee crashed into his ribs knocking the wind completely from his body, hands grabbed his tail and mane to assist those already pulling him on his head collar, and he lost the fight to keep any purchase on the concrete floor beneath his feet. The colt gave a pathetic whicker in the direction of his mother's stable as the rough hands half carried him half dragged him up into the dark stale interior of a trailer. The ramp was closed quickly, an engine started, and Storm sped off into the night.

Mike woke with a start in the middle of the night, his body dripping with sweat, his head befuddled with sleep. He rose wearily from the hospital bed, and without even an inkling of why shouted for the nurse to bring his clothes. After an hour of arguing with the nurse, and the doctor she had called, Mike agreed to a compromise. If he signed a disclaimer, should he feel the same in the light of day, then his clothes would be returned and he could discharge himself. At six am when the sun first peaked its warming rays over the horizon, Mike was again shouting for his clothes. By six-thirty he was hobbling down the front steps of the hospital trying to attract the attention of one of the speeding taxis that sped past, oblivious of his frantic waves. By the time he actually made one of the potential formula, one driver realised that he genuinely wanted be delivered to a destination that would not inconvenience them too much, it was going on seven. He arrived at the villa he had rented at around eight, surprised at how little he remembered the outside, but then the little time he had spent there was in a state of complete drunkenness. His distaste on entering the villa would have been evident to the most ignorant. As he wandered round looking at the dirty clothes, empty bottles, and overflowing ashtrays, his distaste turned inwards. As he entered the kitchen to see the mess resembling the aftermath of a world war, his distaste turned to disgust. How he ever allowed himself to become so degenerate he failed to see and in an effort to make amends and regain some of his self-respect started by making a strong cup of tea and after drinking the reviving brew grabbed the nearest cleaning items. He attacked the cleaning with vigour hobbling around like a demented Long John Silver, clearing up the disaster zone as he did. It was around nine thirty when the doorbell rang, and he had virtually completed his task. He hopped to the front door with as much grace as he could muster. He could already see her form through the frosted glass, the small give away figure fidgeting at her side. His heart raced not from his efforts but from the thought of her. Opening the door he was greeted not by the radiant smile he expected, but the voice of the small girl, "Mummy's very cross with you, and she's going to give you a real telling off!" She said with a sense of both impending doom, and satisfaction. "Becky, how many times must I tell you not to be rude. Now apologise to Mike, and behave yourself."

The little girl mumbled an apology, which Mike accepted with a smile. He turned his gaze to the beautiful woman stood before him, and cast a quizzical look towards her followed by a smile and the word, "Well ?" In reply he received a dazzling smile, and a look of concern. "You know you're being stupid by discharging yourself from hospital. Becky's right I really should be cross with you. Especially after we took the trouble to visit you in the hospital, or should I say attempted to visit you! Not so much as a word of where you had gone! It took a great deal of persuading to get the nurse to give me your address!" She tried to sound firm but it was lost on the boyish expression Mike had slapped on his face. Suddenly remembering his manners, he gestured with his hand for the two to enter and was rewarded with that smile, plus a nod from her very beautiful head. He noticed that as her head bobbed forward, her shoulder length dark blond hair partially covered her face in the most enamouring fashion. Mike also noticed that she passed a critical eye over the now, as he thought, clean villa. "I think that

Beck's and I ought to have a bit of a tidy up? It appears you left your villa in somewhat of a state." Before he could stop himself Mike had replied, and was simply rewarded with the raising of an eyebrow. "But I've just finished cleaning up!"

"Honestly mummy. Men, they don't have a clue do they!" Mike suppressed a chuckle.

The mother and daughter went to work with alarming dexterity and efficiency. Mike could not remember when the villa had looked so clean, in truth Mike could hardly remember the villa! It was only when they had finished and Mike had opened a bottle of wine, and poured a glass of lemonade for the younger of the two, that he realised he still had no idea of this beautiful woman's name. "I'm sorry. I feel terrible..... I haven't even found out your name, and here you are cleaning up the place for me!"

Mike would have given his fortune for the smile that came after his statement.

"No. It's my fault. I should never have been so rude as to ignore introductions. My name is Kate, simple I grant you," she said with that most brilliant smile, "but it's quite effective as names go. I answer to it at least!" Mike wouldn't have cared if she had been called Gertrude. "Now perhaps you would like to explain exactly what all this nonsense is regarding you discharging yourself? I think I deserve some explanation after all the effort Becky and I made to come and visit you!" Mike felt foolish at first. Trying to explain to a virtual stranger that you were getting "funny feelings", that you thought were something to do with a horse, which at that precise moment in time was housed safely in a stud, partly owned by him, some thousand miles away. Much to his surprise both Kate and Becky listened avidly, with only an occasional question from Becky. Most of the questions centred around the horse's colour, if she could come and ride him when they returned to England, and one statement which took the wind out of Mike's sails. "Doctor Doolittle can talk to animals you know! I saw him in London, my aunty took me!" She looked amazingly smug, and altogether grown up as she said it, and even when Kate had reprimanded her mildly for interrupting her expression of absolute certainty remained. Mike subconsciously thought, how ironic it was, here he was desperately trying to impress the most stunning woman he had ever set eyes on. And low and behold her daughter, on listening to him spout off about the subliminal messages he believed he was receiving from his horse, pronounced him in the most positive fashion, the millennium's answer to Doctor Bloody Doolittle! *Good start* he thought. Kate however was intrigued, and questioned him in detail of the feelings he had been experiencing. Not once did she appear to be having a laugh at his expense. She was totally interested in what he had to say. When he finished she was quick to offer any help in sorting his travel arrangements back to England. Mike was uncertain as to whether this was to actually help, or to get rid of him from the scene. Paranoia, lack of self-esteem all kicked in at once, and Mike suddenly became quiet. Kate mistook his change for weariness, and immediately sprung into action. "Where did he keep his clean sheets? Where was his bedroom? Could he manage to put himself to bed?" Answering each question in turn he eventually managed to convince her that even with a broken leg he could just about manage to put himself to bed.

After making sure his bed was comfortable, and one or two more assurances that he could just about manage to lay down without help! Kate and the chatterbox departed. The chatterbox with several thousand orders and one or two pieces of advice gained throughout her vast experience of her long six years, Kate with a smile that made Mike wish she was staying just a little longer..... Without the chatterbox!

Mike put himself to bed, Kate had been right he was tired beyond his body's physical tolerance. Even though his leg was troubling him, he fell almost immediately into a deep restful sleep. It lasted fully half an hour and again he awoke with a start. This time he really did feel that he had finally flipped. He could definitely hear voices. To be more specific, one voice repeating the same thing over and over again in his head. "No time to waste, come home now. I need your help." Mike wearily dragged himself from beneath the covers, grabbed the crutches by the side of the bed and dreamlike made his way towards the kitchen. It was difficult to make tea with one hand whilst standing on one leg and one crutch but eventually he managed. Sitting at the table mug of tea cupped between his two hands, he actually found himself crying as the voice continued to sound deep in the recesses of his mind. His whole being felt emotionally torn as the tears rolled down his cheeks, the emptiness he felt inside could only compare to losing a loved one, even worse the feeling was tinged with a fear so real that he could visualise it. Then his eyes became unfocused and within his mind he found himself looking at a screen which played like a video. His fear grew deeper, when suddenly all went black. Mike didn't have a clue why he picked up the telephone and dialled the airport. All that he did know is there was an urgency within him to return to England, he managed to book a flight for the following day, which all things considered was pretty convenient. It would give him time to get his things together and to organise the funds to purchase the villa, which he had agreed several weeks before in an unusual moment of sobriety. Mike hobbled around the rooms restlessly until the hands of the clock turned nine and he could sit himself on the phone again and organise the Spanish side of his life. At ten thirty prompt, there came a knock at the door and when Mike eventually limped his way over to see who was making such a valiant attempt to karate his front door to death. Opening the door he was greeted by the stunning smile that had had such effect on him the previous day and a very indignant little person that complained vigorously that her knuckles were terribly sore from banging his door. Kate interrupted her tirade. "I am sorry! I'm afraid Beck's gets a little impatient and for some unknown reason she has taken you under her minute wing. I'm afraid your fate is sealed!" She said and the devastating smile she finished the comment with nearly made Mike's good leg buckle. Mike remembered his manners.

"Please come in, I'll put the kettle on."

The statement was immediately seized upon by the little person. "You most certainly will not! Mummy and I will do all that, you have to sit down because we have come to cook your breakfast!" Mike made to object even though the words had brought a warm smile to both his and Kate's faces.

"It's much easier to go along with it believe me. She's a very determined young lady and has in our absence decided she is going to be your nurse. As I said I think your fate is sealed, let's get to the kitchen and sort you out some breakfast." Once again Mike tried to object but his words fell on stony ground. That he pointed out the two were on holiday seemed to count for naught as they busied themselves around his kitchen. Comments like "you should be on the beach" and "lying in the sun relaxing" were cast aside with a simple smile. Breakfast made they all sat down together and Mike told them of his imminent departure, both seemed genuinely disappointed, which he had to admit to himself pleased him greatly. Becky made a great attempt at pleading for him to stay another week and failing this she made him promise that they could come and visit him at the yard when they themselves returned to England. She just had to see the horses it was a matter of virtual life and death. Mike readily agreed. The only down side Mike realised was that he had fallen in love with this beautiful woman the first time he set eyes on her and in his experience love was too painful.

CHAPTER FOUR

Seamus and John stood in the middle of the yard looking completely lost as pandemonium rained all around them. Police vehicles, policemen, insurance representatives, insurance investigators all buzzed around the yard busily looking for clues. John would in different circumstances have found their tenacity amusing. The concern came mainly from the insurance personnel not the police. It wasn't the fact that two of his horses had been drugged with a dart gun and were at that moment under the scrutiny of a caring vet, neither was it because a beautiful colt had gone missing. It all came down to money, twenty million pounds was more than a considerable worry to the underwriters. John would willingly give every penny of his considerable fortune if the colt was still safely in his box.

"Where the fuck, is that Mike?" John said pointlessly.

"I only wish I knew. He'll go mental when he hears of this!" Seamus replied.

"If, he ever bothers to contact us and find out. Which I very much doubt!"

"Trust me, I know Mike Willett well, he'll bounce back eventually and there is nothing on this Earth that you could give

18

me to be in the shoes of the people responsible for this when he catches up with them!"

"I'll believe it when I see it! Mike's behaviour in ignoring his responsibilities has not impressed me over the last few months, regardless of how hurt he is!" John was quite vociferous, the strain of losing his beloved Rockets colt was almost too much for him.

Mike stepped, or rather hobbled off of the plane into the cold damp air of Heathrow, his crutches clanging noisily as he made his way down the steps from the airplane. The ensuing clamour that followed did nothing to relieve his depressed state, leaving so shortly after meeting Kate and Becky plus the feeling of concern he felt for his own mental state had made him withdraw into himself again. Cameras flashed, television reporters harried him. The magical, mysteriously missing trainer of the most famous horse in history had returned and everybody wanted a piece of the action. Mike, still unaware of the missing colt, was a little awed by the attention he did manage eventually to make his way to the checkout after a kindly air stewardess called security for help. Even though Mike was feeling so low he found himself smiling at the security guards comment, "Bloody hell I thought someone like the Beatles had re-formed! So why, if you don't mind my asking, are you so famous?" Mike went on to briefly explain his success with horses and the security guard lost interest, an avid football supporter apparently. By the time Mike had made his way to the car he had booked to drive him to the yard his return was being reported on every news channel in the country. John Cullen sat watching the melee as reporters badgered Mike to comment on his return. Seamus smiled " Told you, I knew he'd come back and I'll bet you he already knows about the colt!" Seamus was looking quite smug as he spoke.

"Don't be silly how the hell would he know about the colt?

The only people that know are the insurance and the police."

"Mike seems to know when something's wrong with Rocket. Don't ask me how but mark my words he'll know something's wrong!"

"I wonder what the police and insurance investigators are going to make of Mike's sudden reappearance.....Just after the disappearance of the most expensive foal in history." John retorted with a raised eyebrow and both men fell into a worried silence knowing not only that it would lead to questioning over the coincidence of his return but Mikes hot temper.

Mike sat back in the comfortable seat of the chauffeur driven Rolls he had hired, opened the conveniently situated cocktail cabinet and poured himself a large scotch and dry. It was a three-hour trip to the yard and he had already been travelling for seven hours if one included the trip from his villa. It amazed him how the press managed to find out the whereabouts of people seemingly before they knew themselves. He pondered the problem deciding in the end that someone having access to the booking list for the flights must have sold the information for a few pounds, it almost amused him he would have paid them a great deal more to keep quiet! Mike put down his glass and drifted into that half state between the conscious and the unconscious. Kate's face flashed before him her imaginary smile bringing butterflies to his stomach. Rocket galloped in nuzzling her neck then looking directly at Mike "get here quickly, no time to waste, hurry" he seemed to say, and Mike's dream of the wondrous woman he had just met was broken. He leaned forward and sleepily asked the driver how long it would be before they reached their destination. "About an hour, you said you weren't in a hurry Sir." He said.

"Do it in half and I'll give you a hundred-pound bonus!" Mike was rocked back into the seat as the driver's foot hit the throttle as hard as it could.

By the time the driver earned his bonus, which he did with five minutes to spare, the television crews, journalists, photographers, Uncle Tom Cobbly and all seemed to be camped outside the drive to the stud. Mike's scowl was replaced by an ironic smile when his driver commented that if Jesus had returned it would be to less fuss!

The car was swarmed by the waiting so called news seekers, Mike thought to himself how ridiculous it was that he should be the subject of such importance when all around the world there were people starving, children being abused. So much that deserved attention to bring home to people the realisation of what was going on and here he was an insignificant item receiving top billing. It was all so pointless and stupid! As the large hydraulic wooden gates that shut the outside world from the stud closed behind them Mike breathed in a sigh of relief, only to breathe it out again rather quickly as he saw the melee enacted at the end of the long drive. There were police cars everywhere, people in suits rushing from one spot to another and in the midst of it all stood John Cullen looking completely lost.

John, on seeing Mike, was unsure how to react. He felt like walking up and thumping Mike as hard as he could and hugging him all at the same time. In the end he settled for gripping him warmly by the hand and saying, "You old bastard I wish I could say it's not nice to see you but I can't. I should fucking well shoot you for the worry you've caused. That aside. Welcome home you don't realise how glad we are to have you back!"

Mike smiled rather meekly, he felt a complete cad for running away as he had but now he was back his immediate concern was for Rocket. "It's good to see you again too John but what the hell is going on." Mike didn't give John time to answer. "I really need to see Rocket for some reason I have an urge to be with him. God knows why it's almost as though I've been drawn back here I haven't been able to get him out of my mind for the last few days. I know it sounds stupid but I swear it's almost as though he's telling me something is wrong."

John looked quizzically at Mike, then spoke as they both walked towards the stable block where Rocket was housed. "I hate to be the one to tell you this Mike but I'm afraid that Rockets foal has been stolen!" John could see the tension in Mike's face appear as the words sank in and his thoughts went to Seamus' comment of how he wouldn't wish to be in the shoes of the persons that had committed the theft. The ice he saw in Mike's eyes confirmed the fact and sent a shiver down his spine, he almost felt sorry for them.

As they entered the stable block a policeman grabbed Mike by the shoulder enquiring who he was, his grip was released swiftly when he too saw the look in Mike's eyes. Mike was allowed to see Rocket who went into raptures as he entered the stable whinnying and rushing across to Mike to nuzzle fondly at his neck. Before Mike even considered what he was saying he spoke. "Rocket says there were two of them one tall very muscular guy and one about average height, the shorter one had a snake tattoo on his right wrist!" The escorting policeman snorted and said to his busy colleagues. "That's a great help" looking round to his fellow workers, "We'll have to call in the carpenters, boys.... To build a stand to house our new witness in court. I'm really going to look forward to seeing this one cross examined. Calling Doctor Doolittle and the star witness. A bloody horse!"

"I think that's quite enough constable." John Cullen said quickly as he watched the ice in Mikes eyes grow, he most certainly didn't' need a confrontation between the police and the stables and whatever he felt about Mike's disappearing act his belief in Mike with his horses was undiminished. "You have to understand constable that if Mike says the horse has told him... He has, though you may find it strange you would nonetheless be well advised to listen!" The constable harrumphed and walked off to join the rest of his friends in their search for real clues. John turned to Mike almost in an effort to placate but also because he actually found himself believing what Mike had said. "I'll speak to the superintendent as soon as we return to the house." Mike didn't even seem to register that he had just informed everyone that a horse had given him the description of the perpetrators.

CHAPTER FIVE

Mike had completely forgotten that Alice was pregnant, his self-inflicted alcoholic blur had wiped most of his memory, at least on a temporary basis. His surprise on walking into the kitchen to be confronted by Alice rocking her new born baby in an attempt to alleviate his whimpering was to say the least a revelation. His surprise was compounded when he saw Ann standing at the kitchen sink apparently warming the baby a bottle. Mike didn't know what to say and when Ann turned and spoke to him it was all he could do to nod his head in acknowledgement. The feeling of bitterness, the emptiness, wasn't as profound as it had been Mike found he could look at Ann without feeling as though his insides were being torn from him. In fact, his mind went wandering to the realms of fantasy and the warm soft smell of Kate's perfume, her blue eyes, blonde hair and incredible smile. It actually made him feel guilty, rather a reversal he thought as she was nothing more than a friend he had met during his brief visit to hospital. Nevertheless, his mind's eye gripped tightly to the overwhelming feeling Kate's eyes afforded him, he suddenly realised that the woman he had met in Spain had bewitched him. Ann no longer held his totality, Kate did and she was married and therefore out of reach. Sadness washed over Mike like a tidal wave, only to be mistaken by Ann as remorse for his not attempting to resolve the problem they had between them. She moved towards Mike and placed an arm around his shoulders in an attempt to hug him only to find she was holding a piece of stone, not the warm humorous person she had been with for all those years. Mike made an effort to smile, his anger having dissipated in the Spanish whiskey but all the smile brought was further tension and Ann moved away an involuntary tear running down her cheek. Mike couldn't believe himself as he blurted out the words. "I've met somebody else," and the lone tear became a flood. Alice looked at Mike with such venom, "You bastard," she said, "you piss off not telling anyone where you are come back and within seconds destroy this poor girl with one sentence. I hope you're proud of yourself!"

Mike felt the anger welling up inside him but somehow managed to subdue it. He looked directly at Alice before turning to leave and said simply "Congratulations he's beautiful." Mike left the kitchen walked over to John and asked him if he could borrow a car to go home. Looking at the pain on Mike's face John decided that it would be wise to take him home rather than to allow him to drive, using the excuse of his inability to drive properly with a dodgy leg. When they reached the car and set off towards Mike's old yard, John started to draw Mike into a conversation but on finding his words hitting empty air he tried a more direct approach. "Mike for fuck sakes, have you gone deaf as well as stupid?" Now he had started his anger at Mike's unannounced disappearance and return erupted.

"You fuck off without a word to anyone, return the same way. Walk into my house upset my wife and Ann and you haven't even the courtesy to answer me when I make the effort of conversation with you!" John knew he had said too much the moment he finished his outburst and managed a brief glance at Mike before concentrating again on the road. The look in Mike's eyes nearly made him pull over in fear. He realised that bringing the subject of Ann up was a mistake.

"Don't you ever fucking talk to me about upsetting Ann. You cheeky bastard! I was okay until she decided to drop her fucking knickers to the first asshole that came along. I'm the injured party in this everybody seems to forget that, well fuck you because the moment this colt is found I'm putting everything I've got up for sale and I'm gone." John made to say something but Mike interrupted. "Don't say a fucking word, just stop the fucking car and let me out!" One look at Mike's face was enough and John did exactly as he was told. Before he turned back for home John sat and watched as Mike limped determinedly down the road.

The pall of smoke hung limply in the large but dingy room stopped only from its escape by the now yellowed yet ornate ceiling. At one time the room must have been beautiful, the home of many parties with pretty young girls fluttering their eyelashes at young bucks looking for a potential mate. Now empty beer cans, spirit bottles and half-finished packaging from microwave dinners littered the worn stained carpet that clung tenaciously to the floor, as though it expected a return to the room's former glory. Sitting comfortably in the middle of the discarded rubbish were two men one average and ferrety, one huge with arms that were only just contained by the material of his shirt sleeves. The smaller man held a half empty can of strong lager in one hand the other held a half bottle of whisky. He offered the bottle to his friend a big man who had obviously seen the interior of many bars and with sufficient scars to indicate that he had he fought in most of them. He grinned and took the proffered bottle from the ferrety little fellow that was his compatriot, took a mouthful and passed the bottle back. "'ere, when d'you reckon 'e'll turn up. I'm getting fed up of waitin' around 'ere. My missus won't be very 'appy if I don't get 'ome soon. I told 'er I was going for a job in London 'an I'd only be away a couple of days….. she'll think I've gone on a bender. She'll go bloody mad if I don't get back home soon." The big man's voice reverberated against the walls of the once opulent room.

"Shut up Nick." The ferrety man snapped. "All you do is moan. Fuck what your missus thinks! She'll be all right when you walk in an' put hundred grand on the table. Go an' do somethin' useful an' check that little fucker outside. Malek said to make sure we looks after 'im well so give the little shit some stuff out of the bag Malek brough⁻ an' make sure he's got some water to drink."

"Ohh come on Al I did it last ti⁻ne why's it always me?"

"'cause I'm the brains an you'r⁻ the muscle. Anyway, Malek might turn up, if 'e does I want to make sure 'e brings the right amount of money, now fuck off an' do what I say".

Nick moved ponderously heaving his bulk from the dirty armchair. He was without doubt a formidable looking fellow but his subservience to the smaller man showed that his intellect did not match his stature. Nevertheless, his size was impressive square jawed head with no visible neck on a pair of massive shoulders with arms and chest to match, his legs had obviously though not been a part of whatever workout the rest of him had endured, they looked almost inadequate to carry his bulk around but were still well above average size. He moved across the room pulling a childish face at this companion when at his back and wandered out to the dilapidated stables which rung the courtyard to the rear of the house. He looked over the door of the first stable he came too. Inside a wretched looking foal stood caked in his own excreta. His eyes had been watering and dried making a white crusty stain on the sides of his face. His look of total dejection made the big man reach his hand towards him, he shrunk back from the approach. "Come on little fella I'm only trying to be nice. I feels a bit bad takin' you away from your mum an all that. Trouble is I got meself in a bit of bother like." The big man continued to hold out his hand as he spoke to the foal. "I ain't really a bad person you understan' fact is I lost me job at the docks. Wouldn't 'ave bin too bad if I could've kept fightin' like, but the missus didn't like me doin' it, an' if I'm 'onest neither did I. I gets a bit fed up keep hurtin' folks. See I've always bin a big bugger ever since I was a kid like." The foal cocked a sad looking head to one side as if he appeared to listen intently to the big man's tale. "Funny really you'd think it would put people off bein' big, but it don't, every bugger wants to 'ave a go at you. Think if they can beat a big bugger like me they end up bein' big themselves! Don't work like that of course, jus' means you get more trouble. Mind you can't think of too many that ever did beat me. See I'm strong as well as big, but I ain't the brightest spark in the box, should've got meself a good manager, gone boxin' proper like, not this bare-knuckle stuff I bin doin'. See I was doin' all right when I was at the docks, bloody good money it was, me an' the mssus like was all right, you'd like 'er you would, soft as butter she is, got a sharp tongue mind you, but good as gold, don't like Al at all mind, reckons 'es a weasely little shit, but I've known 'im a long time, must be gettin' on twenty years now. Clever bugger is Al, an' 'es always looked to me when 'e 'as a problem like. I'd sort it out for 'im, 'ad more bloody fights 'elping 'im than I bin paid for! Don't mind so much though when it's your mate do you. Anyway, when I lost me job three years ago Al said 'ed 'elp me out like, said 'e could make me a few quid. Well I was up for that, didn't want the missus worryin' where the next few quid was coming from. That's 'ow I got into bare knuckle fightin', I did all right too." The big man puffed his chest out a little. "Beat the lot of them, made good money too, Al arranged everything 'an all I 'ad to do was beat the buggers. Then Al arranged this fight for me wiv a 'alf Chinese fella. When I saw 'im I felt sorry 'e weren't no bigger than a pea, I didn't want to fight 'im, didn't think it was fair like." His eyes took on a sad off planet expression. "didn't think it was fair! Fuck 'e nearly killed me. I should 'ave stayed down really, the Chinaman told me too, don't get up big fella 'e kept sayin', but I could 'ere Al sayin' get up you big bastard get up an' fucking do 'im, an' I did get up....lots of times." He laughed. "an' every time I got up I'd just end up goin' down again. I couldn't see 'is hands an' feet they was so fast…Then 'e jumped up in the air… jus' like 'e was on springs it was an' 'e sort of spun roun' as 'e did wiv 'is foot in the air, kicked me 'e did right on the side of the 'ead. Well that was me done I can tell you, funny I can remember that but bugger all else. Nex' thing I know I'm in a 'ospital, the missus sat by me bed like lookin' all worried, give me a right good cuddle she did when I opened me eyes." He smiled. "'an a bloody good bollickin' too, I 'ad to promise I wouldn't fight no more. Al wanted me too but I ain't gonna break my promise to my missus, no way. Wouldn't break a promise to my Vi I wouldn't… D'you know that China fella come to see me when I was in the 'ospital, told me I was the toughes' man 'ed ever fought. Didn't feel like I was though. Anyway, I ain't gonna go back in the ring an' I can't get a job. Al 'e meets this fella Malek who reckons this bloke killed 'is ole man an' got away wiv it. Says 'e'll pay us a 'undred grand to nick this foal… Tha's you." He added as an afterthought. "My share being fifty grand, well I could take me time an' find meself another good job an' still keep the missus 'appy. Trouble is I didn't know you was goin' to be such a cute little fucker. Don't know nuffin about 'orses me like, as a bet now an' again but not very often. I ain't gonna 'urt you tha's for sure. Sorry about you're mum an' that other 'orse but they'll be all right it was only some stuff to knock 'em out. Look you an' me jus' so well be friends an' in a couple of days you'll be back wiv your ole mum. So you eat up that food I give you s'morning an' I'll 'ave a word wiv Al an'see if 'e can get 'old of this Malek an' speed fings up a bit." Storm stretched his neck out and touched the big man's hand tentatively with his velvet soft nose, Nick grinned from ear to ear. "caw you got a real soft nose little fella." And he gently moved his hand to stroke the stained neck of the dejected foal.

It took Mike quite a while to realise that his emotional exit from John's car and his continued stubbornness had potentially cost him a long walk home, his yard was still some five miles away. It wasn't until he'd walked or hobbled the first mile that he realised his mobile phone was in his pocket. Even so it was over half an hour before the taxi he had rung managed to find him. At least his temper resided and the dark cloud slowly lifted from his thoughts, he began again to think of Kate. He fell from temper to elation from elation to guilt and as he sat discussing the problem he was enduring his taxi arrived, Mike was so engrossed as he sat talking to himself he didn't even notice its arrival. "Excuse me, did you call for a taxi?

Mike started. "Sorry I was miles away."

"Don't wish to be rude sir but I did notice. Women trouble I suppose?"

"That's very perceptive!"

"Not at all. Simple really, man looks melancholy, troubled or confused, it's a pretty safe bet there's a woman behind it somewhere! We're all at risk and we all love it, can't live with them can't live without them is what they say and their dead right. Just goes to show you though. We think we're the clever ones but woman rule okay if you ask me. My wife is always telling me that when God made man she was only kidding!" The taxi driver said as Mike settled into the back seat. Mike looked into the rear-view mirror and could just see the upper part of the drivers face and a pair of warm brown eyes. We have all found ourselves in position where the need to talk outweighs any other consideration and a strangers un biased ear of great solace. Mike found himself with a sudden urge to tell this complete stranger what bothered him so. He opened his heart and then his mouth when he had finished the tale of how his previous partner had deceived him and his now dilemma over his chance meeting of a married woman and her child he felt better. The driver deliberately cleared his throat before speaking.

"You know," he began "driving a cab is a bit like life. You

have to make choices, sometimes you choose right, sometimes you don't. Whichever way you choose there are consequences. Turn right when you should have turned left and your passenger misses their flight, turn left when you should have and they catch their flight and it crashes! Or maybe they go away and have a really good time. Bit of a drastic hypothesis I'll admit but it does seem to happen that way for some. What you have to decide is if the odds are worth the gamble do you take a chance? Life is a chance, it's the biggest gamble we face. We all have to throw our money on the table and show our hand. All we can do is hope our hand beats the person sitting the other side of the table." Mike looked totally confused. "Look what I'm trying to say is if you don't take a gamble in life how are you ever going to know if you hold a winning hand? Put it this way if the time I take the wrong turn and the passenger misses the flight the chances are someone else will get the seat, so what's to say that the one in my cab doesn't take a bigger risk with their life because of it and succeed where before he would have failed through never having taken the chance!" Mike thought about the words for a minute before framing a response.

"Are you trying to say that if what happened to me hadn't happened then I wouldn't be able to take a gamble somewhere else?" Mike looked even more confused at his own question. He wasn't sure he understood exactly what or where the conversation was.

The driver pulled into the drive of Mike's yard and turned off the engine. "Right! If your new friend was in my taxi she'd be the one that missed the flight, your partner would be the one that got the seat. Consequences. Your flight was missed when the car hit you and broke your leg, again consequences. If you're playing it's getting near the time for you to show your hand or leave the table. One way or another it seems to me that you have some serious decision making to do for everybody's sake. Most of all your own. That's five pounds twenty for the ride, the advice is free." The taxi driver grinned. Mike gave him a twenty and told him to keep the change.

Entering the house after such a long time away was a strange experience for Mike. Ann's things were still around though most of it had been moved during his absence. The house still smelled of her perfume, there were still photographs, an earring on the dresser. Mike wondered how and what he was to do. Slumping in his favourite chair with a glass of scotch he felt exhausted. So much had happened in the last twenty-four hours, much of which he did not understand, some of which like his meeting with Ann he did but was too tired to deal with. The voice in his head returned. "Stop feeling so bloody sorry for yourself you've a lot to do. Tomorrow you have to find my boy!" Mike went ashen, he had to be going completely insane. He thought Rocket was talking to him telepathically, he had already made himself look ridiculous at the stud by announcing the horse had just spoken to him. "Christ!" He said to himself. "I really do need to sleep."

"Couldn't agree more," the voice said. "You're going to be busy."

Mike rose at 7 a.m. feeling refreshed and after a shower decided to have breakfast at a local café. He made his way to the garage, ironic he thought, he had after winning the Derby with Rocket run off to Spain, yet had ordered the car of his dreams. A Noble M15, British and beautiful. Here he was opening the garage door and he didn't even know if it had been delivered. The hydraulically operated garage door smoothly rose to reveal its contents. There stood Mikes Land Rover and next to it a glorious metallic purple M15. Mike ran his hand over the stunning bodywork noticing as he did the empty space beside it that had once housed Ann's own Noble.

"What the hell!" he said, opened the door of the M15 and turned her over. The 400bhp 3-litre twin turbo burst into immediate life. Mike engaged first gear pumped the throttle and eased the clutch out, the car shot down the drive at an incredible rate of knots taking Mike completely by surprise. He only just managed to stop as the red Mercedes convertible turned into his drive. "Shit!" He breathed more in relief the anything else, "I'll have to watch you girl you're a bit quicker than the old Land Rover!"

"You really shouldn't drive so fast you know, it's very dangerous!" The indignant tone and face of the young lady that looked at him through the open passenger window of the Mercedes made Mike burst into laughter "It's not funny!" she said with great seriousness "Mummy said she very nearly had kittens... and what would we have done with them. My dog wouldn't like kittens running all over the house.!" Mike laughed even louder.

"Becky! I've told you before not to be so rude. You have to learn you cannot speak to adults in that manner. You are only a child!" Kate's voice was firm but not harsh.

"I'm very nearly seven mummy." The short person replied with the indignation back in her voice.

"That really is enough Becky." Kate said with some force and it subdued the little one into wandering around kicking at the gravel drive aimlessly whilst the two adults spoke.

Mike thought he must be imagining things when he saw the diminutive child appear at the cars window and the joy he felt attributed to his laughter but when Kate stood before him and he looked into those deep blue eyes his legs went weak and his very heart sang with joy.

"Are you just going to stare at me all day or are you at least going to say hello." She said raising one eyebrow as she spoke.

Mike stuttered a reply. "S…sorry I'm just a little surprised to see you…When did you get back?"

"Yesterday morning. Becky has driven me insane! After twenty-four hours of a determined Beck's it was easier and a lot quieter to bring her over to see you. I think the horses may have a lot to do with it as well!" She added defensively.

Mike smiled. "Then we had better take her to see some! I expect everyone will be in the yard by now." He looked at his watch, 8.30. "They'll be coming in for breakfast in a minute. If we hang on I'm sure I can persuade one of the girls to show Becky round, maybe we can lead her round the yard on a quiet one. That's if she wants. I couldn't be bothered to cook this morning so I was going to the local café, it's not the Ritz but they do fantastic breakfasts. Would you care to join me?"

Kate melted him with one of her smiles. "Not unless I can drive. That!" she pointed at the Noble "Looks a little fast for my tastes! Anyway, if I am going to buy Becky a horse I ought to have a talk with both its possible trainer and meet the staff. I'd also feel a little safer with someone that has two good legs with which to drive!" Kate gave Mike a critical look as she eyed him attempting to stand without bearing too much weight on his repairing leg.

Mike smiled and limped without comment to the passenger side of Kate's Mercedes. It wasn't far to the café and there was no opportunity for Mike to discuss with Kate her statement about the purchase of a horse and its training, Becky kept up a constant chatter throughout the short journey. It was then time to tuck into the impressive breakfast that was put before them, which both Kate and Becky ate with such relish it brought a smile to the faces of the other customers as they watched them demolish the huge plate of food.

"Hungry?" Mike asked barely concealing his grin.

"Mmm, after the flight yesterday we were too tired to eat! We went straight to bed, twenty-four hours is a long time for me let alone Beck's to go without sustenance!" Becky gave a smile containing the remnants of her last sausage that said all.

"Now let's talk some business, shall we?" Kate said.

Mike looked subdued, pausing before he chose to speak. "Look Kate." He heard the voice in his head telling him to think before he said anymore but Mike ignored it. "I'm quite happy to help you find a horse but as for training …I'm afraid I've given up." Kate made to interrupt but Mike raised his hand a resigned look on his face. "I met you…and I know I shouldn't be talking like this," Becky was looking on intently and Kate told her to go and wash her hands and face holding Mikes gaze until she had made her way to the bathroom so he did not speak. When she was out of earshot Mike continued. "I met you and all the hurt I was feeling inside seemed to disappear, I was at such a low ebb and one look at you seemed to make the world right. I know I'm wrong in saying this, you're married and have an incredible daughter so I can't get involved but you see I am and though I want to take our relationship further I know I'm only ever going to be your friend because you wouldn't have it any other way." Mike did not pause for breath. "That's really got nothing to do with me training horses but I'm alone and sad and have no enthusiasm left for myself let alone training horses."

"Is Mike going to train our horse mummy?" Becky's little voice interjected. Mike looked up at the small face full of excitement and hope.

"Don't be a pratt, it's what you do best," the voice said, "and don't keep jumping in so quick you never know if you're patient you could get a surprise!"

Mike answered Becky. "No, I'm sorry sweetheart but I'm not. I'll help you find a horse and put you in touch with a good trainer but I don't train anymore."

"Then I don't want a horse!" was all Becky would say her bottom lip quivering and no cajoling from Mike or her mother would bring her to speak.

"Sorry Mike but I think I had better go. I'll let you know if Becky changes her mind and we decide to buy a horse regardless." Mike nodded glumly indicating that he would make his own way back to the yard which was only a half mile away. "Idiot!" the voice in his head said and Mike wearily rose from his chair feeling that every eye in the café was on him, which of course they were not, he was just another customer leaving. Under normal circumstances it would have taken Mike ten minutes to have walked back but with the limp it made the effort of walking much harder and it was over half an hour before he ambled back to where he had left the Noble. The roar of the exhaust and squeal of tyres left no doubt in the mind of the stable staff of the mood Mike was in and they hurried to complete their work so they could be out of the yard before his return.

"Go on then nutter, kill yourself by driving like a loon," the voice said "a lot of good you'll be to us then! Get your ass here and find my boy!"

"Oh God!" Mike said "I think Rockets fucking talking to me again. I'm going 'round the fucking bend!"

CHAPTER SIX

Seamus was surprised to see Mike stride purposefully across the yard of the stud. Since his disappearance after Rockets Derby win Seamus had taken control of the day to day running of both the stud and the training yard. The training side had been kept small, training only those horses that Mike or John owned. There were plenty of enquiries from outside owners wanting to have a horse in a Derby winning yard but they had been given excuses why their horses could not be accommodated at the time. Seamus was no fool and in the hope that Mike's unknown sabbatical was to be short lived he had taken everyone's name and number passing them on to John. His surprise was to actually see Mike in the yard as apart from his first visit he had not been near the place.

"Morning Guv." Seamus greeted Mike smiling broadly. "Knew you'd be back. Everyone's missed you!"

"Thanks Seamus but I'm not here to run the yard…. that's your job now." Without hesitation, though he did not have a clue why, Mike added. "I'm taking Rocket for a ride, tell John I'll be back." Mike was wondering to himself what the hell he was doing but he had this uncontrollable urge to ride Rocket, his leg was feeling much better but it wasn't exactly the most sensible course of action to take.

Rocket whickered loudly as Mike entered the stables banging impatiently with his front leg on his stable door.

"Fuck knows what I'm doing here you old bastard!" Mike said. "Let's go for a ride and see if I can't shake off this insanity and please remember I've got a dodgy leg." He added.

"Insanity my ass, get the saddle and let's get going, we've no time to waste!"

"Oh fuck!" was all Mike could say.

"Are you all right Guv?" Seamus had followed Mike quietly into the stables.

"Uhh! Yeh just forgot something." And with that Mike quickly saddled a restless Rocket and led him jig jogging from the stable.

"Careful Mike he looks as fresh as he could be and he hasn't been ridden since the Derby!" Seamus voice was full of concern. Mike smiled as a reply jumped onto Rockets back. Rocket reared, struck the air with his forelegs whickered and took of down the drive as though his tail was on fire.

"Holy Mother Mary!" Seamus said under his breath and ran quickly to the house to tell John what had just transpired.

By the time Mike and Rocket had reached the entrance to the drive Rocket was flat out and Mike for the first time in his life was afraid. He tried desperately to control Rocket but it was useless, Rocket had no intention of stopping. "You stupid bastard Rocket you'll get us killed. Slow down you miserable fucker. Just once can't you behave like a normal horse."

"I've never been normal you idiot, that's why I won the Derby for you. Well when you started to listen to me that is!" the voice was back in Mikes head.

"Oh shit! It is you talking in my head, isn't it?" Mike spoke out loud.

Rocket slowed to a walk immediately he spoke turning his head he nuzzled Mikes leg.

"Takes a long time to sink in with you, doesn't it?"

Mikes hand reached forward to gently touch Rocket on the

nose. "Been a long hard road Mike, hasn't it?" and this time Mike knew he wasn't insane this time he knew it was Rocket!

Seamus banged frantically on the door of Johns house until John appeared in his dressing gown. "What the hell is going on Seamus you'll wake the dead let alone the baby."

"Sorry John, but Mike's just taken Rocket and they've took off down the drive like all the hounds of hell are after them." Although Seamus had taken the initial news that Mike was taking Rocket out when he saw the speed at which they took off mild panic began to set in.

John Cullen stood in shock he found it hard to collate the information he had just been given. Without speaking he offered Seamus into the kitchen indicating that he should sit. John walked over to the worktop, put the kettle on methodically and slowly he made two mugs of tea placed one in front of Seamus and sat himself opposite. The whole process took around five minutes and not a word was spoken by either man during this time.

"Seamus what the hell do you mean, Mike doesn't even ride any more he wouldn't take Rocket " John appeared as though in shock.

"I've just watched him tear off down the drive like a lunatic. No explanation, just tell John I've taken Rocket and I'll see him later."

"What the hell is he playing at." John said as much to himself as to Seamus lifting the phone from its cradle on the table and dialling Mikes mobile number. It rang and John waited.

"I 'fink you and me could be friends little 'un." Nick said as he slowly knelt on one knee to get down level with Storm. Storm nestled his head in the side of the big man's face and blew softly, it was the first sign of kindness he had been shown since he was snatched from his mother and he was grateful, his fear lessening slightly. Nick chuckled. "Caw ain't you a friendly fella now we've introduced ourselves proper like!"

"You're not here as a nanny for that scrawny little shit, just feed him and do as you're fucking told." Nick looked up still holding the little foals neck in a gentle embrace. Malek stood looking over the door of the dank dark stable. He was the spitting image of his late father, he had the same cruel twist in his lips, the same dark shifty eyes. Anyone who had known his father could have no doubt of his parentage.

" 'e's all right boss I'm only making a fuss of him 'e's a bit afraid poor little bugger…. spec' 'e's missin' 'is mum."

Malek opened the stable door and aimed a vicious kick at the foal. Nick showed speed that was amazing for such a big man spinning round to take the blow himself. Malek's boot connected with a sickening thud against Nicks broad back. There was sufficient force to have winded a lesser man but Nick did not even flinch, he rose slowly to his feet anger welling in his eyes. He grabbed Malek's coat at the neck lifting the man clean off his feet at arm's length. "You got that one for free boss but if you ever 'urt that little chap." He pointed towards Storm with his free hand then clenched his massive fist bringing it round until it was inches below Malek's nose. "I swears it on me life I'll kill yuh!" he let go of Malek who staggered both to keep his feet and through shock. Nick went straight back to cuddling and reassuring the little foal who had cowered in the corner. "Don't you worry little un no one's gonna 'urt you whilst I'm 'ere." He stated forcefully.

Al had stood quietly behind Malek throughout nervous to speak in case Nick's anger had been re-directed towards him. He had seen the devastating force of the man when consumed with anger. Now that Nicks anger had subsided slightly Al's confidence returned. "Oi! You watch your mouth and that temper of yours round the boss. Sorry about that boss." His voice became obsequious " 'e ain't to clever boss don't know what 'e's doin' 'alf the time."

Malek showed the same arrogance as had his father before him slyly though it was his words were directed towards Al rather than Nick and in a quiet voice so the big man did not hear. "If that moron ever touches me again he will wish he had never been born!" he placed a hand on Al's shoulder leading him back to the entrance of the stables, when they walked into the neglected ivy-covered courtyard outside and he was certain he was out of earshot he spoke again." When the ransom has been collected how would you like to collect another twenty-five grand?" he paused momentarily and watched the greed pass over Al's face. "And collect the hundred grand without having to share!" Al's face lit up in interest and a broad grin spread across his thin lips showing stained half rotten teeth.

"Sounds good to me boss!"

"Then before you shoot the foal shoot that oversized fuck."

Al's grin became wider, friendship didn't mean that much to him in comparison to money. "Job done!" he replied and they walked back to the house leaving Nick comforting the petrified little foal in the stable.

Mike pulled Rocket to a halt reaching in his pocket at the same time and extracting his mobile. He looked at the screen for several seconds before deciding he would answer. "Yes!"

John voice sounded furious at the other end of the phone. "What the fuck are you playing at Mike? Get that horse back here now!"

"Sorry John can't do. I'll bring him back when I've finished, I need him at the moment."

John had not calmed down at all and Mike held the phone well away from his ear. "If that horse isn't back in this yard by lunchtime I'm calling the police and reporting him stolen. Don't make me do it Mike!"

"Just remember I own 10% of Rocket still so I've got some rights left."

John screamed down the phone. "And I own 90% so as the majority shareholder I'm telling you get the fucking horse back here like I said or there will be trouble!!"

"I'm no stranger to trouble John, the fact that we've become good friends has just saved your ass!" Mikes voice rose to a scream as his anger boiled over, it became almost manic, "don't fuck with me John or I'll show you trouble like you've never even fucking dreamed of!!!" He switched the phone off and put it back in his pocket, feeling sheepish and guilty at his sudden outburst.

"He didn't sound very happy, did he? But then neither did you in the end…you should really learn to control that temper of yours you know, it can be quite intimidating if you're on the receiving end as I can testify myself." The voice in his head said rather smugly as Rocket stared him straight in the eye. "Come on let's go we've no time to waste." Rocket leapt forward, tore across the field they were in, jumped the hedge and galloped on.

"Bastard, how can he do this, I swear he's so fucking stupid at times." John said across the kitchen to Seamus. "What a mess!"

Rocket reached the end of the field they had been galloping in, trotted along the hedge to the gate and walked out onto the road. "Well, where do we go from here?" Mike said looking at Rocket.

"I really don't know," the voice replied, "but I've a feeling we should head this way." Rocket turned and walked uncertainly towards Batcombe Downs.

Mike thought for a moment. "We'd better get off the roads as quickly as we can. I think John is angry enough to carry out his threat and the last thing we need is the police chasing us all over the countryside."

"You're right." The voice said. "We'll need to find somewhere quiet to hold up for the night. I think we should consider some food as well, if we find a quiet village somewhere you can buy something. I presume you had the sense to bring money?" The voice finished off pompously.

Mike winced at this checking his jacket pocket finding his wallet with relief. "Okay let's go." And they trotted back to the road cantering towards the nearest village.

John sat with his head in his hands elbows on the table. Seamus sat opposite looking worried.

"John." Seamus broke the silence. "You've known Mike a while now and you two have become good friends. You know he wouldn't do anything to hurt Rocket, shit he'd rather hurt himself than hurt one of his horses. Look I know his behaviour is a bit erratic but…"

John interrupted. "Erratic I'd say it's fucking erratic, fucking mental more like. He's lost the plot Seamus, you know it and so do I." John had looked up but now worriedly placed his head back in his hands before running his hands through his hair. "No…. he's left me no choice I have to tell the police if there was an accident there would be hell to pay with the insurers. Though I don't know what the hell the police will make of it… they have their suspicions about Mikes arrival anyway…" Seamus went to speak but John held his hand up to stop him. Moving to the telephone he looked once more with resignation at Seamus before picking up the phone and dialling the police.

Kate sat in her lounge in a pensive mood watching her daughter tease the little black and white cat she had bought her in an effort to appease her after the disappointment of their earlier meeting with Mike. Her little dog had surprised them all by taking to the little ball of fluff immediately even allowing it to help itself to his feed bowl. Becky suddenly looked up from her game leaving the kitten looking unsure at the fascinating piece of string that only a few seconds ago had been writhing irresistibly in circles around the carpet and now all of its own volition appeared to be completely dead without any help at all from its sharp little claws, it decided that until it found another live one it would irritate the dog. Which, I might add, it did very effectively by jumping on his back as he was in mid snore. "Mummy when's Daddy coming back?"

"Probably next week sometime darling. He's still sorting out some business in France why?

"I just wondered if he could talk Mike into training a horse for us. He's very good at that sort of thing you know!"

Kate found herself blushing for some unknown reason at the mention of Mike and her husband in the same sentence. "I really don't think that would be a good idea sweetheart Daddy doesn't have much time for horses and if Mike doesn't want to do it there really isn't a lot we can do about it. I'm sure daddy would be happy to try for you but I really don't think there's much point."

"Then why don't you try again. He really likes you, you know! I can tell!" Kate was stunned momentarily by her daughter's perceptiveness. "Please mummy I know you can do it. Just give him one of your smiles that will work he always goes silly when you smile at him!"

"Becky!" Kate's voice was a mixture of shock, amusement and perplexity, "Where ever did you get such an idea?"

Becky's face took on a look of such seriousness it made Kate smile. "Mummy!" she said with great importance and indignity, "I am very nearly seven you know and I do know about these things. Why I'm practically an adult. Please ring him mummy I know you can get him to do it and you know I've always wanted to have a horse... and a racehorse," she added as an afterthought, "would be the bestest thing in the whole world." The tiny adult had changed back half way through her sentence to a little girl again.

Kate looked at her tiny daughters face and it brought such a feeling of euphoria that she caved in. "Okay but if he says no this time I'm not going to ask again, is that clear."

"Yes mummy but I just know he will and I really don't want anyone else to train my horse."

"Okay if that's clear I'll ring him and just remember you haven't got a horse yet and I think young lady you will have to be on your best behaviour for the next fifty years if Mike says yes and you get one!"

"Yes mummy." And on hearing Becky's reply Kate picked up the phone.

Mike was in a small Aladdin's cave of a village shop piling packets of just about everything onto the small counter. He had just realised that he had no utensils with which to eat or drink and having bought a dusty rucksack that had obviously been held in the shops stock for some time to carry all his purchases was in the process of picking up a decorative mug showing a picture of the shop proudly bearing the name of the village from the shelf when his phone rang. Why this made him jump he had no idea but it did and much to his embarrassment he dropped the mug which shattered on the stone floor. "Sorry I'll pay for that." He said immediately and the shop keeper smiled reassuringly. Mike reached into his pocket and looked at the phone not recognising the number. At first he thought not to answer it but somewhere in the dark recesses of his mind the code looked familiar so he pressed the green button and held the phone to his ear, apologising to the shop keeper at the same time.

"Hello." Mikes stomach did somersaults as Kate's voice came down the phone.

"Could I call you back in two minutes?" ... "It's okay I have your number in my phone now... Okay give me a minute and I'll ring you."

Mike turned to the shop keeper who stood with a broad smile on her face.

"Girlfriend?" she enquired.

"Oh no; not at all... just a friend." Mike found himself saying for some unknown reason.

"Mmmm." Was all the grey-haired lady behind the counter said and her smile grew broader.

Mike loaded his purchases into the rucksack and hurried back to Rocket who stood patiently on the grass outside the shop being frantically patted by several small children. The voice in Mikes head piped up. "Nice little things aren't they. That little one even knows me. I didn't realise I was quite that famous!" The voice was rather smug and Rocket nuzzled one of the children bringing delighted laughter from them all.

Mike jumped up onto Rockets back, said goodbye to the kids and they moved off down the road before finding a track that Mike knew ran across the downs. He was sure there was an old barn about two miles up the track, they could hold up there for the night. As they rode along Mike pressed redial on received calls. The phone at the other end hardly rang at all before Kate's voice came over the line.

"Mike what the hell is going on... I've just been to your house in an effort to talk you in to training a horse for Beck's, she's totally distraught you realise!" Kate didn't pause to await an answer to either of her comments. "There are police everywhere, I actually thought they were going to arrest me because I know you! What the hell have you done...?"

Mike took a few seconds before answering. "I can't really explain it on the phone.... Look I'll phone you tomorrow and we'll meet up somewhere quiet and I'll explain." The signal on the phone was lost and Mike cursed as Rocket moved quietly down the track they were following.

After a five-minute silence, the voice in Mikes head came back.

"That young filly has a soft spot for you! You'll bugger it up through your own stupidity and pride though... Just like you always do! You really should learn to listen you know. You're good at giving orders but not so good at taking them."

"Shut up Rocket." was the only reply given. Rocket however was determined to have the last word.

"My very point!" The voice rang rather smugly in Mike's head. "Anyway, who will train Storm. You really didn't think that I would allow anyone else to do it, did you? You see my friend you don't really have a choice!"

CHAPTER SEVEN

Kate sat in her lounge with two blue eyes staring intently at her. The little face they belonged to was screwed up tight in a look of absolute concentration as she trailed the piece of string in front of the frantic kitten. Kate couldn't understand why she felt so frustrated and cross towards someone in truth she hardly knew. "God that man is so exasperating!" she said to no one in particular.

The voice made both her and Becky jump. "Who is?"

"Daddy!" Becky screamed with delight and ran towards the man standing in the doorway embracing him with all her might. "You made me jump!"

"Steady!" he laughed. "I'd like some ribs left!" Becky clung to her dad as he walked over to where Kate was now standing. Kate's face had lit up on seeing her husband and she walked over and gave him a long lingering kiss. "I missed you." She said and he simply smiled at her. "Why didn't you tell me you were coming back I'd have cooked you something, are you hungry? I'll go and do you a snack!"

"Don't worry I had a meal on the way back... so, who's exasperating or am I to be kept in the dark." Kate didn't know why but she blushed and although her husband did not appear to notice, her daughter did. Geoff stood looking at Kate with an expectant look upon his designer stubbled face. Dark haired with greying sides he was not a handsome man but then neither was he unattractive. His eyes were grey and piercing and it was this that would appear to make him attractive to the opposite sex. Geoff was from a very wealthy family though this was something he never showed or bragged of. In fact, most people on meeting him would take little notice of him a fact that normally haunted them when they let their guard down on a business transaction. To say that Geoff was a clever man with money would be an understatement. A pleasant man with a strong personality, Geoff, regardless of his money, was not pretentious but then neither was he frivolous with his fortune. For all of this he still had an air of authority, especially where Kate was concerned, and one could see it now as he looked expectantly towards Kate for an answer. His gaze drew from her face a look of such love and devotion it was impossible to measure but behind it there seemed to be a look of fear. It was a fear of loss, loss of the person that stood before her. Geoff was a nice guy but could be acid tongued when things weren't quite as he wanted and with Kate determined to be herself the relationship was often stormy even bizarre. Nonetheless that Kate loved Geoff was beyond doubt, that he made their relationship harder by never saying where he was going or doing and disappearing for sometimes weeks on end cast a shadow over what should have been a match made in heaven. Kate for her part was no different and although she always said where she was going she expected never to be questioned why and yet seethed when the boot was on the other foot. All this aside there was a subtle yet tangible strain in the hug they gave each other even if the devotion was apparent from Kate.

Becky was dancing for joy literally at her dad's unexpected arrival jumping excitedly from one foot to the other. "You're not going off somewhere again daddy, are you?" She asked her dad in her most pleading voice then without waiting for a reply continued in a most business like and proper manner. "I need you to have a word with someone for me. I'm very cross you know! Why I became very excited at the prospect of owning a racehorse, and of course in going to see it work. I know all the correct things to say you know. I spent hours learning them so everyone would be impressed!"

"I'm already impressed Beck's."

"Please don't interrupt daddy this is very important… well I met this man in Spain… he had a broken leg you know and I signed his cast." Becky's dad raised an eyebrow and smiled towards Kate who returned him a look of resignation and a shrug of her shoulders. "Well would you believe it," Becky continued, "he is a very famous in fact the most famous racehorse trainer in the whole world! He was just what I was looking for so that I could have a horse and we could go racing, it's a very exciting thing to do you know, I've been watching it on the telly. I'll have to borrow some money from you of course daddy but I'm sure you won't mind." At this both Geoff and Kate burst out laughing much to Becky's annoyance. "I do wish you would try to listen and to take me seriously! You don't seem to understand that when I get my horse….and I shall… I only want the best for it, oh and I'm going to call it Sunrise! Well when I asked Mike he's the racehorse trainer you know, can you believe he said he wasn't going to train horses anymore, well it just not good enough and I need you to speak to him for me daddy. Mummy tried but he wouldn't listen but I'm sure he will listen to you! Anyway, we can do that tomorrow if you like but now you can tell me all about where you've been. I bet you've done loads of exciting things!"

Mike spotted a barn set into the side of the hill on the right of the track they were following. It seemed rather a strange place to build any building as there was nothing in view for miles and for the farmer who owned it, it must have been a logistical nightmare using it but for whatever reason the farmer had put it there, Mike was grateful. He pointed Rocket towards the building and they both made their way wearily up the hill. The light was just starting to fade and there was a chill in the air made worse by the breeze that blew across the down. Mike slid from Rockets back with the voice in his head making comment of relief from the burden of the extra weight Mike had managed to acquire during his sabbatical from racing. He checked his phone considering whether or not he should phone Kate now or leave it to the morning as he had said he would. He looked at the missed calls that had stacked up on the screen scrolling through them quickly. Thirteen attempts from John seven from Seamus two from Alice and one from Ann. His heart sank a little as he scrolled down the list again hoping to find Kate's number and realising it was not there. He decided to ring Seamus first but was interrupted by Rockets voice. "Do you think you could take this saddle and bridle off of me before you become involved in anything else? I would like to eat some of that hay over there and perhaps I could then have a lie down! Oh it would be nice if you could find me some water, I'm rather thirsty!"

Mike did as he was bid before he settled down to make his call to Seamus. Seamus answered, obviously recognising Mike's number. "For fuck sakes Mike, why don't you ring John, if you speak to him he might listen and stop all this nonsense with the police! He's worried sick for both of you, not just Rocket! You're not helping the situation by ignoring everyone..." Mike tried to interrupt but Seamus continued unabated. "I know the horse is safe with you and I believe you must have a bloody good reason to have gone off but John doesn't understand horses like us so ring him and explain I'm sure he'll listen."

"You know Seamus as usual you're right, I will phone him but you know me as well as anybody and I can't really explain what's happening to me. I'm hearing voices that I believe is Rocket talking to me, I'm frightened, I'm lonely and I'm so angry inside I think I might explode, and I really thought all the anger in me had been washed away!" Mike sounded exhausted and scared his voice drifting sadly down the line.

"Now you listen to me Michael Willett you phone John then you phone me back, tell me exactly where you are I'm coming to bring you some food I'll bring some for Rocket too then I'm going to listen to what you have to say and if I think you are making any sense I'll come with you and help in whatever it is you're trying to achieve and you have my word I'll not tell a soul!"

Mike paused before replying. "Okay Seamus you've been a loyal friend to me over the years so I give you my word that I will, give me an hour and I'll ring you back." Mike pressed the red button on his phone to end the call. Mike looked at the phone for a minute hoping that Kate's number would flash across the screen but his reverie was broken by the voice in his head. "It's no good looking at the thing it won't make anything happen! You'd be better off ringing Seamus back and getting me some food… I'm starving, it's not easy carrying you around all day…especially as you seem to have put a lot of weight o since you last rode me." Mike was sure that the voice not only held sarcasm but amusement at its last comment. He was stunned when the voice came back

"And you can stop referring to me as it! My name as you well know is Rocket!"

The call was made and they sat and waited.

Mikes attention was drawn to the sound of a vehicle and his frame tensed automatically, relaxing as he recognised the diminutive Seamus behind the wheel of the yard's Nissan Navara effortlessly negotiating the last few hundred yards of the rutted track that led to their barn hideaway. It appeared that Seamus had come prepared looking at the amount of feedbags and hay loaded in the back of the Navara. Seamus pulled the truck into the barn and jumped out walking over to Mike and shook his hand warmly. "Bloody hell Mike you've got everybody worried sick and half the police in the South of England looking for you!"

Mike placed a hand gently on Seamus shoulder but his voice

was curt. "Then they should be looking for Storm, not me!" his voice became softer, "It's good to see you Seamus, thanks for the supplies." He pointed towards the back of the loaded Navara. "We'd best unload and get you on your way."

Seamus pulled himself up to his full five feet and a bit. "Now don't you go thinking that I'm here for the short haul Michael Willett. I'm not, I've spoken to Mary and she agrees with me, so I'm not going anywhere other than with you two until we've got the little fella back! Now I suggest you get me up to date with what's going on, then I think you should ring John and try to get some of the pressure off the situation!"

Mike didn't know whether to feel elated or deflated but seeing the look on Seamus face, resigned himself to the fact that they were now three. They unloaded enough of the Navaras contents to make Rocket and themselves comfortable and with a cup of tea and plate of baked beans made on the camp stove Seamus had brought and settled on some hay bales looking like something out of a western movie. Mike began an attempt to explain all that had happened since his return from Spain.

Kate and Becky watched as Geoff walked across the lawn to where his helicopter stood waiting the pilot already in situ behind the controls. Geoff would normally fly himself but the helicopter he had just replaced for the old one was far larger and required a commercial pilots license to fly. Ernie was usually available when needed and so Geoff had decided he could relax more and be flown, if he ever felt the need to have a go Ernie was there to supervise him as he took control of the Augusta. He turned and waved as he reached the door of the helicopter and Becky frantically waved back, Kate waved but it wasn't with the gusto of her daughter. The Augusta lifted from the ground creating eddies of swirling leaves beneath it, its nose dipped towards the ground as though in salute and it whirled away over the trees and out of sight.

"Mummy?" Becky's voice sounded sad. "Why doesn't Daddy spend much time at home? He's always dashing around everywhere and he doesn't really do a job does he?"

Kate looked down on Becky, there was a look of sorrow on her face as she smiled at the small child gripping her hand she looked tiny and not her normal confident self as she strained to see if the helicopter was still in view.

Kate bent down on one knee levelling herself with Becky's face. "No sweetheart." She said gently "Daddy doesn't really work. He does have to do a lot of travelling though…. You see when you have as much money as Daddy does you have to look after it and Daddy likes to do something he calls deals." Becky looked puzzled, "That is he buys things, anything really and tries to sell them for more money than he bought them for. He doesn't have to but he says he would get bored if he didn't." Kate's voice took on a more sombre tone. "Daddy loves you very much darling and I'm sure that he is always thinking about you. I'm sure that when granddad moves into the new estate and we move there too daddy will spend much more time at home."

Becky looked sullen kicked the lawn and replied as much to the grass as to her Mum. "Only to spend time with granddad not with us!" Breaking free of her mum's hand she ran across the lawn to the house disappearing through the French windows. Kate sighed and went after her.

Becky sat with her back to the French windows, her little brown terrier pup held tight in her lap enthusiastically attempting to attack the toggle on her jacket. Kate knelt beside her and attempted to placate her, explaining again that once her grandfather moved into the estate he had just purchased she and her father would see much more of each other, not because her father wished to spend the time with her granddad but with her. Becky was having none of it, her petulant mood not swayed at all by her mother's explanation. "And what about you and daddy? Will you stop shouting at each other when you think I can't hear!" Kate's hand automatically snaked out in more shock than anger slapping her daughter sharply across the leg immediately regretting her reaction. Becky jumped up anger and hurt flushing her face. "Wait till I tell Mike what you did!" She ran to her bedroom slamming the door behind her. Kate stunned by her retort strode after her. She opened the door to find Becky sobbing face down on the bed. "Now you listen to me young lady. What I have just said about daddy is true and as for us shouting all grownups do that. Now I love daddy just as much as you do but that doesn't mean to say that we always see eye to eye and I'd like to know what this has to do with Mike? You hardly even know him besides which if you had known him for a long time our life is our own and has nothing whatsoever to do with him. So don't you dare say anything like that again and most certainly not in front of daddy or he will go nuts! Is that quite clear? Now I'm sorry that I smacked you but you really did deserve it, I know you think you're grown up but you're not and there are limits to what you can and can't say. Now give me a hug dry your eyes and come into the kitchen breakfast will be ready soon."

Breakfast was eaten in virtual silence and after Kate had cleared away the dishes she told Becky to go and change as they were going out for the day. Becky sulkily complied only replying to her mother when absolutely necessary. Walking to the car Beck's kicked at the gravel drive as she slowly wandered around to the passenger side. "Becky do stop sulking and get in the car you're going to make us late." Becky gave in and moved more quickly climbing into the passenger seat and fastening her seat belt.

"Mummy. I'm sorry if I was rude but no one ever listens to me! I'm a lot cleverer than people think you know and you say I should always say what's on my mind and have an opinion!"

Kate looked sympathetically at her daughter. "I know sweetheart but there are ways of saying things to people without being rude and unfortunately you aren't quite old enough to realise that yet."

"So why won't you tell me things?"

Kate smiled. "Like what young lady?"

Becky hesitated for a moment then looking directly into her mother's eyes spoke. "Like why you and daddy argue so much and why you look at Mike funny and why he goes silly when he looks at you?" then accusingly "I'm really not silly mummy it's no good saying I wouldn't understand!"

Kate sighed started the car and pulled out of the drive before replying. "Okay I'll be as honest as I can and hope you understand. Daddy and I care very much for each other, we've been together for a long time, nearly fifteen years, I still love daddy you understand and he still loves me but in a different sort of way. This is very hard to explain Beck's."

Becky interjected. "It's okay mummy." She said reassuringly.

Kate smiled at her, she was much brighter than even she gave her credit for.

"Daddy isn't the sort of person to show his feelings he isn't what they call demonstrative. That means giving people cuddles and things. When you grow a bit older you'll understand that sometimes you need a hug and every now and then for the person you love to tell you they love you. So you know they care. As I say daddy's not that sort of person and so I get cross with him because he seems more interested in money than in me sometimes and then we argue. I'm sure though that we'll sort it out in the end. Does that explain it a little to you?"

"Yes, but you haven't answered me about Mike?"

"What is this fascination with Mike?" Kate said almost crossly.

"You said I could ask and you'd be honest mummy and anyway Mikes good fun, a bit moody sometimes but he does silly things and makes me laugh!"

"Okay let's see! I like Mike even though I don't know him very well he makes me laugh too and it's important to laugh. As for why Mike goes, as you say, silly when he sees me I don't know, perhaps that just what he's like, I really don't know him well enough to be honest. Does that answer your questions?" Kate ruffled Becky's hair playfully

"Mmmm, sort of. I don't understand one thing though." Kate looked quizzically at her daughter. "The lady in the café said to the other lady when I went up to get a drink that there was electric between you…. You must get an awful shock!" Kate burst out laughing much to the annoyance of her daughter. "You see you just think I'm silly!"

"No darling I think you're the cleverest little girl there ever was!"

Kate slowed the car and turned into a magnificent drive. Becky's attention was immediately diverted. "Mummy it's a horse farm!" and every other thought went out of her head.

John Cullen smiled and walked over to Kate warmly shaking her hand. "Pleased to meet you Mr.s Stokes, would you like a coffee?"

Kate smiled. "Thank you I'd love one but perhaps we could look at the horses first? If that's okay with you?" and John led an exuberant Becky and a smiling Kate around the stables. As they did John tried his best to give them an insight into the horses they were looking at. "I do apologise, I expected Seamus to have been here. He's normally so reliable but no one seems to know where he is this morning. I'm afraid my knowledge of horses is quite limited, Mike or Seamus normally deal with this but anything you like the look of we can get them to sit down and go through with you as soon as we can."

Becky was desperately trying to attract the attention of a pretty chestnut two-year-old filly, who was looking back at her frantic attempts with uncertainty. "I'm really not going to do anything horrible I only want to stroke you silly." She said and the filly seeming to realise that the pair of eyes and waving hands that had appeared over her door were not a threat after all took a few tentative steps towards the diminutive human. Stretching her neck out she sniffed the top of Becky's head exhaling to breathe in again the hair on Becky's head blew across her face making Becky laugh. The filly stuck her head right over the door to see what the rest of this small creature that made such a funny noise looked like. "Oh mummy look at this one it really likes me. See it's giving me a kiss!" Becky was ecstatic as the filly put her muzzle to her face and wiggled her lips. John smiled at the joy shown by Becky. "I'm afraid I can't really tell you much about the pedigree or potential of the horses like Mike but I do know that filly is bred out of one of Mike's favourite mares, My Tika. Mike hasn't even looked at her since he's been back, yet I know he had a real soft spot for her. In fact, I don't even know if she's for sale and if she was how much she'd be! I'm not being very helpful, am I?" John's voice held an apology but before he could utter another word a very excited short person grabbed her mums hand and did an impromptu dance on the spot.

"Please mummy ring Mike and ask him if he'll sell Sunrise."

John looked a little bewildered so Kate proceeded to explain. "Sunrise is the name Becky chose for the horse she wanted and it looks as though she has found it! Let's just hope that Mike wants to part with her!"

"Oh mummy please ring him. Please..." Becky's jig from one foot to the other continued as she begged her mum's indulgence. Kate smiled at her daughter, it was that same devastating smile that lit up Kate's face and melted icebergs, and John suddenly realised that he was before the person Mike had so callously announced to Ann he had met. Though he was uncertain from his brief meeting of her as to whether she herself was aware of the fact. John felt guilty though he was unsure why, he was fond of Ann, she was a good friend to him and his wife's best friend, but his true loyalty was to Mike even though they had fallen out over the removal of Rocket from the stud. His thoughts were thrown aside as Kate took her mobile phone from her bag and scrolled down for Mike's number. She pressed a button and held the phone to her ear. "Hello, I thought you were going to ring me back?" she paused for a reply, "Okay you're forgiven, now please listen. I'm at the stud." Mikes voice came down the phone loud and clear. "What!"

"If you're going to shout I shall hang up!" Kate waited as what seemed a mumble apology was issued. "Okay as I say I am

at the stud and Becky has taken rather a liking to a filly by....
sorry John what is the mothers name?" She waited for John to
answer her question ignoring his pleas to speak to Mike himself.
"My Tika and John would like to speak to you." She paused,
then turned to look at John. "Mike says please bear with him he
promises he'll phone you later." Again she paused, "he'd like to
speak to you." She said passing the phone to Becky. Becky took
the phone and held it to her ear listening intently. "Yes...I think
she's very beautiful and she really likes me.... she gave me a
kiss...yes, I'd love her lots... I'd never sell her, never!" Kate
and John looked on with puzzlement as Becky spoke down the
phone in reply to Mike. She went quiet for a minute delving into
her pocket and bringing out her purse, counting the contents
with total concentration. "Fifty-three pounds and twenty-seven
pence." She said quite proudly. "Do you mean it? ... oh thank
you Mike.... love you!" Becky was squealing with delight as she
passed the phone back to her mother. Kate listened then asked
if he were sure, thanked him, said she would and switched the
phone off. "Well I'm a bit stunned to say the least." She said to
John.

John answered. "Believe me Mike could stun an elephant,
however nothing Mike does anymore could stun me!"

"He's just said that Becky, no one else mind you but Becky is
to pay you fifty-three pounds and twenty-seven pence, and the
filly is hers!"

"That's Mike, the old Mike!" John said breaking out a smile.

Becky was ecstatic passing the contents of her purse to her
mum to give to John she ran back to the stable door shouting.
"She's mine, she's mine. Why Sunrise is going to be the best
racehorse in the whole world." And just as though she
understood Sunrise nodded her head and whickered.

Seamus had listened carefully to all that Mike had said
without comment. Now that Mike had finished speaking

Seamus rubbed his forehead with his hand.

"Jesus Michael that's one helluva tale. Don't misunderstand me mind, I'm not saying it's not right just that it takes a bit of getting used too! I always knew you were a bit special with the horse but one talking to you…. well…. it's a bit hard to take in! Still if you say it then I guess I have to believe you! So you say that Rocket me lad here can find Storm? Well we best make the most of what he knows then. I'd suggest that you don't give John the details when you ring him…. for sure he'll never believe it and he'll have every man in a white coat chasing us both from one end of the country to the other. If I was you I'd just say that you think Rocket might be able to smell Storm him being a horse an' all with a horse's good sense of smell. It might just work….and it's all we've got…. but you must still ring him then perhaps we'll get some peace and can get on with the job."

"Listen to him." The voice in his head said. "He makes a lot more sense than you do!"

The three of them settled down for the night, grateful for the cover of the old barn as the rain pelted down outside.

Morning came, sunny, clean and with the fresh newness that follows rain. Mike had risen before Seamus setting the kettle on the camp stove and brewing tea, neither bothered to eat but Rocket tucked into his bucket of horse nuts as though he had never eaten. They tidied up the improvised camp site, Seamus loading the possessions into the back of the Navara agreed that he would follow in the truck until they came off the downs and then would decide how and where they would meet up before evening fell. As Rocket covered the ground effortlessly with Seamus bumping along in the truck behind they soon came to an end of the track they had followed and joined a small country lane. Mike sat on the back of Rocket with a look of absolute concentration on his face. Rockets head was held high studying first one direction then the other. "It's that way." The voice in Mikes head said as Rocket turned left onto the road. Mike deliberated on his surroundings, he knew the area fairly well but it had been a long time since he had been there.

Suddenly it dawned on him. "Seamus!" he shouted with excitement, "I know where Storm is!"

Seamus jumped from the truck and ran to where Mike sat on Rocket. "This lane leads to Malek's old place. I stake my life there's a connection!"

"That makes sense, Malek's boy wasn't slow in coming forward to blame you for his dad's accident. Let's think about this for a minute, before we go steaming ahead. It would cause all sorts of problems if we were wrong."

Mike agreed and during the passage of the two men's conversation agreed that now would be the time for him to ring John. He was surprised when he eventually got through to Johns mobile. The edge was still in John's voice but it had mellowed. It was decided that on Mike's insistence the police should be left unaware on the compromise that Mike told John exactly where he was so that John could join them before any further action was taken. Mike and Seamus settled down in the entrance that joined the track to the road. Rocket contentedly chewed the lush grass that grew thickly beneath the hedge that bordered the track. The sun had risen high by the time John reached them and it was with trepidation that he walked towards the pair from his Jag. Much to his surprise Mike held out his hand and smiled warmly. The past few days of dissention it seemed had been put aside and forgotten. They all leaned against the side of the pickup as Seamus and Mike explained to John the theory of Malek's son. John looked guilty as he listened to what the two men had to say before explaining that they had received a ransom demand for two million pounds for the safe return of Storm. The police he continued had insisted that no mention of this be made to anyone including Mike, it appeared that he was still one of the main suspects. John told how he had explained to them that the logic of their argument was totally flawed but they had been determined that the information be kept secret in case a slip was made by mentioning the ransom with supposed knowledge. Mike actually found it quite amusing, a little hurtful but amusing none the less and thought to himself that perhaps he might consider his own implication having arrived without word from Spain at exactly the correct moment, just after Storms disappearance. Logic decreed that with the wealth he had accumulated over the last twelve months he would have nor did have any need for further finances. He put his thoughts aside and they started to discuss the course of action they would take. John desperately wanted to call the police in to deal with things but neither Mike nor Seamus would have any of it. "They've cocked things up so far, what makes you think they won't do the same now?" Mike asked John and John could not find an answer. The three slowly moved down the road in a line, Mike leading on Rocket who was now jig jogging excitedly, Seamus in the pickup and John in the Jag. It made a strange sight and Mike looking over his shoulder had to smile. The three musketeers he thought to himself a bit on the motley side but the three musketeers nonetheless. The drive to the late Malek's was overgrown and unkempt as though the air of neglect that the house gave off had begun to creep its way into its surroundings. The three men looked at each other without comment the foreboding atmosphere apparent to all. Rocket was standing with his ears cocked. "Storm's here." The voice in Mikes head said and Mike nodded assent to Rocket. "Seamus you come with me, John you stay here and keep an eye on things. If you think things seem to be going badly you'll have to decide what course of action to take. I'm afraid we are going to play this one a little by ear! Seamus you knock the front door and say that you've broken down or something, any excuse to distract whoever's in there. I'll go 'round the back and poke around, see what I can find. I know it's a little vague but it's the best I can come up with at short notice!" Mike smiled to his friends, jumped on Rocket and they forced their way through the undergrowth heading towards the back of the house. John leaned against the pickup trying to look casual, though he wondered why as there was no one to be seen, the lane was as quiet as a graveyard, perhaps it was this that un-nerved him slightly. He looked at his watch for what must have been the tenth time. Seamus and Mike had been gone fifteen minutes only though it seemed as though they had been gone for days. At first the sound didn't register with John, it made him jump but for some reason it didn't register, the second time it did. Gunshots!

CHAPTER EIGHT

Becky's eyes filled with tears as she passed the phone to her mother, Kate's eyes were no different at seeing her little girl so obviously upset. She listened as the voice at the other end of the phone came clearly. "Who's going to pay for keeping the fucking thing? If I'd wanted a racehorse I'd have bought one myself. It's not going to happen do you understand?" Kate's voice went up an octave before her reply. The tears were now streaming down her face at the onslaught she had just received from Geoff. "No! For once you are going to listen to me! It's not your horse and you can keep your precious money...I'll pay the costs of keeping it. I'm disgusted it's your daughter!" Kate's emotions had left her lost for words. "How dare you upset her like this." And Kate slammed the phone down. Becky was inconsolable, sobbing so hard that Kate had difficulty getting through to her.

"I....thought....daddy....would .....be....happy...we could...have...all gone...to the...races together." She sobbed into her mother's shoulder. Kate in tears herself not only because of the contretemps with her husband but also in sympathy with her daughter's state tried to smile.

"Don't you worry sweetheart, I'll pay for keeping the horse

and we will go racing and leave mean old daddy at home."

Becky managed a half smile through the sobs and the tears waned. "And I jolly well will leave him at home and he'll be really sorry when Sunrise wins and he's not there!" The two hugged each other fiercely as only a mother and daughter can when a successful plan has been hatched between two like beings.

Kate sat in front of the television that night wondering what was happening to her life, the more she thought about it the more her head spun. She had met Geoff when she was fifteen and had fallen in love with him. She was sure she had but somewhere deep in the inner recesses of her sub conscious she wondered whether it was the man she had fallen for or the lifestyle he offered! Her mother had encouraged the relationship thinking Geoff to be a knight in shining armour that could do no wrong, in truth just as Kate saw him. Her dad he was a slightly different story, nice enough to Geoff for his daughter's sake but nonetheless reserved in his judgement. There was something he couldn't quite put a finger on but it was there. Not pretension, because that was definitely not Geoff's way, but Kate's father always felt there was just a little look of smugness from Geoff, as if he wanted to say look at me I'm far wealthier than you and that makes me such a better person, but he never did and so Kate's father started to believe he was making an error of judgement simply on the basis that another man had walked in and taken his daughters life over. Kate thought all through the past, how many times Geoff had made some excuse when there was none and worst still her belief in him. Her anger at their earlier quarrel made all the things that popped into her mind crystal clear reality. Even those things that weren't she started to believe. She fell into a fitful sleep, dreaming of long summer days walking across emerald green fields with Becky skipping happily beside her as she held his hand tightly a feeling of warmth spreading through her body. She woke with a start....the hand she had held in her dream was Mike's!

"Becky Stokes, you get yourself out of that pit and get down here for breakfast right now! We have a very busy day ahead and I'd like to get going." A sleepy little face appeared from under the duvet yawning first then talking. "Where are we going mummy? I didn't think we were doing anything, except swimming in the pool if it's sunny!"

"If you got your lazy little butt out of bed young lady you'd see that it's a lovely day but that doesn't mean we have to spend it lazing by the pool…. Especially when you have a horse to buy things for." The words had hardly left Kate's mouth before that yawn became a smile and the child became a tornado of action. Becky was dressed in record time and was told off several times for trying to wolf her breakfast down as quickly as possible. "Can we go to a shop where they sell really nice horse things please mummy. I have some money saved you know. Well quite a lot really. Fifteen pounds and I only want the very best for Sunrise. She's very fussy about what she has!" Kate tried to stifle a smile but couldn't quite manage it she hugged Becky kissing the top of her head. "I love you Beck's," she said.

"And I love you too mummy…..can we please go now?" The pair walked out hand in hand to the garage, Becky skipping with delight and Kate skipping because unknown to herself she had undone a link of the chain that fettered her.

By the time the two of them had finished their shopping spree for the by now infamous Sunrise, Becky having told everyone she came into contact with about the horse and its potential, they had hardly any room left in the Range Rover that Kate had sensibly decided to take in favour of the Mercedes and were considerably lighter financially. The journey to the stud was undeniably joyous, any negative feelings were forgotten and the two sang their way through several C.Ds as they wound their way around the country lanes. The moment the Range Rover pulled into the yard Becky sprung from the passenger seat like a gazelle and ran as if her life depended on it to Sunrises stable. Sunrise stuck her head over the door pleased to see the little creature that had made such a fuss of her the day before. She was even happier to re unite with the miniscule human when a packet of Polo mints appeared as if by magic in the tiny hand. Anita who was walking across the yard with a grooming kit smiled, she had been introduced to the new owners the day before as Sunrise, as she was now known instead of just plain filly, was her lot. "Good morning Mr.s Stokes. I see Becky's made friends with our Sunny already!" she greeted.

Kate smiled, "Yes and she's already cost me a pretty penny!"

"She'll be worth it, that old mare of Mike's hasn't produced a bad one yet! I'm just about to groom her, maybe Becky would like to help?" The look of glee on Becky's face foretold that nothing would stop her regardless and before Anita could open the door properly Becky was in the stable.

"Be careful Becky and listen to what Anita tells you. Just remember you've a lot to learn about horses yet." Becky didn't hear she was far too busy brushing the front leg, which was about all she could reach, and giggling every time Sunrise snorted as she sniffed her hair and it tickled her nose. Kate wondered at how unerring it was that something so large and young could be so aware around something as young and so much more delicate. Children and animals for the most part seem to have this unspoken bond that each protects with absolute precision.

Kate walked across the yard to the back door of the house and knocked. She waited only seconds before a very pretty blond woman with a small baby in her arms answered the door with a smile and one hand outstretched. "Hi, I'm Alice and this," she nodded towards the bundle in her arms proudly, "is Michael." Kate smiled looking down at the toothless but smiling face of the bundle.

"He is gorgeous, could I hold him?" Alice gestured for Kate to come into the kitchen.

"Please, come in my friend is here I'm sure she'd like to meet you. Oh, and you're more than welcome." She said gently passing the smiling bundle to Kate.

"Thank you. Oh goodness I'm so rude." She said on entering the kitchen and meeting Ann. "I haven't even introduced myself. I'm Kate, I'm sure you know what it's like when something as delicious as this little chap is put in front of you, everything else goes out of the window for a few minutes! Though I have to say he doesn't smell too delicious at the moment." They all laughed and Alice moved over towards Kate. "Really I don't mind… if you have a clean nappy I'd be more than happy to change him… it's been so long since I've had to change a baby…'" Kate looked wistfully off into space the thought of those chubby little legs kicking away as she attempted to secure them for long enough to place clean apparel bringing a sorrow that she only had Becky yet grateful that she and her daughter were so close. The three women sat chattering finding they had much in common each being patient with their men and the fixations they had, John for horses and Geoff for business. Mike was hardly mentioned and when he was Ann glossed over the problems that beset her at the moment and changed the subject. Over all the conversation was light, centring around Alice's new arrival which each woman seemed incapable of ignoring him for more than a couple of seconds. Kate proudly described her own daughter, with the odd reminiscence of when Becky was a chubby little munchkin like Michael.

After several reassurances that Anita would care for Becky and keep her safe, Kate stayed for half an hour before making her farewell before going off to find Becky. She found Beck's animatedly telling Anita how Sunrise was going to be the greatest racehorse that had ever lived, astutely adding that even if she didn't win many races she would still be the greatest in her eyes and would have lots of babies by the very best stallions there were. She would she concluded have to speak to both Mr. Cullen and Mike as she was sure they would like to allow her to use Rocket, her horse being so fantastic. Anita and Kate who had not disturbed her daughter but stood slightly to one side of the stable door listening avidly to her daughter simultaneously burst out laughing. Becky was most put out. "You see what adults are like! They just don't listen when we say something… they think we're stupid!" and as if in agreement Sunrise blew down her nostrils making a raspberry sound. Kate still chuckling entered the stable and put her arm around Becky. "We don't think you're stupid at all sweetheart do we Anita." she said.

"Just a little over enthusiastic perhaps. You have to remember Sunrise is only a baby, she won't I shouldn't think be doing anything for a while." She looked towards Anita for statement support.

"Mum's quite right you know. Sunrise isn't even broken yet, it will be at least four months before we even start to do some work with her." Becky looked at Anita quizzically and Anita bent down to her height and explained exactly what she meant. Becky took it all in then replied that regardless Sunrise was and would be special even if she was last in every race she went in but she added with great authority that neither she nor Sunrise believed she would be. Kate eventually pried Becky away from her horse on the promise that she would be back the next day with an even greater supply of Polo mints and they waved to Anita and drove off. Kate felt she had been rude in not finding John and saying goodbye but on the other hand felt a little bit miffed that he had not found them either. It seemed he had disappeared into thin air almost so Kate assumed he had gone off around the stud somewhere and been distracted by something. She decided to ring Geoff and see if their earlier conversation or shouting match could be reverted. Becky was snuggled down in the passenger seat sound asleep and obviously dreaming she was riding her horse in some important race from the way her hands gripped the imaginary reins and feet kicked frantically. Kate knew she could sleep through a world war and so decided that she would use the time to phone Geoff. She pressed the key on her mobile to bring up his number and pushed dial.

Geoff answered the phone with a casual tone not giving away his mood and the first few words they spoke were testing like two gladiators circling each other to test the other's strengths and weaknesses. Kate was stunned when Geoff made a partial apology for their last phone call, she also felt a warm glow deep inside for the man she loved. It was the first time in all the years they had been together he had even come close to saying sorry. Kate was even more surprised when Geoff told her he was at home and would speak to her in depth when she returned there. It was with some trepidation that Kate woke Becky without telling her, her father was at home and they made their way into the house. Geoff was waiting, walking up to Kate and hugging her, another first! Kate responded each holding on to the other tightly. Geoff relinquished his hold and stepped forward to hug Becky who stood as though made of stone as he picked her up and held her. "Hello Daddy." Was all she said and the moment Geoff released her she determinedly walked into the kitchen, sitting at the kitchen table with a pencil and paper upon which she wrote with rapt concentration. Geoff followed closely behind. "What are you writing squirt?" he asked as he leant over Becky's shoulder to take a look. Becky covered the paper with her arm. "Nothing that would interest you Daddy… it's a list of things I'm going to buy for my horse if you must know. Now I'd like to be left alone so that I can get on with it please."

"Becky." Kate's voice was firm, "you do not speak to your father like that. Now apologise immediately, and then you can go to your bedroom for an hour to consider your attitude."

Becky made a mumbled apology and scuttled off to her bedroom close to tears. Kate turned to Geoff. "It doesn't matter how upset she is with you, she still has to remember her manners and certainly shouldn't talk to her dad like that."

"Well perhaps I deserved it?" Geoff said with a shrug of his shoulders. Another first for Geoff, deserving retribution. "I was a bit hard on both of you, look put the kettle on and make some tea and we can sit down and talk."

John fumbled wildly with his mobile, hands shaking as he attempted to dial 999. the sound of the gunshots had freaked him out completely. His voice shaking as he eventually managed to get though. The operator answered and John thought how stupid and just shouted down the phone.

"Get an ambulance and the police there's been a shooting, I'm at a place called Thirsk Manor, Batcombe." And after switching off the phone started carefully up the overgrown drive.

Mike felt a searing pain in his leg and remembered thinking what a sod it was because his leg had healed up nicely, now he was back to square one. The ferrety looking chap that had stood pointing the gun at a wretched looking Storm must have seen him from the corner of his eye and had turned to fire without questioning. The huge man that stood in front of Storm protectively had probably saved his life, immediately diving toward the ferret and striking him a crushing blow across the arm that held the gun. Unfortunately he was not as quick as the bullet but at least he had disturbed the others aim. Mike was catapulted backwards as the bullet hit and now as he lay on the ground in agony he watched first the crimson stain that spread from his leg to the floor then the two men as both scrabbled towards the gun the ferret had dropped as his arm was hit. The ferret being closer had the advantage and reached it first. "You overgrown fucker." He screamed at the big man. "Now you're going to pay." He pointed the gun at the big man and pulled the trigger, just as a hoof struck him in the side of the head. Rocket had come galloping around the corner just in time. The bullet pirouetted the big man making the whole scene appear surreal, like ballet dancers acting out some tragedy, he fell to the floor with a groan blood oozing from the wound in his upper chest as he lapsed into unconsciousness. Rocket nuzzled Storm in reassurance then went immediately to Mike. "Don't you go giving up on me and doing something stupid. I've a long future planned for us." The voice in Mikes head said and Mike managed a smile. John arrived at that moment and eyed the scene with consternation. "Oh shit." He exclaimed. "I've called an ambulance!" and he knelt to help Mike, placing a handkerchief over the spreading liquid that spread through the circular hole in Mikes upper leg. "John you'd better see what you can do to help that chap." He inclined his head towards the big man that lay slumped against the wall "Stuff him." John said shortly.

"No help him, he saved my life." And Mike slumped into unconsciousness himself.

John was engrossed, leaning over the big man and trying to stem the flow of blood from his wound. He gagged as he tore away the man's shirt and saw the shards of bone that glistened white in the crimson gash. The wound was completely different from Mikes it was as though someone had taken a hatchet to the man's upper chest. John gently placed a wad of his shirt on top of the wound unsure what else to do. He decided it would be best if he ran back down the drive to wait the arrival of both the police and the ambulance. He didn't want them going straight past the drive and causing further delays in getting help for the injured men. He rose from his crouched position and as he did so froze in fear. He had been so engrossed in helping the big man that he had not noticed the small dark-skinned man that had crept up on him. As he turned he recognised the man immediately, if the fellow hadn't have been younger he would have believed a ghost stood in front of him. It was Malek. No, a younger version, Malek's son held the gun that had been dropped by the ferret and it was pointed directly at John's head.

"You're that piece of shits mate… I've seen you with him at the races… well I think you're about to regret it. You should choose your friends more carefully in future, that's if you had a future!" He laughed, it was hollow and mirthless, John thought there was a tinge of madness in Malek's voice. "Now you'll see your friend die." He laughed again. "Then you'll die yourself." He started to turn the gun towards Mike and a small arm of steel looped around his neck from behind. John found himself laughing, whether from relief or Seamus miniature Irish imitation of Arnold Schwarzenegger will remain a mystery but he laughed nonetheless as Seamus in his Irish accent spoke those immortal words. "Fuck you asshole!" Kneed Malek in the small of his back and as he doubled up forwards as the wind left his body Seamus cracked his fist into the side of Malek's head and all went dark for Malek. The sirens wailed and a sea of armed response police pointing MP5's and screaming for everybody to lie on the ground appeared. The next hour passed in a haze as police, ambulances, forensic teams and inevitably the press arrived, who with credit to the armed response team were dealt with without any sympathy whatsoever.

Mike woke with a feeling of deja vous, crisp white linen sheets and an excruciating pain in his right leg. Been there seen the film worn the tee shirt, only this time it was not through his doing. Mike struggled to pull himself into a sitting position but the pain soon stayed his attempt. He decided discretion was after all the better part of valour and pressed the button on the bell cord that had been considerately placed on the side of his bed. The effect was immediate a nurse came through the door smiling broadly. "We wondered when you were going to wake up." She looked at the position Mike had manoeuvred himself uncomfortably into. "Mmmm... they said you would be a difficult patient and I see you've already started," she said sternly but the smile did not leave her face.

"Now let's have a look and see if we can't get you back to being a little more comfortable." She busied herself helping Mike to sit up putting pillows behind him for support. When she had finished ensuring Mike was now settled she spoke again. "There are some people waiting outside to see you. You're a very popular man you know they've been there for over five hours waiting for you to come 'round! Shall I tell them to come in?"

"Please." Mike said wincing slightly at the pain as he leaned forward for no reason. Mike looked hopefully at the door hoping to see that smile walk through it closely followed by bossy. He wasn't disappointed when he saw it was Seamus and John but his heart sank a little. John had a piece of paper in his hand and leaned forward placing it in Mikes hand, Mike opened it and read the words. He looked up at John's face not knowing what to say. "Christ John! What can I say... thank you so much!" John grinned broadly.

"Well I have to admit that I didn't trust you when you ran off with Rocket and friends like us three." He put a hand on Seamus shoulder including him. "The Three Musketeers! All for one and one for all! So I have divided Rocket and Storm equally among the three of us, however Seamus and I agreed that it will be down to you to decide on whatever they do. We both agree that we would be stupid to go against your knowledge." Seamus walked forward and grabbed Mike by the hand. "Now how are you feeling Guv... Or should I say partner? Can you imagine the look on Mary's face when she finds out I've a third share in those two? You always said I'd be a millionaire one day Mike and there was me thinking you'd been watching too much Only Fool's and Horses, well I'm buggered if you weren't right," he grabbed John's hand also.

"Thank you both I swear I'll somehow make it up to you!" Seamus was almost in tears.

Mike spoke. "Get away you daft fucker, you made it all right from the first day I met you. Christ, it should be the other way 'round. Never once did you complain when I couldn't pay you, or took my misfortune out on you by being a miserable bastard, and from what I hear you saved both John's and my life. Seamus, you deserve more than that for all you've done for both of us and old Irish bugger I can afford it, so I'm going to make you a proper millionaire, as soon as I get out of here your bank manager is going to fall instantly in love with you because I am going to pay exactly that into your account for all your support. I owe you more than that!" Seamus couldn't hold the tears back, he laughed, he cried, he sang, he danced a jig as the other two musketeers watched and grinned.

The nurse came in to see what the fuss was all about and

asked Seamus after being told of his good fortune if he fancied a wife. Seamus smiled, "Ahhhh, me little darlin'? But I already have the woman of me dreams and several miniatures to go along with her." The nurse laughed.

John and Seamus left leaving Mike alone. He laid in his bed in that state of limbo when sleep is just on the horizon but doesn't quite reach you. Not the irritating state, but the peaceful relaxing state, where dreams are always pleasant. He dreamed of Kate and her smile, her blue, blue eyes, her blond hair resting softly on her shoulders, her lithe body walking catlike towards him and the limbo state became a deep and restful sleep.

Kate sat at the kitchen table with Geoff while Becky rummaged enthusiastically through the package in the hall that contained the present Geoff had bought her. Becky was very polite to her dad but still a little offish, happy though as she tore the paper from the items contained in the box. Her offishness was soon gone when she saw the colour coordinated rugs, bridles and grooming kit for her new horse. She ran into the kitchen. "Oh, thank you daddy, Sunrise will love it." Geoff laughed to see his little girl happy. "That's okay Titch. It's what I do, I'm a dad. It's my job," he said and Becky gave him a crushing hug and kiss. Geoff pried her off of him. "Go and look in my inside jacket pocket, there's another present for you in there...oh and bring the other one with mum's name on it." Becky ran off excitedly to her dad's jacket, returning it seemed before she had left. "I love presents daddy," she said as both Geoff and Kate smiled at each other.

"Okay you can both open your presents and then you, young lady, can go and play. I want to talk with mummy. Grown up stuff."

Becky looked at her dad with a knowing air. "Kissing and that I suppose," she said as though she was hosting the Trisha show.

Geoff looked serious for a moment and Kate felt her stomach turn in trepidation. "No sometimes sweetheart mums and dads have to have a little time to their selves, just like you do. Now open your presents and skid daddle."

Kate and Becky opened their presents. Kate carefully unwrapping hers, Becky tearing the paper with abandon. The beautifully wrapped packages contained identical boxes. Kate and Becky opened them, Kate gasped and Becky said, "Cool!" The necklaces that were displayed on the burgundy red velvet were astonishing. Central teardrop diamond of about five carats on a snake link gold chain into which was set four of the most beautiful emeralds, each a teardrop again and set half an inch apart, two each side of the diamond. Kate stood and went to Geoff hugging and kissing him. Whilst Becky held hers to her neck, saying, "I think I will wear this to show Sunrise if we go to see her today! She'll think it's very pretty!" Kate laughed. "I don't think you will my darling, that is far too expensive and precious to wear out every day. You can wear it when we go somewhere special. Maybe the races or something, I'm sure Sunrise will be just as happy to see it then as now. Right young lady, put that back in the box. I'll put it in a safe place then run along and play."

"Can I write my name on the box mummy so it doesn't get muddled up with yours?"

Kate smiled. "If you must, though they're both the same you know."

"I know but yours is yours and mine is mine!" With that Becky went to one of the kitchen drawers found a felt tip pen and with great deliberation wrote her name upon the small cream case and happily skipped off to again organise her presents for Sunrise.

Kate spoke first. There was an air of trepidation in her voice. "Thank you, this is so beautiful and very expensive, you shouldn't have.... What's this all about Geoff?"

"I should have. I've been a total shit lately. I been so pre-occupied with my own stuff I've totally ignored everything else.

I been so busy helping the old man sort out this estate and running about overseas I'd almost forgotten I had a life! Anyway, one of the things I've done is to build us a new house on the estate. It's not overly big, six bedrooms but it's very spacious and I think you'll like it. If it's okay I'd like us to go over today and look at it. You can sort out the décor and as soon as you have it how you want it we can move in. I've spoken to the old man and he's quite happy to build the two of you a stable yard behind the new house. Says he's quite looking forward to seeing the horses. Between you and me I think he's considering buying a few for Becky and the old lady. Anyway, I think it's time we started spending time together as a family… I've missed you!" This was probably the nearest Geoff would ever get to saying how much he cared for Kate and Becky and even though it fell a little short of knight in white armour, it was enough for Kate, she threw her arms around Geoff's neck buried her face into his shoulder and cried with joy.

Kate and Becky ran around the undecorated house Becky as a child and Kate as a child for that moment. Becky staked claim to her bedroom saying how she was intending to hang pictures of horses, especially Sunrise all over the walls and Kate engrossed herself working out how she would design the interior. Geoff watched them both with a smile that had not been on his face for many a month, everybody felt relieved and happy. The house Kate declared was beautiful and by the time she had finished her interior design it would be incredible. Geoff had no doubt that Kate's artistic flare would again bring envy from all their friends. He chuckled to himself thinking that it may be going to cost him a small fortune but it would cost their friends more when the wives tried to compete with Kate. The upshot was that they never actually managed to succeed and they all knew it.

Mike woke rested from his deep sleep, exhaustion and pain have a way of making the body shut down to recuperate. His stomach rumbled and he pressed the bell to call a nurse in the hope that he could get something to eat. The bacon and eggs slipped down better than any meal that Gordon Ramsay could have produced. It was late afternoon before the surgeon came to see Mike, sitting on the edge of the bed he explained that the bullet had luckily missed the major blood vessels but had hit the bone. Fortunately, he told Mike it had hit the steel rod that had previously been used to repair his leg in Spain. There was not too much damage but he had, had to change the rod, which was rather bent. Mike would be okay but it would be sore for quite a while but a full recovery was inevitable. He could leave if he wished, that was if he could remember how to use crutches and realised he would need to be driven around for a while. Mike started to get out of bed keen as he was to return to his own life rather than live a hospital regime even though they made it as informal and comfortable as possible privately.

Near death experiences have a way of giving you a completely different perspective on everything, some are good some become selfish, in Mikes case it was good that he started to think. He had phoned John and agreed to stay the first night at least at the stud, he would, he insisted return to his own home the following day. John sent a car to collect him from the hospital. As Mike waited for the car leaning on one crutch to roll a cigarette his thoughts wandered from speaking to Ann so that he and she could get to speaking civilly to each other and sort out their finances to what he was going to do about Kate. He knew there was nothing to sort out because nothing had happened, but he also knew that he had fallen deeply for Kate and he, for his own sanity, would have to deal with it. He smiled at the thought of Kate, Becky and himself walking hand in hand through the town together and he felt pride and sorrow all at the same time, pride for thought sorrow for reality and the reality was he was standing alone and most probably would be for a long, long time. He wanted to be friends with Ann and she wanted more, which would he knew make for a very strained friendship if it could even be that with Kate he wanted to progress to more than a friendship and she wanted no more, another possible recipe for disaster. Mike laughed out loud to himself, perhaps he should just stick to horses? "Don't you worry Mikey boy." The voice in his head said. "Life is short but not that short I have your future planned!"

"You think you're such a clever bastard Rocket, don't you? Keep throwing me a curver every now and again!" The voice laughed and the woman that had unknown to Mike stood next to him to await her taxi asked indignantly. "I beg your pardon!"

"I'm so sorry madam, I hadn't realised you were there." Mike said submissively.

"Obviously not young man." She huffed and moved several feet away.

The voice in Mikes head laughed again and Mike this time quietly to himself so that no one else would hear, said. "Oh, shut up you cocky sod!"

Mike hobbled into John's kitchen to be greeted by a beaming Seamus. "Ahh to be sure and who's the Long John Silver now then, I s'pose you'll be ooh arrhin all over the yard or should I say yard arm, well in your case yard leg!" and Seamus, John, Alice who was busying herself cooking what appeared to be a whole cow but was actually a steak for Mike 'to build his strength up' all fell into paroxysms of laughter. Mike laughed too, if you take the mick you have to be prepared to become the brunt of it as well. "You're a lot of unsympathetic miserable buggers taking the piss out of a man that does the same leg not once but twice." Mike said with a huge grin. For all the trauma that the three had seen in the recent past it was good that they could still laugh and joke, especially at themselves. Alice intervened ushering Mike to the table where she placed the cow in front of him with an order to eat. "Jesus Christ!" Seamus said. "I'm off before Alice makes me eat, I'll never understand why you're not t'irty stone at least." He aimed at John, Alice aimed the dish cloth at Seamus with unerring accuracy. They all laughed as Seamus peeled the cloth from his face, grinned at Alice and said a prompt farewell.

CHAPTER NINE

It had been three weeks since the incident at Malek's house the police had it seemed spent most of it at either John's house or Mike's yard questioning both the two of them and Seamus. There had been some amusement caused when a young over enthusiastic police officer had said that he thought the offender responsible for the death of the ferret should be held accountable. The sergeant that was with him suggested that he should 'take the collar' and arrest the subject forthwith. It was with great amusement that they led the young officer to the stables, and of even greater amusement to Mike when the voice in his head pronounce unceremoniously that he did not find it at all amusing. The young red-faced officer would take a long time to live down the story and especially when his colleagues took to calling him Ned and saying neigh that's not right every time they saw him.

The police however did have a cast iron case against Malek and Nick but were surprised to say the least when Mike insisted that the big man had been there to help him not in cahoots with Malek. He had much to their divergence insisted that Seamus and John go along with his story and so it was that Nick appeared at the gate of the yard immediately on being released from the cells. Mike had the advantage of hearing the tale from Rocket of how the big man had looked after Storm the best he could.

"I'm sorry to bovver yuh Guv but I wanted to come an' fank yuh. By rights I should be banged up for a long time. An' I deserves to be really. I jus' wanted to come an' fank yuh an' say how sorry I is for getting' involved wif them two likes I did." Mike held out his hand to the man and it was nearly crushed by his enormous strength! "I knows it's a bit of a liberty asking like but I don't suppose I could come in an' see the little un could I?" Mike opened the gate and offered the big man in taking him round to the stable block that held Rocket, Storm, Silver Dollar and of course JC. Rocket and Storm whickered loudly as Mike and Nick walked into the stable block. Storm was obviously pleased to see the huge man, he was frantically trying to get out of the stable in the direction of Nick. "I think you'd better go in and see him!" Mike said, "Before he pushes his way through the door and does himself some damage." Nick walked tentatively through the door only to be swamped by the excited little colt. Nick burst into tears as the colt nuzzled him. "Well I never!" he sniffed as he knelt in front of Storm and Storm pushed his muzzle into his neck.

"Great leveller's horses." Mike managed but could say no more as the lump in his throat threaten to choke him.

"Thanks Mike." The voice in his head said but this time it was slightly different, younger higher pitched. Mike looked quizzically at Rocket. "Wasn't me." Rockets voice said with laughter.

"Sometimes you're thick Mike Willett, didn't you think when I said we have plans for your future?" Mike stood dumbfounded and the higher pitched voice laughed. Mike never would know why the words came out but they did. "Do you have a job Nick?" and on receiving a negative reply offered Nick the responsibility of looking after Storm under Seamus tutelage. Nick couldn't accept quick enough and Mike heard the voice of Rocket. "Good man, everyone deserves a chance!"

Mike shrugged his shoulders in a resigned fashion telling Nick to join him in the house when he had finished fussing Storm. "And make sure the stable door is properly closed... I don't want to lose him again." Nick looked sheepish then realising Mike was taking the micky puffed his chest out. "Don't you worry Guvnor with me around nuffin' bad will ever 'urt this little fella, why not even the Chinaman could get to 'im." Mike looked puzzled and the little voice said in his head.

"Don't worry I know what he means. I'm perfectly safe now."

Mike had not seen Kate for over a week. She had called in a couple of times to see him but in the last week he had missed her. As soon as he had heard her voice his heart had leapt only to fall through the floor when she departed.

So when he heard her voice on the answering machine inviting him to a house warming party he very nearly floated on air, he could hear a very insistent voice in the background saying, "tell him he has to come mummy I've an idea that he has to listen too. I'll be very cross if he doesn't and I'll never speak to him again." He heard Kate say to her daughter that, that might just encourage him not to come and he visualised the little grownups look as she retorted "That was not a very nice thing to say mummy!" and Kate's laughter fading as the phone message ended. He stored the message tape in his desk drawer.

Mike walked out albeit with a slight limp to watch the horses as they circled the pond in the centre of the yard before walking out on the gallops to work.

"Morning Guv. Nice to have you back." Was the cheery greeting he received and from Anita the addition. "Yeah, that leprechaun we call an assistant trainer is such a grouchy old sod." Everybody in the yard chuckled including Seamus. The yard was back to its old self.

Mike watched the horses go out on the road leading to the gallops with Seamus proudly in the lead. "Don't you worry guvnor I'll make sure this scruffy lot of numpties are better turned out tomorrow." And was treated to a string of expletives. "Now will you listen to that and me assistant trainer an all!" And received another light-hearted string.

"Come on you idyll buggers, I thought you might have pulled yourself together and got to work whilst I was away." Mike said joining in the banter and everybody smiled.

The horses reached the bottom of the gallops and they waited for the sounding of Mikes car horn to start the mornings work. As always everybody had a lot to say, their horse was going to kick the ass of the others, each and every one of them as proud as could be of the horses in their charge. Mike's horn sounded and Anita, Hannah and Nicky jumped off upsides each other. Seamus had told them to touch irons until the five pole and then to let their horses race the last two furlongs. He was bringing up the rear on a green two-year-old and would use them for a lead until they got down to serious work, he'd let his lad canter behind so as not to ask too much of him too quick. Mike fell in love again with the job, watching such magnificent creatures, their coats glistening in the sun, muscles rippling as they pushed every ounce of effort into getting ahead, the girls shouting encouragement to their horses, the warm breeze on his back. He was at home, yet still he wasn't whole. It was at that very moment that he realised that he never would be until he held those blue eyes and dazzling smile close, and that he thought to himself is very unlikely!

Mike enjoyed being back especially as he was under no pressure, Seamus had taken the reins with amazing alacrity turning the yard into an incredibly well-oiled unit. The yard was good before but with all the strain Mike had been under in trying to train Rocket, the death of Malek, problems at home he had missed things that should have been done and were not, Seamus was under no such pressure and soon got everything back in tip top order. It was easy for Mike to leave Seamus in charge to carry on and to come in occasionally to make sure all was still well. Happy that all was in order he walked across to Rockets box and sat with him for a while. "Well old lad, I guess I'm pretty superfluous now, Seamus seems to have everything under control. What say you and I go for a ride, just a walk 'round the place, see how the grass is growing!"

The voice in his head sounded. "It would be nice and I promise I'll look after you with your wonky leg and all! Come on you're starting to look sorry for yourself and that will never do, go and get my saddle and let's get a move on."

Rocket and Mike appeared out of the stable turned out onto the road and wandered down the lane at a leisurely pace. They came back about two hours later at peace with the world and each other.

Mike looked at his watch for the hundredth time as he paced impatiently up and down the kitchen, it was seven o'clock and the party didn't start until eight and it was only a half hour drive to get there. Not that Mike was driving, he had ordered a taxi so he could have a drink and enjoy himself. He wished now he had told them to pick him up at seven thirty rather than seven forty-five. He didn't want to be the first there but he didn't want to be late either. God, he thought to himself, why was he getting so paranoid about a house warming party no one would arrive on time it was a party. Nothing formal drinks and a buffet. He looked at his watch again it was five minutes past seven. He decided to have a tea to pass the time. Sitting down with the mug of tea relaxed Mike a little and he began to consider where his life was going and exactly where he wanted to steer it. Perhaps he should just live a little for a while, just take life a little less seriously. Perhaps he would drop his high moral stance and go with the flow. "Yeah go with the flow Mikey boy." He said aloud and looked at his watch again.

The taxi drew up in front of a beautiful stone house with manicured lawns and gardens lit by subtle low level coloured lights. It gave the house an appearance of having been taken from the front cover of a fairy-tale. Mike knocked the front door and the beautiful fairy queen answered closely followed by the fairy princess. "I was beginning to think you weren't coming, I'm desperate to talk to you." The princess said impatiently.

"Becky!" Kate said sternly "How many times have I got to tell you about minding your manners?"

"Sorry mummy, sorry Mike…. But I really do need to talk to you it's very important…. I've got the most brilliant idea."

"Becky I'm sure Mike won't mind spending a bit of time with you once he's had time to get a drink and something to eat. You can take his coat…. Without the attitude! Then when I've introduced Mike to the other guests I'll let him come and speak to you… if you want too that is." She added towards Mike. Mike nodded his ascent and dutifully followed Kate into the lounge where about forty people chattered and laughed. There was music playing in the background and a few had taken themselves to the adjoining conservatory to dance.

After introducing Mike to most of her friends Mike decided it was time he went to see what Becky had been so desperate to discuss with him. He grinned to himself he remembered when he had first got a horse all he wanted to do was to discuss every hair on its body and he made a guess that it was even more important for Becky as she was determined to obtain Mike's services as a trainer. He had already come to terms with that fact although Becky did not yet know. He excused himself telling Kate that he was going to see Becky and left Kate grinning as though she knew what was coming. Neither of them did!

"It's about time I've waited ages and there's loads of very boring people that keep coming up and ruffling my hair. I absolutely hate that. Anyway, I've been watching this film. It's brilliant I'll lend it too you if you like? There's this man in it he's just like you. Well he doesn't look like you if you see what I mean but he's just like you around horses. He does all these things with funny stuff they find…. Well anywhere really." She paused momentarily for breath. "Anyway, he gets this horse that is a real problem and he… Well…. Just sort of cures it. You see he knows it's really good… just like you did when you bought Rocket." Another momentary pause for breath. "Anyway, it gets so good it becomes the best in the whole world and what do you think there's one horse it has never raced and the owner of that horse thinks his horse is better but of course it isn't."

Mike interrupted. "This film wouldn't be called Sea Biscuit by any chance, would it?"

"Oh wow, have you seen it too. Isn't it brilliant! Anyway, that's when the idea came to me!"

Mike smiled patiently as he waited for Becky to come up with her master plan.

"We," Mike wondered where the we had suddenly come from, "write to all the papers saying that we," again the we, it was starting to worry Mike! "Challenge any horse in the whole wide world to race against Rocket! Why he could beat any of them!" Becky looked up at Mike's face expectantly, Mike was speechless. "I'll give it a go!" The voice in his head said without giving him chance to answer or even consider and Mike knew it would be pointless to argue.

Reluctantly he gave Becky the answer she had hoped for. "Okay I'll see if I can get it organised!" Though his own thoughts were the complete opposite. "Oh yea of little faith." The voice in his head said. Mike sighed. Becky was ecstatic running in to tell her mum loudly what she had 'arranged' with Mike. Within ten seconds everybody in the room was talking about it. There was not a person in the country horsey or not that didn't know the name of The Rocket. One chap made a bee line for Mike. He was the editor of one of the most prestigious newspapers in the country; he immediately offered a huge sum of money as sponsorship if Mike would allow his paper to be first with any story connected to the imminent race. Mike agreed in principal and the editor ran for the door frantically calling his office on his mobile as he went. There was no doubt in Mike's mind that it would be front page news in every paper in the country within two days and front page on *The Times* the following morning. Things were going at break neck speed Mike rang john to tell him. "Have you taken leave of your senses? You've just agreed to race the most expensive horse in history on the whim of a child? For God sakes Mike, what if he gets beaten?"

"No Chance!" the voice said and Mike repeated it, even if he doubted the statement a tad. Becky was told it was time for her to go to bed and she did without argument, walking over and giving Mike a hug and kiss before departing. "You're honoured!" Kate said to Mike. "It's almost impossible to get her to give anyone a kiss normally let alone a hug as well!"

The party had become obsessed with the news of the proposed race and groups of people aired their views, some thought it was a foregone conclusion, others thought that this time The Rocket would be put out. Kate picked up her drink and wandered into the now empty conservatory with Mike following. "Would you care to show me around the garden? It's beginning to give me a headache listening to your friends debate my horse!" Kate smiled one of her devastating smiles. "In the dark?" she said.

"It's only dark if you want it to be." Mike replied and took Kate's hand and led her into the garden. There was no objection when Mike took her hand and so he slipped an arm around her waist as they strolled through the coloured lights towards the summer house that stood at the bottom of the lawn partially screened by an ornate hedge. "I love it here." Kate sighed. "I quite often come here when I'm on my own. You can sunbathe without fear of anyone interrupting you. I love the feel of the warm sun on my skin. It's soothing I always think." Mike still had his arm around Kate's waist and on impulse he pulled her close so that her face was directly in front of his. They stared at each other for a moment Mike noticing how Kate's lips opened slightly and how her breathing became deeper. He bent his face towards her touching her lips with his, her tongue darted out searching his mouth then linking their tongues together. Passion welled up in Mike and he slipped his hand beneath Kate's summer dress feeling the light silk as it slid across his arm her legs parted slightly as his hand found its way between her long slender legs cupping her, gently massaging the warmth that lay beneath the small white G string. He pulled the material to one side feeling the soft flesh of Kate's shaven Venus mound, his fingers searched further pushing her legs further apart sliding his hand slowly between her lips and into her wetness. Kate moaned as his fingers played with her, her own hand pulling ardently at his flies, urgently pulling them down. Mikes erection sprang free and Kate's hand grasp his penis slowly working it up and down. Mike gently laid her on the ground pulling her dress over her head to reveal her firm round breasts and hard dark nipples, he looked down at her lying naked but for the white G string, she writhed slowly and sensuously as her nearly naked bottom touched the dewy grass her slender body tanned from the sun. He let his trousers fall to the floor reached down slowly, pulling the G string down Kate's legs, admiring her clean-shaven body as he did. Kate reached up to him and he went to her willingly as she spread her legs allowing him entry. She groaned as he thrust his hard penis deep between her legs, grinding her pelvis against him, she felt the head of his penis swell and moaned as it pulsed inside her filling her with warm sticky fluid, she came. They laid in each other's arms, Mike stroking her nipples fascinated at the beauty of her, he rolled to one side kissing and licking her nipples, she sighed, her head sliding down to his lap, she gripped his penis lifting it so that it was directly in front of her. She slid her lips over the head slowly moving her head up and down its shaft, her tongue flicking from side to side as she crew her head upwards. Mike laid back as his penis became fully hard again. Kate swung her leg over the top of him without inhibition and Mike thought how incredibly beautiful she was, reaching down she grabbed his manhood and slid it between her legs forcing it into her body as deep as it could go. They both came again. They made love for over an hour, then Kate, realising that they would be missed, pulled on her dress and told Mike to wait for five minutes then come into the house. Mike was a bit confused, happy but confused, only a few seconds ago she had been in his arms, now she almost pretended that they had literally gone for a walk around the garden. He did as he was bid. No one had noticed their absence, they were all too busy talking about the race. Mike was the last to leave the party, as he reached the front door he made to put his arm around Kate but she pulled back. "I'm sorry Mike that should never have happened. Please don't say anything to anyone." She looked vulnerable and panicked. "I'd had too much to drink and was angry with Geoff for not being here. It should never have happened." She said again. "You're a lovely guy and very sweet and I'm a married woman. I love my husband. I feel terrible." And she burst into tears. Mike didn't try to console her. He was afraid she would think he was trying to take advantage, instead he spoke to her softly. "Kate, I promise you I will never tell anyone. I think you are the most beautiful creature I have ever seen and I've fallen for you big time and I would never do anything to hurt you. I wouldn't want to lose your friendship even though I want more than that. I'll never tell a soul you have my word." And with that he left walking to the end of the drive before phoning the taxi to pick him up.

Mike slept in his favourite armchair that night waking up stiff and cramped before the sun rose.

Seamus was at the door at first light closely followed by John. "Jesus, Mother Mary." Seamus exclaimed. "I thought it was one of your wind ups when John phoned me, you're mad so you are? I know the horse is brilliant but don't you remember what a sod to train he was before? Have you seen the paper?" Seamus pushed the paper towards Mike. The headline read COME ON BABY MY FIRE IS LIT! *By five o'clock tonight we predict the biggest influx to the bookmakers in history. Why? Because they've fired up The Rocket.* The story went on to say how Mike Willett had announced at the party of Kate and Geoff Stokes that The Rocket would take on all comers in the biggest race of all time, forget Pharlap, forget Sea Biscuit this race would over shadow the announcement of World War Three! John chipped in. "Mike, I know we said we would follow your decisions where the horses were concerned but this should have been discussed with us first. Can we get out of it?" John asked in false hope.

"No, and even if we could, I wouldn't want to. Think about it, we know Rocket's brilliant, awkward but brilliant, and you were the excited one." He looked at John. "It was you who insisted we run him over fences as well…. Now that was madness I thought but in fairness I was proved wrong…. Just think if Rocket wins how much would he be then to cover a mare, a million? Two million? Christ they'd be trying to give you oil wells to get a nomination to him. Now just think what we could do with that? There are lots of good causes out there and let's be honest, we'd have a job to spend what we've got already. So you see, there's no real downside, except maybe my pride. Even if we lose, and I don't think we will, we've plenty enough ourselves and there will still be plenty of people who would want to use Rocket! Come on guys one for all and all for one?" Seamus and John looked at each other saying together. "Ahh what the hell." Each man placed their hand on the others and Rocket was set to race.

Later that morning Mike received a call from a very pompous and irate member of the hierarchy of the Jockey Club. He was informed that he must stop this talk of racing all comers there had been no such race planned on any of the racing calendars, no permissions granted, no request made, they had had hundreds of calls from trainers all over the world wanting to enter their horses in the race, it had to be stopped. Mikes reply was simple he calmly informed the official that if it was so imperative to stop the race then the Jockey Club had better do it …. and say why. The Jockey Club was he informed the speechless official a dinosaur and if they did stop the race it could possibly cause their extinction, on the other hand if they threw their weight behind it, it might just be the first step in their evolution! The official hung up only to ring back half an hour later to inform Mike that after careful consideration the relevant committee had decided that it would for the good of racing champion the race. How very kind Mike thought but didn't say suddenly why they are championing the race and he was sure that somehow it would be recorded as their idea. He thanked them for their support and with a wry smile hung the phone up. He wandered over to the window that overlooked the yard and looked out, he had forgotten just how many reporters there were in the world.... and they all appeared to be at the gates of his yard. He looked out the card that the editor of *The Times* had given him and dialled. "I have some breaking news for you but if you want it and the rest of the exclusives I want you to put up another million to the charity of Becky Stokes' choice and I want it on the front page, that is what you are doing. You're more than welcome to take the credit for the donation, but I want that young lady to be given credit to... okay fine... I have your word?... good. The idea for the race was thought up by seven-year-old Becky Stokes after watching the film Sea Biscuit. She owns a racehorse herself called Sunrise, which she has to run when it is old enough under her mother's name because of her tender age. She is a racing enthusiast even at her age and because of this worked out that a race of this calibre would be of huge benefit to racing itself. You can then say how you are going to donate a million pounds to the charity or charities of Becky's choice as a thank you to such a young visionary. Word it however you like but I do want it said that Becky thought this up, not anyone else. Oh and I would ring Major Alfred Mapperton at the Jockey club as I believe he may have some news for you as well." Mike was quite pleased with himself, just for this one time he had got the better of them. Whatever claims the pink gin brigade as Mike so fondly called the Jockey Club made at least the right person would get credit on tomorrows front page of *The Times*. He also knew they would soon get the 'donation' back through advertising and by selling the rights to overseas papers. Unfortunately, he hadn't considered the papers themselves and when the story broke Kate's house became besieged with journalists. Becky thought it was great but her mother made it quite clear to Mike that he was not only totally stupid, thoughtless for others privacy, but downright incorrigible.

Mike went out and informed the pack of news hounds who

blocked not only the road but the lane as well, that they would have to liaise with *The Times* as they had exclusivity.

Mike, John and Seamus were inundated with letters, phone calls, telegrams in fact about the only thing they didn't receive was a carrier pigeon! Sitting down to discuss the why's and wherefore's Mike suggested that although the major tracks had approached both them and the Jockey Club they should try to do something for their local tracks. The Jockey Club had said they favoured holding the race at Newmarket or Epsom and as the three agreed it would have to be one of the bigger racecourses to accommodate the expected crowds they also agreed that they should at least take Rocket to their local course as a P.R exercise. The discussion went on as to exactly what Rocket should do on his appearances and for a work regime the race did not even have a venue yet but there were already provisional entries from America, Japan, Australia, Hong Kong, France, Germany, Ireland and the U.K. it seemed that no one wanted to miss out on the opportunity to compete against The Rocket. Rockets first run albeit a disaster had been at Salisbury and so it was decided that he would have his first public appearance there followed by Wincanton then Taunton. The race itself the three agreed should be held at Newbury. Mike phoned the Jockey Club to discuss it with them. Although they had favoured Newmarket, it being the home of racing, they eventually after a long debate agreed to Newbury, a date to be fixed in the next two weeks, but as Mike stressed it was not to be for at least eight weeks to give him time to prepare Rocket. With that agreed and an army of personnel brought in to deal with the day to day running of the proposal Mike relaxed and started to consider what he should do work wise with Rocket. There was no voice in his head as he pulled Rocket out of his box and legged Seamus into the saddle. He was sure Rocket grinned at him, sure they still had that contact but there was only silence. Rocket was taken out on the gallops where he bolted for a furlong casually slowed down put his head to the floor and chewed contentedly on a dandelion! Mike put his head in his hands, "Not now Rocket please not now." There was no reply and Rocket nonchalantly carried on eating his dandelion.

The feeling of elation that had precluded the first mornings work with Rocket dwindled rapidly and Mike thought back to the time when John had first come to him, sure that Rocket would be a great horse. Well he was, of that there was no doubt but he was older now and Mike believed he would need every ounce of stamina and speed to compete with the best younger horses in the world that were queuing up to take a swing at him. Rocket stood in his stable chewing a mouthful of hay. Mike looked first at him and then at Storm. "Well somebody say something!" He said. Silence reigned!

It was a long night for Mike he had read the papers, which seemed to contain page after page of permutations of the forthcoming race. One small photograph at the corner of one story caught his eye and he read the paragraph that adjoined it. Ex-girlfriend of Mike Willett today announced her engagement to wealthy business man Brian Penny. When asked if a date had been set for the wedding she said they were looking to have a long engagement and no wedding plans would be made in the near future, she was far too busy with her own successful partnership with millionaire John Cullen's wife. Asked if she thought The Rocket would win she replied that with the best trainer in the world she would certainly hope so! Mike laughed it was typical of Ann to defend and support him even though they were not together. He felt happy for Ann, pleased that she had found someone, he hoped that she would be happy herself.

Mike eased himself from his chair and walked to the kitchen opening a cupboard taking out a bottle of Jamesons and a tumbler. He wandered aimlessly back into the lounge looked at the answer machine, no flashing light, no message from Kate. He poured himself a drink sipped the amber liquid and thought of Kate's caress and as he did he realised how futile the thought was. He thought of Rocket and what to do, had he been mad, were the voices a figment of his imagination? He found himself slipping into a deep depression which he fuelled with the whisky. He slept dreaming of Kate riding toward him her blond hair flowing behind her, her body naked, beckoning him and he could not resist. In the distance he saw a small figure grasping the hand of someone larger. Both were waving and saying something he could not quite make out, he reached out as Kate came near, he heard her laugh as she circled Rocket around him then galloped of in the direction she had come. He called after her but her back grew further away, a tear escaped his eye running slowly down his cheek and he awoke! He automatically ran his hand across his eyes to rub the sleep away and found his finger were damp. "I can cope with Rocket but I'm not so sure I know how to cope with these feelings for Kate." He said out loud and moved off into the kitchen.

John arrived at the yard around ten that morning. "Well how did our fellow work?" He asked patting Rocket on the neck. "Do you really want to know?" Seamus and Mike said at the same time.

"Come on don't take the mick! This is far too important for all of us. What was he like!?"

Seamus turned to Mike. "You or me?"

"Your the assistant trainer and a third shareholder in Rocket… it's time you earned your keep!" Mike said smiling despite the severity of the answer. "I guess as we're the three musketeers we should be able to deal with a small stumbling block…. and before either of you say a word I know whose idea it was, stupidity was always somewhere in my signature!"

Seamus proceeded to give a resume of Rockets sojourn on the gallops. Although John was still a member of the, I love Rocket fan club, he went pale. "Oh fuck! You reckon your names stupidity. I hate to think what mine must be! Mike could we go into the house, I could do with a drink!" Mike looked at Rocket, heard nothing, saw nothing. The three musketeers walked dejectedly to the kitchen of Mike's house each settling at the table as Mike poured three generous measures of Jamesons. There was a moments silence then Mike spoke. "All right John, what have you done?…It can't be that bad…. Surely?"

"Oh, but it can! I don't know how I could be so fucking stupid. I laughed when Alice's father got into trouble through greed and I've done exactly the same!"

"It might help if we knew what you were talking about," Seamus interrupted.

"I think I can make an educated guess!" Mike stated

"And you'd probably be fairly close to the truth. I've taken some serious money on Rocket not being beat!...Not for my own gain as it happens though it looks that way. I didn't have the slightest doubt that Rocket would go to work properly again, never considered he'd go back to his old self and I thought well I could safely take any bets that contradicted my belief in the old fellow. The money I'd intended to give to charity. Christ, I stood to pick up fifty million if Rocket won, just think what good that could be used for, the trouble is I stand to lose four times that if he doesn't win. I saw what Alice and Ann had done with that complex of theirs and thought it was time I did something more for those less fortunate than me. If Rocket loses I'll be skint and I'll have to take Alice with me. Shit what a fool I am!"

Mike looked over at Seamus. "Are we the three musketeers or what ?"

"To be sure we are that. It's only zeros. I've not got as many by far as you but...!"

Seamus replied slamming his hand hard into the centre of the table looking first to Mike then to John. Mike reached over and placed his hand on top of Seamus, both men looked at John and with a weak smile he placed his hand on top of the pile.

"Like I said the three musketeers, all for one and one for all. John goes for broke we all chip in to help even if it takes us all down."

"I'm for that." Seamus said holding his glass in the air before taking a long swig.

John broke down, disbelieving of the bond he had with these two men. "Shit John, I was broke when you first came to me and you saved my ass. Seamus was broke when he came to me and I saved his ass. Then Seamus came along and saved both our asses. Being broke ain't as good as being wealthy but it ain't that bad. Anyway, I hear you're a pretty good painter, I'm not a bad trainer and Seamus well he's just Irish!" They all three laughed at this each happy that their friendship was far more than mere money.

Adversity is a great test of character, it seemed to Mike that here he was living almost a dream, millions in the bank, and along comes adversity and does her level best to kick the legs from right under you. He did what he had always done before he let her drag him down to Spain and the bottle he went to his horses. She wouldn't get him this time! Rocket stood looking over his stable door. He reached out his hand and stroked the soft velvety muzzle and was rewarded with a whicker, but no words. Perhaps he had imagined it all. "You son." He said. "You are without doubt the best and most cantankerous bugger I've ever met. Christ knows why I thought I could talk to you, maybe it was the whiskey? But I'll tell you this win or lose we'll still love you and I swear even if this stupid race does break me I'll get you Storm Silvy and JC away so they don't get you. I know you're back to being an old sod but if you this one more time just do your best I'll never ask for more and like I say we think you're the greatest whatever the result." Mike stroked Rockets nose bent forward and kissed the soft muzzle.

"Night old son!" and he left the silent stable.

CHAPTER TEN

Kate pulled into the stud drive just as Mike walked across the yard leading Sunrise towards the lunging pit. She looked skitty and worried as she looked round at the strange thing that had been placed on her back. There was froth from her mouth where she was chewing frantically at the metal bit that had been put between her teeth. Becky jumped from the car and ran towards them before her mother could bring the car to a full stop. Mike held up his hand. "Whoa young lady. Rule one, we never run in a yard when there are horses about. Rule two, you stand right where you are, this little filly is feeling a bit worried this morning and she' a bit skittish. Just you go quietly and stand over there you can watch and see how she does but I don't want to hear a peep out of you. Okay?" Becky nodded passively and Mike noticed that Kate had watched from far enough away so as not to be brought in to the conversation, though she did smile and raise her hand.

Mike took the filly into the lunge pit and there were suddenly several members of staff eagerly watching. "You watch this." Anita said proudly to the others, which by now included Kate. "I love to see him break a horse in ready to be backed. It's fantastic, he's a bit tough on them sometimes but before he finishes they'll love him and follow him anywhere!" she said to Nicky, proud of her knowledge, "You'll notice that he doesn't use a round pen and once he's done five or ten minutes with her he'll take her off the lunge and free school her." Becky was in raptures here she was watching the bestest trainer in the whole world do things with her horse and all these people saying how wonderful he was and to top it all she was learning loads about horses. She sat her tiny bottom on the floor and avidly watched everything.

Mike started by walking over to where the filly stood wide eyed, normally this would not have bothered her but today this man she had trusted had put strange things on her and there was no way she was going to go near him now. She tried to pull away but Mike held her on the lunge line talking in soft tones all the time. "You can't get away from me little one why I've had horses try twice the size of you and they couldn't so I'm sure you can't!" He moved to within touching distance of the wide-eyed filly slowly reaching out his hand and caressing her nose and she began to relax, the wildness leaving her eyes. "Okay sweetheart let's go to work shall we. Now if you're good to me I'll be good to you if you're bad it'll only go hard for you." And with that he stepped back pushing the filly away as he did. The filly having stood still had forgotten the saddle on her back as she moved she felt the girth under her belly tighten and she jumped forward narrowly missing Mike. Becky shot up from her sitting position with a gasp as the filly now went into a bucking fit. Mike was at home laughing as he gently flicked the end of the lunge whip across the filly's back to encourage her to buck. "That's my girl you chuck in as many of those in as you like." Mike laughed, "You'll get tired before I do, and when you do we'll sort you out so you know what to do." The filly squealed and bucked for a full five minutes before realising the thing on her back wasn't going anywhere and she was stuck with it, she slowed to a trot, puffing loudly, the sweat dripping from her belly. "That's a good girl now trot on nicely." After Mike had been in the lunge pit for about half an hour the filly was following him around like a puppy, listening to every word Mike spoke. "Stand!" and she stood. "Walk!" and she walked. He gently caressed the filly as he did so. "Go tell that miserable little bugger we're ready for him Anita." Mike shouted and a smiling Seamus came 'round the corner. "I'm only miserable because I know I've got to get on a horse that's been started off by an amateur." He retorted and walked casually into the school pulling his skull cap on as he did.

"What do you think Mike?"

"She'll chuck a couple in but they shouldn't be too bad she's totally bucked." He said quietly and they burst out laughing.

"Dopey bloody Englishman." Seamus said as Mike legged him up onto the filly's back. The filly stood stock still for a minute. Then Seamus turned to Mike with a huge grin. "Let's light the touch paper, shall we?" And he dug his heels into the filly's ribs. The effect was electric the filly leapt forward feeling the weight of Seamus move on her back she went into another bucking fit. Kate and Becky looked on with horror as the girls watching and Mike shouted with amusement for Seamus to 'ride him cowboy'. Eventually the filly tired of trying to remove the irritating little human from her back and began to settle, it was not long before Seamus had her turning circles, stopping when asked and trotting. "She'll be ready to go on with now Mike." Seamus remarked as he gently slipped from the saddle. "Couple of buck's my ass!" Seamus said winking, "I think she might make a decent thing you know Mike," and turning towards where Becky now stood gripping the side of the pen breathlessly he shouted, "you've got yourself a good one here young lady you look after her mind!"

"I will!" Becky beamed hugging everybody in sight.

Sunrise proved a willing student and with Becky on her school holidays Kate was badgered into bringing her virtually every day. Geoff even came with them on occasion and though Mike tried hard to dislike the guy he couldn't and his guilt at what had happened between him and Kate deepened, even more so as every time he looked at her he visualized her beautiful naked body straddled across his. Kate was pleasant enough to him but remained at arm's length avoiding any opportunity for Mike to talk to her on his own.

Rocket had become a nightmare. Because of the importance of the race, Mike Seamus and John had decided that they would work Rocket with his race jockey. This was when the nightmare began, they brought in William who knew the horse well, was in fact the only person that had ridden him on the track but he never got further than the start of the gallops before Rocket dropped him then either blasted up the gallops at blistering speed or simply chose to eat by the time they had tried another fifteen jockeys and there was still plenty in the queue waiting for a chance to prove that they were the one to ride the Rocket it was decided that Seamus would go back to making the attempt of getting Rocket to work. It was like watching Freddie Kruger turn into Cinderella. Rocket never dropped Seamus in fairness but then neither would he work. The most he was ever seen to do was a gentle walk up the gallops with an occasional stop to graze on a particularly succulent dandelion he had happened to spot. Different scenario same nightmare! Mike spent at least half an hour every evening with Rocket talking through life's problems the race, Kate, in fact everyone and everything and there was only silence in return. Mike came to the conclusion that the whole voices in the head thing had been nothing more than a form of temporary insanity. He began to see the rest of his life that had become so good oozing slowly down the proverbial drain.

Mike sat up for the umpteenth night thinking about Kate and pondering his problem with Rocket. At the moment the only person who could even sit on the horse was Seamus and that was at a walk. An idea began to form in his confused brain.

At eight thirty the following morning the police rang to say that the court case would begin in one week's time and Mike would of course have to be there. He wasn't looking forward to it, there was a lot of mud that would be thrown in his direction and there were still members of the gutter press that would love to catapult it at him. He knew it was going to be a rough ride. Thinking about the court case pushed all other thoughts aside and it wasn't until twelve thirty that he remembered his idea. Mike picked up the phone and dialled the Jockey Club. Major Alfred Mapperton was not a happy man, he had been enjoying a rather sumptuous lunch with his colleagues. "Outrageous, totally out of the question. Never in a million years!"

Mike stayed perfectly calm as the Major nearly swallowed the phone as he raved at Mike. He forgot one golden rule Mike in this case held the trump card. "Okay sir! Thank you for your time and I'm sorry to have interrupted your lunch." Mike was as close to being obsequious as he had ever been. "I'll get *The Times* to announce it in the morning."

"Announce what!" the Major blustered.

"That the race is off of course, we can't race without a jockey and Rocket won't race at all without this one. It's a shame really the Jockey Club took two steps into evolution and ten back, because of their own pomposity. I'm sure *The Times* will make an excellent headline from the idea!"

"That's blackmail Willett, you can't do that!" Mike pictured the Majors face at explosion point and smiled.

"I think you'll find I can sir. Not only can, but will. Anyway I've a busy schedule today so I must run."

"No, no wait Michael." What had happened to the Willett? Mike thought and grinned even more.

"Look I'm sure we can arrange it somehow. Totally irregular, totally but then I suppose one could say the race itself is totally irregular?" the Major started to unwind a bit realising that he had been played like a fish hooked landed and on the plate. "I have to tell you Michael." He said. "I always thought you a bit of a loose cannon and when the idea for this race came up I disagreed with it completely, but you have a point, we do need to progress, don't we, and I also know when I've been beaten," he managed a short chuckle, "well I know I'm bloody well beaten now. You'll get what you want and by the way I hope you're going to kick the ass of the competition, I must admit to looking forward to this race myself!?"

"I'll do my best sir and thank you!" Mike put the phone down well and truly satisfied with his work. The Jockey Club had taken their first evolutionary step.

Mike wandered out into the yard pleased with his efforts, he saw Seamus walking towards Rockets box and called after him. "Oy Clint Eastwood!" Seamus turned to Mike with a broad grin, knowing that every time a horse was broken the same banter would be forthcoming for a few days. "You must be Tonto then?" and both men chuckled.

"When you've done pop up the house for a minute will you please? I need you to go into town and I have something to discuss with you first." Seamus put a thumb up and Mike moved off round the yard looking into each box as he did ensuring that each horse was as it should be. Going back to the house he phoned John and told him his news. John was thrilled. After their previous evenings meet John felt much happier. Obviously still worried but relieved that the problems that beset him had not only been shared but divided in a friendship that millions could not break. Friendship of that ilk can feed most men fuelling them to achieve. John had spent most of his morning pouring over his accounts, although it was of little consolation he realised now that the panic of possibly losing such a great deal of money had been relieved sufficiently by his friends offer of help. Looking at his assets he realised that should the worst come to the worst and with Mike and Seamus help he could survive without losing the stud or asking Alice to touch her assets. He felt as though an elephant had been lifted from his shoulders and as he spoke to Mike it was noticeable. "Bloody Hell Mike what a good idea. At least we'll know that there'll be no skulduggery. How has he taken the news?... Oh, fantastic I'll come straight over I can't wait to see his face.... don't tell him until I get there... thanks." The phone call ended. Seamus came into the kitchen after organising the morning lots and John arrived five minutes later joining the two men at the table for the obligatory tea. Seamus spoke first. "Well now young Master Michael what would be so important that I'd be having to come up to the big house?" he said cheerily, pulling at his forelock with mock timidity. They all laughed at this.

"Well boy!" Mike said keeping up the banter. "I've important news, I've manage, brilliant chap that I am, to solve the problem of Rockets jockey!"

"Now that really would impress me." Seamus replied with gravity. "Who have you found that can sit the old bugger?"

"You!" was the short reply.

Kate had resisted the insistence of her daughter to go and see Sunrise, the day had dawned warm, the sun rising quickly spreading a warm cloak across the ground and she had decided to relax in the garden for the day. Geoff was wandering around the estate with his father and Becky had tagged along. Geoff's father insisting that his granddaughter be given the opportunity to see all that they had done including the placing of a small motorised boat on the lake which they were now sampling. Becky was delighted as they splashed each other over the side of the boat.

Kate led in her favourite spot by the summerhouse the sun warming her body. The summerhouse was totally secluded, even if a member of staff was doing something on the house they had no view of that part of the garden. There was no one around the house or garden today and Kate felt utterly at ease. She turned so that her front could absorb the sun's rays the tiny black bikini bottom she wore accentuating her shapely body, confident in the knowledge that there was no one around she slid the bottoms down her long slim legs so her whole body could benefit from the sun. She reached over to the small table that stood beside the sun lounger, taking the sun oil spray to liberally coat her slender frame. She rubbed the oil into her skin ensuring that the small white triangle where her bikini bottom had been was well coated. As her hand caressed the top of her thighs she thought of that night with Mike her hand straying between her legs, she could feel the wetness and her stomach began to tingle, then guilt kicked in and she cried. They were not the tears of true guilt, though there was guilt there, they were the tears at the loss of something found. Kate's feelings were in turmoil. Two people, two loves, one old, one new, both difficult, what was she to do. Kate stood up her lithe form catlike, she walked to the pool and dove in the cool clear blue water temporarily washing away all other thoughts.

Seamus sat with his mouth open unable to speak. "Christ." Mike threw across the table at John. "That's the first time I've seen an Irishman lost for words!"

"Fuck!" Seamus eventually managed. "Me with a licence again!" he jumped up and did an impromptu jig around the table as he squealed 'diddly diddly diddly dee' he sat back down breathlessly as the other two looked on with amusement.

"It looks as though your fitness level needs a bit of work the way your puffing. Christ looking at you now you'd be knackered before you reached the start!"

"You don't need to be worrying about that young Michael I'm plenty fit enough to ride ten races!" then more seriously. "You've set me a bit of a task though my friend. I think I'll be needing every bit of horsemanship you've got if we're to get Rocket to work! I'll need to ride in a couple if I can before the big one, just to get back into the swing of things like."

Over the next few days Rocket showed himself to be as cantankerous as ever refusing point blank to do anything other than walk even when they took Storm to the end of the gallop in the hope it might encourage him. Seamus was concerned, Mike didn't have a clue what to try next and John went back to being the chairman of The I love Rocket Fan Club, saying "He'll be all right Mike just you wait and see!" Though Mike wasn't quite so sure this time that John believed completely in what he was saying.

Monday came around all too quickly and Mike, Seamus and John sat on the uncomfortable plastic seat sweating in their suits as they awaited the usher to call them into the court room. It would be a simple case the investigating police officer had reassured them and shouldn't last more than a day. Malek was pleading not guilty but the evidence was so stacked against him that the judge would have no choice but to sentence him to the maximum term. The press had been stopped from entering the courthouse and awaited the carcass of Mike to appear in the car park so they could have the opportunity to pick his bones clean. Most of the journalists would report the case fairly and honestly but as always there were a couple that were looking to twist the whole thing on it is head for the chance of seeing Mike in a bad light. Mike thought even they would have a hard time turning this one around to lay any responsibility at his feet.

The Judge called in Mike to give evidence and as he stood looking directly at where Malek stood in the dock he felt sympathy. Malek looked as though he wasn't aware, Mike thought that his sanity must be in question but the judge, prosecutor and police obviously didn't because after exactly five hours and twenty-seven minutes Malek was sentenced to fifteen years in prison. Though Mike's sympathy for the man remained his relief that there was at last closure to this part of his life was tangible. Now all he had to worry about was Rocket.

CHAPTER ELEVEN

Mike picked up the phone to hear the voice of Major Alfred Mapperton. The change in his attitude towards Mike was reversed since their last discussion. It seemed as though the Major was relieved to be less formal and his air was that of a man far removed from the pomposity that he had first showed. "Michael?"

"Speaking."

"Jolly good my boy! Look we've managed to get a date for the race. It's quite exciting really isn't it!?" the Major continued no waiting for an answer. "We've had three hundred... three hundred entries mark you! Can you believe it!? Amazing! Anyway, we've whittled it down to thirty-five possibles, a list of which I shall fax to you this afternoon, as of course I shall to all entrants. We've initially set a safety factor of twenty-five so one or two will have to come out still...oh yes sorry the date for the race, so much to do to organise this you know, never expected quite the response we've had. I digress today is the, let me see the 3rd of July the race is set for the 14th of September. Are you happy with that?..... Good, good. I'll leave you in peace then. See you at the races old chap!" the major was gone. Mike thought it wouldn't have mattered if the race was next year at

Rockets present work rate he would never be ready. He walked out to watch Sunrise work and was pleased with what he saw. She wouldn't be the best he had ever seen but she worked well and showed spirit, Mike thought it would be lovely if she could win her maiden. He imagined how excited Becky would be but he knew just how hard it was to win first time out. Still she was nearly ready for a run so he would have to start looking through the Racing Calendar. He walked into the office calling Seamus to join him as he did. "What do you think about that little filly of our young Becky then?"

"She'd be fairly sharp but I would think she wouldn't quite be sharp enough for five. If you're asking me I think she should run over six and then if it's too quick for her step her up a furlong. Though I think she'll run well over six."

Mike replied. "Then that's what we'll do then. Let's have a look through the calendar, I think we should try to find a maiden that's not too hot." And Seamus agreed. They poured over the pages discounting some and marking others as possibles.

"This is the one!" Seamus declared. "Six-furlong maiden at Wolverhampton. She's a handy little thing so it might well suit her, entries close tomorrow."

"I'll phone Kate and see if they're happy with that." Mike said rather too quickly and Seamus smiled to himself. "Oh dear trouble brewing," he thought. "For sure it will end in tears one way or another!"

Kate voice sounded like silk to Mike as she answered the phone even if it was somewhat strained. The first few sentences were spoken with an awkwardness that bordered between the guilt of their passion towards each other and the desire to admit there were underlying feelings as yet unspoken. Mike spoke of the race that had been planned for Sunrise and Kate dropped her guard slightly, she began to speak animatedly about how excited Becky would be and at how much she was looking forward to it herself. She asked Mike what the normal dress code was for the races and Mike commented that if she wore a sack she would still be the most glamorous thing on the course. Kate responded, flirting a little bit Mike, each of them talking like school children that are trying to build up the courage to ask the other on a date, neither brave enough to take the one step that would finalise the question one way or another. Mike heard a small voice in the background though he couldn't make out what it said apart from his name.

"Can I speak to Mike mummy please?"

"How did you know it was Mike?"

"Easy!" Becky said smugly. "You go all googly and squishy when your talking to him…. And your eyes sparkle!" Kate was stunned her daughter was she decided far too astute for a child of her age.

Becky spoke to Mike and after she spent two or three minutes without pause enquiring after Sunrise she drew breath long enough for Mike to get a word in edgeways. "I've entered your horse in a race in a weeks' time, well six days to be precise." The miniature at the other end of the telephone went into raptures and Mike had to hold the phone away from his ear as she screamed more excited questions down the phone. After a few minutes Kate's voice came back on the line.

"Sorry about that but I have one very excited little girl and when she gets going it's like a tornado picking up speed. You never get a chance to speak until she runs out of puff. Do we have to do anything before the big day?"

"No, you've already signed all the necessary paperwork. So all you have to do is to turn up, looking very beautiful in your sack!" Kate laughed.

"You're a very cheeky man Mike Willett I just might wear a sack to spite you!"

"I don't think anything you could ever do could spite me." Kate's voice went quiet.

"Mike, I don't mind having a bit of harmless flirting with you but you must understand that's as far as it will ever go. The other night… well I think that's best forgotten… by both of us."

Mikes heart was springing around his chest like a frolicking lamb until the last words from Kate, now it plummeted through the floor to disappear. He knew though that Kate was speaking total sense, she was married he was an unknown quantity. She was level headed, he had a head like a butterfly, a force ten gale.

"Fair enough... but that doesn't mean to say I regret anything or will stop having feelings for you!"

"I know!" Kate's voice was wistful. "I can't say that I regret it either but ours can only be a friendship. I'm sure we'll cope hard as it will be, you see I have feelings for you too." Mike knew that he was straw clutching but he couldn't help hoping that those last few words were a ray of hope. He drew himself up and became more sensible.

"Yeah, I know, but I can't help it if I think you're beautiful. I'm sure as you say we'll cope. We are adults after all we have enough control to keep our hands to ourselves and just enjoy each other's company." Although Mike spoke the words with conviction deep down inside he wasn't at all convinced.

Kate dutifully drove Becky to the yard, Sunrise now being in training had become a boarder at School... Mikes school, she took the transition in her stride and went about her work with pleasing willingness. Becky watched her horse every day not daring to let her eyes stray in case she missed one stride. She helped Anita groom her and even Anita had to admit they had never had a horse that looked so pristine. Kate had brought Geoff with her and he shook Mike's hand warmly, Mike felt a pang of guilt as he did. When the filly had worked Mike invited them into the house to discuss the forthcoming race Becky having gone her usual route to groom her horse, Geoff went to help her after Becky had determinedly harangued her father to do so, Geoff saying he was happy to leave all the arrangements for Kate to sort out and that he would join them in a while. Kate walked with a skip in her step excited at the prospect of racing with Mike understanding at her excitement but amused, still he thought even after all these years I get that stomach churning buzz when race day comes close and I'm sure if I could remember I was the same for my first race, probably more so. As they reached the kitchen door Kate's hand accidentally brushed against Mike's leg and they both jumped as though they had received an electric shock. "Sorry." Kate was demure. Mike on the other hand was confident and as they entered the kitchen he replied. "That's okay you can touch my leg any time you like!" Kate laughed nervously but Mike noticed that her breathing had become a fraction quicker her eyes a more startling blue and as she now stood looking at her, her lips were moist and slightly parted. He knew he had promised, he knew he was wrong but the feeling he had for this sensuous, lithe young woman was almost over powering. He took a step towards Kate so that their bodies were only inches apart, Kate looked the picture of innocence her eyes modestly looking towards the floor. Mike cupped her face in his hand lifting her chin, each now feeling the warmth that was radiating from their bodies. Mike bent forward very gently kissing Kate's lips and they both exploded. Mike lifted Kate so that her bottom just rested on the worktop and urgently thrust his hand between her legs, pushing her hands with a giggle down the front of his jeans and grabbing his hard penis. "Hello!" they both leapt back from each other Kate, scratching her hand on Mike's waist button as they did. John wandered down the hall to the kitchen.

"Thank God he came through the front door." Mike thought. Kate had managed to arrange her short mini skirt, though her hair looked a little dishevelled. John looked at Mike then at Kate realising that something had been interrupted and looking for something to say. He noticed the small stream of blood on the back of Kate's hand, it was the ice breaker he was looking for. "You've cut your hard Kate." Kate flustered at the lack of control she and Mike had just shown and at nearly being caught in each other's arms gave a stuttering excuse. "Can you believe it! I was helping Mike make the coffee and there must have been a chip on the mug and it scratched me!" Mike stepped forward with authority. "That's what you get for buying cheap mugs!" he picked up the nearest mug and threw it a bit too ceremoniously into the kitchen bin. John watched him do it, it was no cheap mug, it was the best Royal Doulton one could buy. Kate went to the bathroom with the plaster Mike gave her and returned a few seconds later, her hair again immaculate, her deportment now back to normal. Geoff and Becky arrived and Mike, John noticed, shaking, made drinks for everyone. "What's this horse of Beck's going to do then? Should I put the family silver on her?" Geoff asked with levity.

Mike laughed. "I wouldn't do that, you never know what they're going to do first time out! I think she'll be worth a couple of quid each way, but don't go too mad on her and as for you young lady." He looked at Becky. "Don't go raising your hopes too far, I'm sure she'll run her heart out for you but if she finds it all a bit too much don't be disappointed. She's got a bit of company to travel with as Seamus has entered another in the race before Sunrise."

"Even if Sunrise finishes last I shall be very proud of her." A very serious seven-year-old declared. "I know she'll do her best!"

It was a happy entourage that filed from the kitchen to wave their farewells though John couldn't help but notice that the kissed cheek from Mike to Kate cause a pink flush to creep up the face of Kate.

Nick had asked if he could bring his wife over to see the horses. "My missus ain't never seen a race horse close up like, an' I bin tellin' 'er all about the little fella like. She's says to me, 'she wonders who I finks more of 'er or the little fella, did make me laugh she did, she knows I loves 'er to bits!" Mike was happy to have Nick's wife over. He had more than proved himself to be worth Mike's faith in him. Steven had stayed with Alice and Ann's business, which Mike was happy with. Steven's interest laid more with the cars than horses and he did well since operating the repair side of the car business. With Mike's sudden departure and Steven's absence the everyday maintenance of the yard and surrounding fields had been partially neglected. Nick had done a fantastic job, working hard to make sure there was never a door that wanted painting, a fence that wasn't perfect, a trough that leaked and it was a brave weed that popped its head through to glory in the sun!

Mike's house was reasonably tidy but never quite reached the standard that women seem to be able to achieve no matter how hard he tried. There always seemed to be something that needed tidying, somewhere that the hoover hadn't mysteriously reached, just little things. Mike thought how many times he had heard a man say there was nothing to it, housework was a doddle, now as he sweated with the hoover he realised just how difficult a housewife's job is. When Nick arrived with his wife and she presented him with the most delicious chocolate cake he thought he might just have found the answer. Mike found her a delight, she was bossy in that motherly sort of way and when Mike went to put the kettle on she immediately ordered him to sit down as she would do it and he did much to his surprise without question. "You men are no good around the kitchen. Never was, why my Nick couldn't boil an egg 'e couldn't, useless in the 'ouse 'e is. Big lummox." She walked over and patted Nick warmly on the face and Nick grinned like a schoolboy given his first ice cream. "I fink what you done 'as bin the best fing that ever 'appened to us an' I'd like to say fank you, 'specially when you fink 'ow you met the big fool!" She continued to Mike. Nick looked embarrassed, Mike modestly shrugged her thank off.

They sat together at the table with Nicks wife Violet, Vi for short, force feeding Mike her chocolate cake, Mike thought he could get used to this if he could manage to control the inevitable weight he would put on with cake this delicious. Mike impetuosity kicked in again and he made a spur of the moment decision. "Do you work at all Vi." Vi answered that she 'charred' for a woman about fifteen minutes bus ride away from their house but only for an hour, which didn't really make sense because she paid half her wages in bus fares. Mike took the bull by the horns. "I don't know if you'd be interested but I need a housekeeper and I have an empty cottage at the bottom of the yard, it would need decorating mind you, but it would go with the job. I'll pay you a small wage and you can have the cottage rent free for as long as you like. If you wanted to you could rent your house out and earn a bit extra through that."

"What be a proper 'ousekeeper in this posh place?"

"I'm not so sure about the posh but yes a proper housekeeper. You'd be responsible for the cooking, cleaning, making sure the window cleaner did a good job and was paid on time, in fact you'd be responsible for the complete upkeep of the place. Nick has done a good job around the place so you can always ask his advice if you think there's something that needs doing. You would only need come to me if it started look too expensive!" You couldn't have made Vi happier if you'd have given her the winning lottery ticket. She accepted the proposition with only a small hesitation, a look at Nick who was beaming from ear to ear.

"You're in for a right treat, she'll look after you better than your ole mum!" Nicks comment heralded their exit and Mike sat wondering if he could manage just one more slither of the chocolate cake.

John tapped the kitchen door and wandered in. "They look like the proverbial cats that got the cream?" it was framed as a question rather than a statement. Mike explained what he had done and John smiled at him. "I didn't like to say old man but it is about time the old homestead does have a bit of a lack lustre look about these days!"

"Bollocks!" and they both smiled.

"Mike can I talk to you about something personal."

"Of course you can, you know I'll always try to help."

"No this isn't about me… It's about you." Mike looked surprised but nodded in agreement.

"Now don't go getting the ass ache and saying it's your life and all that shit! Seamus and I are worried about you. It would be pretty obvious to a blind man that there's something happening, and I mean that in the emotional sense between you and Kate." John saw Mike's shoulders square. "Now hold on

Mike you said you would listen without getting the hump! I'm only here saying it because the three of us are friends and we're concerned.... For you, no one else. Please Mike she's married, I presume happily, it looks like it from where I'm standing, there is electric between you that's patently obvious but think about what's happening if you fall for this woman it can only end in tears and I think they may well be yours!"

Mike seemed deflated. "I know you're right that's the stupid thing John but I can't help it I've already fallen for her and you know the crazy thing? I know that what you say is perfectly true but I've never felt like this for anyone, not Ann, anyone and to be frank I don't know what the Hell to do!"

John told Mike he should try to avoid contact with Kate in the hope the fascination would wear off. Mike knew it was no fascination and would be far easier said than done. John left Mike to his own devises and made his way home to spend some time with Alice and little Mike. He had been gone only five minutes when the phone rang. It was Kate. "Mike its Kate would you be a sweetheart and see if I left my ring in your bathroom?" Mike hurried to the bathroom.... "That's okay I don't expect you to do that, look I supposed to be going to see a friend tonight for a drink. I virtually pass your place so if it's okay with you I'll pop in and pick it up?"

"No problem!" the pair both sounded very casual but Mike's stomach was doing somersaults. He put the phone down and ran like his life depended on it to the shower. Throwing his clothes in a heap he washed his hair and showered quickly, grabbing the discarded clothes and throwing them in an already overflowing laundry basket. He took deep breaths and tried to calm his stomach walking back to the kitchen he poured himself a Jamesons, went through to the lounge and sat listening to the stereo. He must have sat for an hour before the knock on the door came and when he opened it he thought how breathtakingly beautiful she was. He invited her in and she walked through to the kitchen and accepted the offer of a glass of wine. She wore a light summer dress, Mike could see she wore no bra as her nipples pressed proudly against the material. He was thinking of what John had said earlier and knew the moment he thought it that the words had fallen on stony ground. He moved closer to Kate and she turned towards him her lips slightly parted and moist. Mike took the glass from her hand placing it on the table and she made no effort to resist, he cupped her face in both her hands leaning down to kiss her eyes, she sighed lifting her face to his, opening her mouth and kissing him passionately. Mike lifted her onto the worktop sliding her dress above her waist as he did, he stood back admiring her, she was completely naked under the dress. Her head tossed back in abandon she showed no inhibitions, as Mike never taking his eyes off her tore the clothes from his body. They made love with total lack of control, each exploring the others body, savouring the taste and feel of each other's bodies as they pleasured each other.

Their love making lasted until one o'clock in the morning and as both lay completely spent, neither then daring to look at each other for what had just passed, Kate rose but this time with a coyness that spoke volumes, her embarrassment at what had happened between them obvious. Mike spoke in an attempt to ease the situation and Kate burst into tears, sobbing into her hands.

"What have we done?" she asked, still not daring to look at Mike. Mike rose and there was an awkward silence as he searched to find his jeans before answering. He put an arm around Kate's shoulders in an effort to console her but she pulled away quickly looking to find her own clothes.

"I'm sorry," Mike said inadequately. "This is all my fault. I should never have…."

"Oh God …it was both of us…. I can't believe I've been so stupid… I love Geoff and I can't believe I've put my marriage in jeopardy." Mike looked into Kate's eyes as she spoke and saw the pain and indecision that led deep in those beautiful and tearful blue orbs. Sorrow for the pain Kate was feeling welled up inside him like a black cloud rising from his stomach to his chest. How could he hurt this precious thing, he thought, how could he not touch her she was so beautiful. He had never felt like this it was like being pulled between two horses at any moment they would tear him down the middle and he would be ripped apart. He had to forget himself and concern himself for the feelings of Kate. "Let's put it down to the wine!" Mike said almost choking on the words knowing as he spoke them it was the one excuse he would never accept himself. "Perhaps we both needed to feel there was someone else in our lives that cared on whatever level, sometimes we need to know that other people still find us attractive, sort of an ego boost I suppose." Mike knew the words were coming out wrong, knew he really wanted to say he had fallen in love with Kate, knew it sounded as though it had just been sex and nothing more but knew from the look on Kate's face that the situation was giving her so much trauma and he didn't have a clue how to ease her pain. Kate had pulled her dress back on and now clothed pulled herself up and became almost business-like. The words came out sharp and painful to Mike. "Well I'm very pleased I have notched your ego back up! You must think I'm so bloody stupid.... And I must be to have come here. Please don't call me again unless it's to do with Sunrise and if you dare say anything about what's happened between us you'll regret it." There was a coldness in Kate's eyes that Mike hadn't seen before, a hardness that did not go with this beautiful creature at all but it was there nonetheless.

"Kate I'm sorry, look, that came out all wrong, I would never do anything to purposefully hurt you and you weren't an ego boost. You're something special." The words were still coming out wrong.

"Special! I'm so glad I'm special!" Kate spat the words at Mike. "You're just a typical man Mike Willett, get what you all want and that's it!"

"No, I'm not." Mike started, "I never have been and never will be. I don't know why this has gone so wrong... I'm in love with you!" the words were lost to Kate's back as she stormed out of the house. "Shit!…. fucked that right up Rocket!" Mike said automatically but there was no voice in his head to reply. Mike sat in his chair, glass of amber liquid emptying and refilling until he fell into a restless sleep dreaming of Kate, Becky, and what seemed an impossibility. He was woken by a gentle shaking and opened bleary eyes to see Vi standing before him. "Right young man," she said as a mother speaks to a child, "by the look of you and this place you 'ad a war 'ere last night. Now you go and get yourself in the shower and freshen up an' I'll make breakfast, then I'll tidy up my kitchen, there's stuff knocked on the floor an' all. Come on off you go!" she stood with her hands on her hips determination on her face and Mike obediently did as he was told rising and unsteadily making his way to the shower with Vi tutting and puffing as she made her way towards the kitchen.

Mike stood in front of the bathroom mirror talking away to himself. He could feel himself slipping into a deep depression and did not know what to do. He didn't want to allow himself to fall back to the situation that had spurred his Spanish moment neither did he at that precise moment feel like throwing himself at life. He laughed as a memory flooded back to him, he remembered John comparing Rocket to Jimi Hendrix. What was it he had said… "Don't look so concerned Mike! The horse will be all right, he's just a bit temperamental. All stars are, look at all the greats, they all had foibles. Look at Jimi Hendrix…brilliant guitarist but a complete nutcase in life!" Maybe this was the foible he had to bear for being what everyone now classed as a great horseman. To Mike it was just natural, nothing less than common sense. "Oh well." He thought. "Perhaps I should take up the guitar, learning to play that would sure as hell be less painful than trying to get to know Kate, I might even learn to play the right note. Feeling dejected still but managing to smile at his situation he made his way to the biggest plate of bacon and eggs he had ever seen. "I want no 'scuses 'bout not bein' 'ungry. You makes sure you cleans that plate 'fore you leave this table mind!" Vi ordered and Mike quite enjoying the attention smiled again despite the black cloud that determinedly clung to his chest.

Mike did not see Kate or Becky for two days, the race for Sunrise was only two days away and Mike his stomach doing cartwheels and hand shaking picked up the phone, he dialled Kate's number and as the phone at the other end rang he thought what a stupid fool he was standing at the end of the phone like a schoolboy ringing a girlfriend but this wasn't his girlfriend, she was to all intents and purposes not even his friend any more, his regret was tangible in his voice as it held that 'lost' quality. His heart jumped when he heard her voice answer the call. Mike tried to sound chirpy but it didn't really work. "Hi, it's me!" silence, "I've rung about Sunrise she's done a nice piece of work this morning and should go fairly well I hope. I've arranged for your owner's badges to be left at the owner's entrance. If you need any for your friends let me know and I'll arrange it."

The voice was formal without emotion. "Thank you we'll just need three badges for Becky myself and my husband." Mike was sure there was an inference on husband. "No doubt we'll see you at the races." Again with inference. "Geoff will meet up with you so that we can follow the correct protocol, I'm sure you've done a marvellous job on the horse," the softness came back into her voice. "I'm really looking forward to it…. It will be nice to see you… and everybody else… it's been strange not coming to the yard these past couple of days." Mike's heart missed a beat then rose so high in his chest he could have swallowed it straight back down again.

"Kate…. I've missed you guys too…. I know things sort of went wrong… I mean I'd love for things to be different… but." Kate interrupted him.

"It's okay I was awful to you the other night. Perhaps we can start again… but this time remain just friends?" Mike quickly agreed putting the phone down with far more flourish than he had picked it up. "You looks pleased wiv yourself." Vi said as she entered the hall, spray polish and duster in hand. "You go to the kitchen an' on the top is one of me chocolate cakes, an' if you don't fancy that there's a fruit cake in the tin on the side. Don't you go eatin' it all mind or you'll be sick!" Mike laughed.

"Vi you're like having my old mum back!"

Vi beamed. "Not so much of the old or you'll get this 'ere duster wrapped roun' your ear'ole!" Mike's smile grew.

CHAPTER TWELVE

Race day dawned and the yard became even more of a hive of activity. Seamus ran around shouting orders at everyone. It was always the same and everyone knew it. If it wasn't Mike it was Seamus, if it hadn't of been those two it would have been someone else. Race days were never any different no matter how many times they came. There is normally so much pride in not only the yard but more so the horses and no one who worked in racing and lasted wanted their horse to go without every single hair in place and every single piece of equipment in perfect order. Anita as always produced her horse immaculately and she proudly walked Sunrise out to the lorry. Mike walked over from where he was standing talking to Seamus. "Well done Anita, she looks a picture…. Here." He said putting fifty pounds into her hand stick that on each way, if we have a result you can treat the yard, if she doesn't you've lost nothing." Anita thanked him loading the horse and quickly informing every one of the bet before leaving for Wolverhampton. Mike knew that the local towns bookie would be swelled to bursting point by the time of the race, there would be no way the rest of the 'lads' would miss a chance to see one of the yards horses running and for the time of the race, especially the finish, each and every one of them would be on board riding the horse for all they were worth. He often chuckled to himself as he watched them viewing a race. Their concentration was total, oblivious to those around them except their companions. Each and every one of them would crouch as though in the saddle urging the horse forward and each and every one of them would be exhausted at the end of the race such was their love for the game. To an outsider it was hard to understand, racing is in your blood it courses through your veins like a drug, ties your stomach in knots, you learn to love it.

It was a three-and-a-half-hour drive to Wolverhampton, John did his usual thing and order a chauffeur driven car to take them. As they were driven along the two looked at *The Racing Post* looking to see what had been said about Sunrise. The comments were rather more than they both realised they would be, the comments referred the reader to a full-page article, including a photograph of a very haggard looking Mike stepping from a plane after his Spanish sojourn, they read. Sunrise out of an unraced but well-bred mare is the first horse to run from the stable under Mike Willett and not his assistant trainer since his unexplained disappearance after The Rocket made racing history. Whether Willett has retained his ability to get the best from a horse will be better left judged until after the race. Whilst Willett did make leading trainer when The Rocket was running this was only through the amazing ability of the horse (and the success from Silver Dollar which Willett was lucky enough to procure for his owner Mr. John Cullen which rumour has it he did by default). However, Willett's stable did not previously produce anything that would lead one to believe a top trainer was arriving. It will be interesting to see whether Willett is the trainer his main owner John Cullen says he is. The horse faces a stiff task here today against more experienced and better-bred horses though she is bound to be supported by the hardcore followers of The Rocket being from that stable but I do not believe this will be reflect in the price which should start out at around the twenty-five to one mark. A word to the wise and to

Mr. Willett, who I am sure will read this article. The Rocket is a great horse, I do not deny it, but from what my spies tell me he isn't working very well at all and he hasn't been given much time to prepare either, he's a year older and a year slower and to top it all he is up against the best and most of them younger horses in the world, all of them eager, no, hungry to take his crown. Now, who would you put your money on, top trainers with younger fitter horses or a two-bit trainer who had a bit of luck with two horses and doesn't even seem able to get the good horse he had fit? I know where my monies going, the mortgage for me, goes on All Aglow who has already been travelled from Australia, was unbeaten as a two-year-old in his own country, then came to Europe to beat all comers. I have watched him work and he is devastating. For the each way backers I would go on Orange County Blues because for my money, All Aglow will start odds on favourite and has to be the win bet, for the money he will take all the beating. This is not just the race of the century, it's the biggest thing to ever hit racing. For me the sad thing is that our representative is not only an unproven trainer but a horse that is unfit, unprepared and from what I am reliably informed, unwilling to race. If I were Mike Willett I think I would count my blessings for the luck I've had and leave the proper training to the big boys!

John was fuming and surprised all at once fuming at the article, surprised at the calmness with Mike read it. "They fucking well said the same sort of things about all the greats you know.... Take Jimi Hendrix..." John was stunned into silence as Mike burst out laughing, tears rolling down his cheeks as he gasped for breath. It was infectious and soon both of them falling about on the back seat in paroxysms of laughter. Mike because of his thoughts in front of the bathroom mirror and John without a clue why. When the laughter had died John still gasping for breath spoke with seriousness. "It looks as though he's got a lot to lose as well if he's putting the mortgage on the Australian horse. More fool him Rocket will come through you wait and see!" But although John was still a fully paid up member of the I Love Rocket Fan Club he didn't sound quite as convincing as he had prior to the Derby.

"Look John." Mike said with the same serious tone. "I know you think a lot of Rocket just as I do. I love the old bugger to bits, he's not just a racehorse to me but he's my friend, silly as it sounds and please don't take offence because it's present company excluded." Though John knew that Mike's best friend would never be human, and he understood and was in fact grateful for the close bond the two men had. "Rocket's my best friend. I tell him more than I would tell any man. He knows me better than any man or woman alive. He never judges me, never turns away from me, he listens. I know it sounds stupid but it will break my heart to see him fail and if he does well he'll still mean as much too me as he does now... and I'll be there for him, same as I am for you!" Mike felt emotion wash over him from somewhere deep inside, it was so strong that a tear escaped his eye though after the laughing fit it went un noticed on his tear stained cheeks. He called out in his head, "Rocket?" there was silence. "I must be bloody mad!" he said unintentionally out loud.

"You must be to support me after I've been so bloody stupid!" John said believing Mike meant in his standing by him. Mike was quick to reply.

"No, you daft sod, not mad for supporting you." John was his close friend and he didn't wish to jeopardize their friendship. It was far too important to him he recovered quickly. "Mad for not seeing the answer to your, our problem regards the bet you made!" John's face took on a quizzical expression. "How many bookmaker's shops do you own now." John answered seven. "Your business name is well respected and known in the industry now even if you're actual face isn't?" John answered. "You know it is and I've always been very careful about keeping my own name and face private from the business, as far as most people are concerned I'm just a very lucky horse owner."

"Okay does the guy you've taken the bet from know of your involvement with the bookmakers?" John answered in the negative. "Then we have to hedge our bets so to speak and this article," Mike threw the paper back on the seat of the car, "is just what we needed." John looked puzzled and Mike looked smug. "Give your shares in everything you have to Alice in theory, if you haven't had the sense to already. That way no one can come after it if this fails. I know it's naughty and you like to play it straight but it isn't anything that everybody else wouldn't do to protect their interests. Okay?" John nodded dumbly. "Right you do an interview with the paper making sure they are fully aware that not only do you own the bookies but that you believe the horse is unbeatable. Make sure they get a really good photo of your ugly mug! You shorten the odds so much on Rocket it will be almost impossible to bet him, open up the odds on All Aglow to 2-1 and Orange County Blues to 5-1, they are at best evens at the moment, and the money will flood in."

John spoke, "But how the hell is that going to help? I still need Rocket to win!"

"No, you're not thinking straight. None of us are, we became so concerned and tunnel visioned all we could see was a massive loss, not the case, a loss maybe but not as massive as we first thought, in fact we could come out okay and at worst with a loss that can be coped with. The guy who wrote this article will have a field day and that's just what we want. I can see the words being typed right now. He'll slate you for a fool, or he'll have to admit to being very wrong and if his column is anything to go by he's far too far up his own backside to even consider that! You've got fifty out to this other chap, if and I don't know why I still think that old sod can win this race," Mike felt his stomach churn and his eyes fill as he said it, "but if he doesn't you just might be able to pull in enough to stand the loss, you've taken four to one and you're giving two to one and thinking about it putting Rockets odds so short won't actually make him that hard to back, so you will bring in some of the big hitters on that and if he does win the payout won't be that great but the returns on the money from the others will. If the one of the others wins you should pull enough in to not only cover the bets but also to throw a bit at your problem. I don't know, it's a bit of a long shot but it might just work…. And if Rock's pulls this one off charity will be jumping sky high because there will be more money than you can shake a stick at! Oh and I think if we do manage to come out of this evens we should donate something decent to the rehabilitation of racehorses and the injured jockeys fund."

"Mike." John said uncertainly if this comes off and I or we come out with only a small loss I'll buy another yard for injured horses and not only will I staff it with lads and jockeys who have been injured or are down on their luck I'll make them think they've died and gone to heaven. I'll even buy some ambulances for the jocks and the horses!" The two settled back feeling happier, though it was John this time that had a nagging doubt and Mike that felt a confidence he hadn't felt for ages. Wolverhampton is a pretty little track stuck in the middle of a mass of houses, compact and well-groomed it offers everything for the owner that the bigger tracks profess but on a smaller scale. Mike liked Wolverhampton because you never had to walk very far to get where you wanted to go. He saw Kate before she noticed him. She looked fantastic in a cream summer frock cut about five or six inches above the knee, her slim legs and lithe figure accentuated by the swish of the light material causing every male that passed her to cast a sideways look in her direction, a few even received a dig in the ribs from disgruntled partners! She stood her arm around Geoff's waist, her other holding what looked like a very excited Becky's hand, she was doing her normal shuffle from one foot to the other, Mike noticed she did this every time she became energized with something. He smiled to himself at her imitation of an Irish jig but his heart dropped a foot at Kate's arm around Geoff yet pounded at the thought that he was soon to be in her presence. She turned and noticed him and the smile nearly knocked the knees off Mike. "Hi! Nice to see you." She said, Geoff offered his hand shaking Mikes warmly. "They've given you a bit of a slating in the press." He said.

Mike smiled. "Oh that's nothing new, they always do, then I always think if it's me they're leaving some other poor beggar alone!" Both chuckled at this. Becky stood with her hands on her hips impatiently. As soon as Mike and Geoff finished their sentences she grabbed Mike's hand and pulled him away. "We're off to the stables mummy to see Sunrise." Mike bent low so that he could look directly into Becky's face. "You can't I'm afraid sweetheart, they won't let you in. I'm afraid you don't have a stable pass and you're not old enough." Becky harrumphed but took the news very well. "Then I shall just have to wait until she comes out to the parade ring!"

"I'm afraid you won't be allowed in there either you have to be twelve. But what we'll do is take you to the entrance where the horses come from the stables… as long as you do exactly what I say and it's okay with mum and dad. Some of the horses will be a bit skittish and so you will have to listen to me carefully. We don't want to get you trodden on do we?" Mike emphasised. Mike looked towards Geoff and Kate and after Kate telling Becky she must behave and Mike's assurance he would look after her, both her and Geoff agreed to Mike taking Becky off. As Becky skipped along beside Mike he turned and shouted back to Kate and Geoff to meet him in the bar in ten minutes where he would buy them both a drink. Becky was thrilled when Anita walked out of the stables with Sunrise, she fussed the horse telling her she would be fine and to do the best she could, then delving in her pocket she held out a fifty-pound note, Anita resisted taking it. "It's okay, mummy said I had to give to you." Becky chuckled and lowered her voice conspiratorially.

"It's not even mummy's she pinched it from the money daddy left on his dressing table." She laughed again to be a part of such a masterful scam. "Mummy said he wouldn't miss it." Anita laughed to taking the note gratefully. It would buy her the very flash cap silk and chaps she had seen on one of the stalls.

Everyone stood glass in shaking hand in the owner's bar. Mike noticed that Seamus shock more than normal, the adrenalin rush is awesome. The horses were loaded Becky standing between Mike and Seamus watching the television screen. Kate laughed to herself as she noticed that all three were in harmony 'doing the Becky shuffle'. The gates opened and twelve glistening bodies leapt forward in unison. "And they're off... it's Marlin that takes the early lead followed by Hocus Pocus then comes the favourite Moyotaka closely followed by Sunrise and the rest trail by ten lengths.... Coming to the two pole and Moyotaka kicks taking the lead by a length over Marlin and Hocus Pocus starts to struggle Sunrise is making steady progress on the outside heading Marlin and closing the gap to Moyotaka," Becky screamed Mike and Seamus rode a finish Kate jumped on a table Geoff pushed his way to the screen to watch more closely. "...and Sunrise is still making ground, they're head to head as they cross the line together... that was too close to call, it's a photo... rather the judges than me." The commentator shouted breathlessly.

Seamus turned to Mike. "Shit that was close, what do you think?"

"I reckon the favourite got it on the nod but it was a bloody good run!" he turned to Becky who was jumping around her mum and dad saying to her dad. "Didn't I tell you she was the best....did you see her ....she's fantastic... Mike swore a lot but he's really pleased!" Kate couldn't believe it tears of joy were streaming down both her and Becky's cheeks they hugged each other as if they would never let go. Mike came over to them with Seamus. "I think we got second, I'm sure the favourite got it on the nod!" he said, "but for first time out that was one helluva run, I think you can look forward to a win or two with this one!"

"Well done Mike, you did a marvellous job on her!" Geoff was almost hoarse from shouting at the finish of the race.

"No, Seamus did a marvellous job, he's the one that deserves the credit and all the lads in the yard!" Mike said quickly and Geoff walked straight to Seamus shook his hand and thanked him warmly. Seamus flushed unused to being at the forefront.

"My pleasure." He replied. It was several minutes before the announcement was made Moyotaka by a nose, second Sunrise but the party was still well underway. It was a happy if somewhat inebriated group that made their way back from the races that evening. Mike received a massive hug and kiss from Becky grateful thanks from Geoff and the thing he savoured even more than the race a gentle kiss on the lips from Kate, just a small kiss but a kiss nonetheless, it was like giving a man in the middle of the Sahara a drink of water. That night Mike polished off three quarters of a bottle of Jameson's and slept soundly and happily.

The following morning John arranged his interview with *The Racing Post's* columnist. Seamus checked Sunrise over with a fine-tooth comb reporting to Mike that she had come out of the race without injury and the sun shone. Mike stood alone in Rockets barn, looking from Storm to him a quizzical look upon his face wondering just how insane the whisky had made him. "You know old fella, I actually believed you two were talking to me. That Spanish whiskey must be some potent stuff! Christ, I even told Seamus and he believed it too, mind you." He laughed. "That silly bugger believes in leprechauns! I do wonder about you though Rock's, I swear you're taking the piss on purpose and not because you're an awkward sod! You're the best thing I've ever seen, or come to that I'm ever likely to see, you've that much ability it's frightening but if you don't get to work I'm worried you'll be made a fool of!" It didn't surprise Mike to hear the silence, annoyed him as it was he believed no less than a miracle when he had finally got used to hearing the voice of Rocket in his head but not surprised, he had got used to his own idea that his horsemanship had transcended to a higher level and the magic he saw in Rocket when he bought him was real.

"Oh well son." He said sarcastically. "I guess there's no fool like an old fool. Who am I kidding to even think I'm that good I can truly understand a horse's thoughts! Mind you I enjoyed thinking it for a while!" He walked away with Rocket and Storm watching his back disappear through the barn door. It was with surprise that he found Geoff walking alone across the yard towards him, and it has to be said a little trepidation. "Hi Mike." Geoff greeted him and the trepidation left him.

"Geoff, how are you? Unusual to see you here on your own?"

"Yeh, I just wanted to thank you for yesterday. I didn't realise how exciting this racing job is! I've also come to ask you something!" the trepidation crept back.

"Don't look so worried," Geoff said picking up Mikes vibes. "It's nothing horrible, I just wondered if you weren't too busy tonight you'd care to join us for a barbeque. Becky is insisting that we have one in 'honour' of her horse, everyone will be invited of course, it took me and Kate all our time to convince Becky that the horse couldn't come. She very nearly had me fencing off a piece of the lawn. I can see this is going to cost me a fortune. Becky's already chatting up her granddad to give her a paddock and build her some stables. He's as soft as soft can be with Beck's and I'm sure his reticence is only to make her work on him a bit harder. He adores her, she makes him laugh. I think it's because they're so much alike, both as stubborn as can be but both as kind to someone they get along with as you could imagine." Mike was taken back somewhat but gratefully accepted the invitation and at eight o'clock that evening joined the barbeque where the rest of the stable were already well entrenched. Becky pounced on him the moment he arrived insisting that the second he had eaten and obtained a drink he just had to, had to mind you, come and see the paddock granddad said she could have to keep Sunrise, when she won lots of races of course and where the stables were going to be built. Mike quickly grabbed a cheese burger and bottle of very cold Rolling Rock and was promptly dragged off towards the bottom of the beautifully landscaped gardens to be shown a paddock which was already being re fenced in post and rail. A digger sat in the right hand top corner where Mike could see considerable work was being done. He smiled at Becky as she clung to his hand waiting desperately for his approval. "How big is this stable going to be then young lady?" the site being cleared was enormous Mike judged it would be a complex of at least twenty boxes.

"Granddad said that if we're going to do a job we should do it properly!" Becky said proudly. "He's thinking of buying me another horse and even one for himself!"

"Well I should think you should count yourself very lucky to have such a kind grandfather. It looks like you'll soon be in competition with Hartslock!" Becky was gleeful as they walked back towards the house. Mike fascinated at the tiny hand in his clinging on grimly as though life itself depended on not letting go. He thought of John and Alice and their pride in his namesake his thoughts wistful as near regretful as one can be that he never had nor never would it seemed have the opportunity to be dad himself. Becky's tiny voice snapped him from his reverie.

"Honestly Michael you really should pay attention." She said. "That's mummy's favouritist flower in the whole world. She's going to be very cross with you!" Mike's foot landed right on top of a beautiful flowerbed crushing a stunning specimen of a white rose with peach coloured edging on its petals. Unfortunately it looked more than sorry for itself now, snapped off at ground level and decidedly worse for wear in the flower head department. "Whoops!" Mike said pulling a funny face and they both laughed conspiratorially. "Don't worry I'll explain to your mum that I trod on it. If you do something and are pretty well caught you're always better off admitting it, it only gets worse if you don't and get found out later!" They rejoined the barbeque with Becky yawning frequently enough to give her mum cause to suggest bed. Becky though reluctant to give in to sleep at such an exciting party with everybody talking about the race and horses agreed on the condition that Mike told her a bedtime story. Mike thought that it made total sense after seeing the miffed expression on Kate's face when told of his collision with the rose, so after Becky had cleaned her teeth snuggled into a pair of pyjamas covered in ponies she came and took Mike off for a story. Mike sat trying hard to think of a story to tell. "Come on slowcoach. If you don't tell me a story soon I will fall asleep because I'm bored!" Mike laughed Becky was cheeky but it was in such a charming way.

"Okay your choice," he finally said, "you can have Storm or the Stallion."

"Ooh! Can I have both, please, please!"

"No only one then I'll have another to tell you some other day."

"Oooh, okay then I'll have…. I can't make up my mind… you choose."

"Okay then I'll tell you the story Storm." Becky pulled the covers up to her neck settling her tiny head on the pillow staring at Mike with rapt attention. "I shall begin." Mike said rather dramatically.

"The mare stood in the centre of the box, foam flecked sides shivering, eyes white with fear, nature had told her what to expect, but that didn't stop the fear of the as yet unknown. Michael's voice made her feel better, knowing he was there was a relief. She had known Michael since she was a baby, all through her illustrious racing career he had been there, his soft country accent whispering reassurances in her ear. At times she had been a "little toad" as Michael put it, she had to admit, even when she had been really badly behaved and Michael had given her a reprimanding slap she or he had held no grudge. Michael had been there for her always it seemed, and here he was, drinking his tea from his plastic thermos cup telling her not to worry it would all be okay. "You'll have the prettiest little colt anyone has ever seen, and he'll be as fast as the lighting that's frightening you, nothing to worry about, just you be steady old lass". Mind you he was no angel, he was quick to lose his temper, normally over something silly, but when a crisis came Michael always took charge, and stayed calm, though he shouted at the others a lot. Michael had a past, she knew for he had told her, he told her everything, if anyone crossed him he would get his own back tenfold. But seldom did they see the side of him that she did, kind and gentle. You think he's hard but he's as soft as butter underneath, you think he's daft because he talks to the horses, but they understand him, and he understands them, she had heard his girlfriend once say. She felt a little guilty for all the times she had aimed a hoof at a stable girl who had been getting too much attention from Michael, she wasn't really that jealous, she just thought she deserved his undivided attention. A warm feeling overwhelmed her as she remembered Michaels words on such occasions, "All right I'll do her, come you jealous old bitch you can have me to yourself now" always the smile and the caress of her long sleek neck to accompany the words. The crash of thunder made her start, she turned to look for Michael. He was still there waiting patiently. The pain made her groan as another contraction racked her body, and she knew the time had come. She whickered at Michael knowing he would understand, "Alright lass let's get to work" was all he said as he came up beside her, but she knew that he would hear, making reassuring croonings throughout her ordeal. Nature would wait no longer and the urge to produce her baby took over. With an effort that made the need to lie down irrepressible her knees buckled beneath her, and she lay in the straw on her side, back legs stretched rigid as the contractions became stronger still. With an enormous push, the foal's front legs appeared. With an effort, she stood and pushed again, Michaels strong hands pulled gently on the foal's legs, and with one last push the foal slid on to the straw. "What did I tell you", Michaels face beamed with happiness as he gently lifted the foal to her head, "If you like we'll call him Storm" he said as he looked down on the beautiful black colt, and she had whickered her approval. Five years had passed since that night, four more children, all helped into the world by Michael. Storm was now one of the country's best stallions, unbeaten on the racecourse, his favours were sought by the smallest owners to royalty. She was so proud, and there was still Storms brothers and sisters. Michael's familiar face appeared at the stable door,

"Tea up lass", and her thoughts returned to the need to eat....
For two." Mike looked down on the tiny face whose eyes had
not left his for a second.

"That was brilliant. The bestest story anyone has ever told
me. Thank you." Mike smiled and thought what a delightful
child and so well mannered, he bent down and kissed the top of
her head. "Now you go to sleep young lady and dream sweet
dreams of when you have a Storm of your own!"

"I've got the Sunrise." Becky said through a yawn, there
really wasn't an answer to that.

Mike tip toed out of the room quietly closing the door
behind him. He marvelled at how in one second flat her eyes
had closed and she was fast asleep. "It's okay you don't need to
creep about Becky could sleep through a rock concert. We've
never pussy footed around, I think if you do that you are only
making a rod for your own back in the future." It was Kate.
Mike couldn't help himself starting at her beautiful blue eyes, he
swept his own eyes down across her body, as always she looked
stunning. She was simply attired but it was very effective. Tight
cream lacy top that showed just a hint of dark nipple through
the opaque material, three quarter length tight trousers that
clung to the curves of her body. Mike could feel the reaction in
his groin and thought that Kate had to for she smiled a knowing
smile. "Mike will you come and sit with me on the patio? I'd like
to talk with you... talk mind you." She added defensively. Mike
nodded and silently followed Kate back through the party goers
to the patio where it was quieter. Sitting on a swing seat there
was an awkward pause before Kate spoke. "Look Mike," she
said hesitantly. "This is very difficult for me.... More than a
little awkward if I'm honest... embarrassing even! I.... Oh how
can I say this without appearing an absolute bitch...?" Mike
went to speak but Kate put her hand up to quiet him, "I can't
say that I don't have feelings for you because I do... more than I
would care to admit and I can't say that I regret what happened
between us," she blushed and Mike thought how enchanting it
was. "but I am married and I do love my husband. If I wasn't

married it would be different but I am, I don't want to jeopardise my marriage and I don't want to lose your friendship. Becky is so taken with you, Geoff likes you and me well I should know better. I am so confused but I do know I want my marriage to continue and don't want some sordid affair... I'm not saying that what happened was sordid but it would be if we allowed it to continue, it has to stop and now... please if you think anything of me you'll respect my decision and never be any more than my friend in the future." She looked first at the floor then at Mike's face, waiting for his reaction. Mike looked sadly back at Kate but there was no surprise in his eyes, it was something that he expected, he was not a fool and had seen the way Kate was around Geoff it was obvious how much she cared for him. Mike managed a smile, "I would never do anything to cause you pain, if that's what you want then that's exactly how it will be!"

"It is." She said simply and leaned forward to kiss his forehead as if he were a little boy about to sleep. Mike's heart was in his boots but he bravely managed a smile, walked around the party goers for half an hour then made his excuses and left for home.

CHAPTER THIRTEEN

The Racing Post arrived on Mike's doormat the following morning and he avidly read the headline: The Rocket becomes favourite with Musgrove's! The article went on to say that John Cullen part owner of The Rocket told The Racing Post exclusively that he had owned Musgrove's for some time and believed so steadfastly in his horse that the bookmakers chain had opened up the odds on All Aglow to 2-1 and Orange County Blues to 5-1 and had closed he odds on The Rocket to 1-4 on, he was taking win bets only. The writer went on to expound the virtues of taking the better prices of the other horses, it seemed a ridiculous price and was he a said a plot to get the bigger punters to bet on The Rocket at 1-4 on and that he thought John Cullen's convenient confession as to the ownership of Musgrove's was a ploy to get bets in on The Rocket by shortening the odds to such a degree that it was only worth putting a massive bet on , the ordinary punter wouldn't look at the horse at that price. Because John Cullen knew he couldn't win this race. His advice was bet on All Aglow or Orange County, as he had advised in his previous article. By noon John had received several worried phone calls from the managers of his shops expressing their concern over the amount of money they had taken on All Aglow and Orange County, John instructed them not to worry and to continue taking money if it came though his stomach churned with anxiety over the whole situation. "God Mike, I hope your idea is going to work or we'll all be homeless and broke." Unbeknown to John Mike was feeling the same, depressed that he and Kate could only ever be friends he threw himself back into training the horses, Seamus still holding the reins but with Mike back in the saddle. Seamus would bow to Mike's superior knowledge of training and concentrate on his forthcoming race on Rocket. Mike stood at the side of the gallops watching Rocket meander aimlessly along as other horses flew past him. If anything he had become worse over the last few days and showed no interest in even taking as much as a brisk walk for exercise.

It was a subdued bunch that sat down to breakfast, the race was now only a few weeks away and on Rocket's recent performances he would not be fit for the race. With everybody back to work Mike wandered over to Rocket's barn. "Hello son." He said as he reached for the bolt on Rocket's door and Rocket pawed the ground impatiently. "What am I going to do?" He stroked the horse's sleek neck surprised at how muscular it was considering the lack of effort that Rocket showed in training. Rocket nuzzled his pocket and it made Mike laugh. "Oh you want a mint now do you? Well I suppose, you don't bloody well deserve it mind you, you old bugger." Mike took out the mints and fed Rocket looking closely in the eye of the horse hoping against hope that he would see or hear something, but there was nothing. "You know son. Sad as it is I actually liked the idea that you and I could talk.... I don't mean me talking to you but you talking back as well. Just for a moment I felt so special it was an amazing feeling. Once I got used to what I thought was happening. Silly really, humans are so vane and me I must be about as vane as they come to think I should have a gift that thousands have wished for. You've done a lot for me." Mike continued stroking Rocket as he spoke running his hands over Rocket's shoulder, the feel of warm was comforting. "I was skint and unknown virtually and you gave me money and fame. When I was down you listened, well I'll tell you now son if it all goes tits up I've made sure you're okay, and the little fella," he said nodding towards Storm in the next door box. "John's transferred the stud into Alice's name just in case and you'll go there. John will be all right of course because he has Alice and she's wealthy in her own right now, turned around a bit I suppose but then that's life. Me I don't know I can't let a friend down and I'll do all I can to help John even if it does break me. I suppose what I'm trying to say is thanks for giving me the chance to get there, even if I did fuck up a bit on the way. I'm not sure where I'll go yet, if you do get beat that is, but I promise you I'll come and see you whenever I can." And with that he leant forward kissed the velvety patch on the side of Rocket's nose and left the stables. Rocket watched his back disappear through the barn doors.

Mike wandered back across the yard his shoulders slumped, eyes cast towards the floor. The voice made him jump. "Hello Mr.. grumpy!" It was Becky, she laughed. "Why do you look so cross this morning?" Mike cheered up straight away, he looked around for a glimpse of Kate, she wasn't there. "Hi Mike hope you don't mind us coming over unannounced, but this…" he rubbed the top of Becky's head much to her annoyance, "wouldn't give me any peace until I did." Geoff laughed "And to top it all she's talked her grandfather into taking an interest in horses so I didn't have much of a choice really." Geoff introduced the man standing beside him who held Becky's hand proudly. Mike could not only see the similarity but also the bond between them. He reached out his hand as he was introduced shaking hands with Becky's grandfather. It was Becky who spoke. "This is my grandpa Pete." She said with pride and formality.

"So you're the chap my granddaughter has not stopped talking about for the past few weeks? I feel as though I already know you!" Peter said with a broad grin.

"My granddaughter believes that as my 'favourite', which is

something she tells me she is on frequent occasions I should spend more time with her. At the races I'm reliably informed," he paused to affectionately pat the top of Becky's head, much to her chagrin, Mike stood watching and listening with an amused air. "Personally I think it could be cupboard love and the reason I am being showered with affection from this nonetheless delightful bundle is that she knows granddad is a bit of a softy underneath and he might just buy her another horse, seeing as how her father seems to have his hands stitched into his pockets." Mike laughed out loud and noticed that Geoff blushed slightly at his father's words but soon found himself laughing as well.

"Are you saying I'm tight dad?" he asked with the smile from laughing still in place.

"Let's just say careful!" His father replied with a similar smile.

"Then Becky might just have a lucky day because I've just become very un- careful as long as Mike here doesn't try to take advantage!"

"Do you mean I might get two more horses?" Becky was beginning to get more than a little excited. Her grandfather and Geoff spoke at the same time.

"Let' see what Mike's got first shall we?" Her grandfather adding. "Can't see a lot of point building all those stables if we're not going to use them, can you?" and Becky shot off like a bullet from a gun towards the stables. "I think now might be a good time for you to show us around Mike!"

The three of them hurried after Becky, she had found Anita who was just tacking up Sunrise and was animatedly telling both Anita and Sunrise of the imminent expansion to her immediate as yet enterprise of one. Of course she explained to Sunrise she would still be number one but she was absolutely sure the new members would be very nearly as good as she was. Mike had suggested to Peter and Geoff that it might be an idea for them to look at one flat horse and one maybe older horse to give them a potential hurdler or jumper. The two men readily agreed both seeing the merits of having the chance to go racing in over the winter months if they chose to do so. It meant Mike explained that they would give themselves the option should the others not go well on the all-weather tracks, something that with the modern surfaces was relatively unusual but did occasionally occur. Both men seemed satisfied with this and after an hour of looking at different horses they whittled it down to a choice between three. There was a dark bay gelding and two fillies one a bright bay and one grey. Mike explained that the grey was a bit of a gamble as he had bought her from an old lady who was giving up. She occasionally bred a really good horse but had been very sentimental so even those that weren't quite up to scratch she kept and raced. "I," he said. "Am probably as sentimental as she was, or stupid, I'm still not quite sure what! I bought this horse," he pointed to the grey, "over the phone. Bloody daft really because in all honesty I would never have bought her if I had seen her! She's well-bred enough so I was going to keep her to breed from…. Possibly…. Look, I'll show you why I'm a bit reticent for you to have this one." Mike walked into the grey mare's box, beckoning the two other men to follow. He spoke softly stroking the mare's neck and turning her so that her rear end was visible. "Look," He said pointing at her hock. There was a vivid circular scar about three inches across and the joint itself looked slightly larger than the other legs. "Some pratt of a lad apparently came 'round the corner of the old girls yard in a four-wheel drive trying to impress one of the girls and slid, unfortunately this poor bugger was right in the way! They never even told the old girl it had happened, turns out it was the old girl's favourite nephew, was, being the operative word. Anyway right or wrong I'd done the deal so I stood by it. She's coming right but I don't in all honesty think she'll ever be that good. Maybe win a little race somewhere over hurdles, she's got a big heart that's for sure but she'll never be a world beater, but she wouldn't break the bank either."

A tiny voice interrupted them. "How much is she?"

"Oh she wouldn't be dear sweetie, two thousand pounds would buy her."

"That's an awful lot, Sunrise was only £53. 27pence, and she's the bestest horse in the whole world!" The three men laughed uproariously as Mike between gasps for air tried to explain that Sunrise had been a sort of gift. Becky became very serious addressing her comment to her dad.

"Daddy I've decided what I would like to do when I leave school." They all looked on with amused surprise at the definitive comment. "I'm going to be a racehorse trainer and I think it would be nice to have my foundation stock in place." Geoff thought to himself how grown up Becky was, she knew words he hadn't even heard of and absorbed information like a sponge. She had obviously heard someone in the yard talking about foundation stock and had been quick to pick up on the expression. "Granddad?" she said in her most persuasive voice. "Would it be at all possible for you to lend me some money until I get older and can pay you back?"

Becky's grandfather beamed, if there was one thing he could not resist it was the diminutive person stood in front of him. "Oh I think I might see my way clear to helping you out a bit. What do you want shorty?" he said with love for this little one obvious in his words.

"Well I'd like to buy Cloud but I'd also like Dusk and Dawn." The three men looked totally confused.

"Sorry Titch you've lost us a bit there! Who are Cloud, Dusk and Dawn?"

Becky put her hands on her hips cocking her head to one side in feigned exasperation.

"The three horses silly!" she said. "Isn't it obvious? That's my theme." She announced proudly. "Cloud because she looks like a cloud!" she pointed at the grey. "Dawn because I already have a Sunrise of the same colour and Dusk because she's darker!" The three men looked at each other in stunned silence. It all made absolute sense.

The deal was done and three horses joined the Becky Stokes

string. Becky mythered her dad for his mobile phone and was in the process of telling her mother as they walked back to Mikes office to collect the necessary papers to sign before adjourning to his kitchen for the inevitable tea and probably breakfast. Vi in full flow insisted that everyone should be fed the fatted calf before leaving what was now her kitchen and as they sat eating the prodigious platter that was laid before them Geoff's father made several unsuccessful attempts to re-deploy Vi to his own kitchen. Becky loved it Vi having no children of her own spoilt her rotten ignoring the protestations of all as she fed Becky enormous lumps of cake. It was four very stretched but happy stomachs that left the table that morning. Mike watched them leave in the Range Rover that Kate drove quite often with mixed feelings, he really liked Geoff and had taken to his father straight away, but there was still a feeling of guilt for his duplicity with what was fast becoming a friend, yet an aching for another moment in the company of Kate. He knew he had fallen totally in love with the fair haired blue-eyed beauty, almost every waking moment there was some thought of her in his mind. He even found himself comparing her lithe body to the sleekness of his horses as they passed him on the gallops. He longed for her but knew that the longing would never become reality. "Oh well." He said like my old guvnor used to say a taste of something is better than a taste of nothing at all and at least I have her friendship." He turned and walked back towards the stables in particular to Rocket's barn. He could sit and tell Rocket his troubles and not be judged. Seamus was already there vigorously rubbing Rocket down with a damp chamois. He shone like gold, his coat so sleek that it looked as though some inane hairdresser had crept in and highlighted it with burgundy. "He looks an absolute picture Seamus." Mike said admiring the fantastic job Seamus had done. Seamus smiled in appreciation of Mike's compliment.

"Shame he doesn't look like it going up the gallops." He commented. "But then," he slapped the backside of Rocket who laid his ears back in mock anger at this indignity. "I suppose he did manage half a show up the gallops this morning. Annihilated the others, left them for dead so he did, then the old sod decides he'll stop put in a rear and fire off in the opposite direction." Seamus became tentative. "Mike maybe you could have a word with him like, you being able to communicate and that?" Mike flushed, Seamus was being deadly serious, there was no trace of a mickey take in his voice at all. Now he had to admit that it had all been a figment of his imagination, he would try one more time just to satisfy himself. He asked Rocket to answer him in his head and again there was nothing except silence. He sighed regretfully that he had just proven a point to himself that deep in his heart he didn't want too. He turned to Seamus. "I'm afraid that was all a figment of my imagination Seamus. God knows I wish it wasn't but I haven't heard a thing since we decided on the race and you know what I fought so hard not to believe what I thought was happening in the beginning... now I wish to who knows that it was. For the first time I really thought I understood and that Rocket was my friend. I'd never enjoyed speaking to someone in my life as much as I did speaking to him and to get an answer... and such bloody logical ones too...." Mike's voice tailed off. Seamus walked over and put an arm round his shoulder he could see that Mike was as close to tears as he had ever seen him. Rocket pushed his nose against Mike's neck as though he understood and the action brought laughter from both men.

"Well I'll be... perhaps he speaks to you after all Mike.... Just not in the way you thought? I'll tell you Michael I've met some horsemen in my time but never anyone that could even stand in your shadow. You're the best man with a horse I've ever met." Mike smiled, no one could have paid him a better compliment and coming from Seamus an expert horseman himself it was praise indeed. Mike still worried, it didn't matter to him how good he was, the race was down to Rocket. He had no lack of faith in the horse whatsoever but he didn't see how a horse, even one with the ability Rocket seemed to possess, could possibly beat the best twenty-three horses and one wild card, that it was decided should be given a chance at such a big prize, without putting any effort at all into training and to boot Rocket was now older. Rocket hadn't seen a race track for over a year and Mike as much as he thought of the horse began to have even more doubts about whether he made the right decision in agreeing to Becky's idea of a race. "Hollywood's got a lot to answer for." He said aloud and walked back towards the house. Mike looked at the flashing light on his answer machine and the liquid crystal display it read fifteen messages. He picked up the handset pressing play on the machine and listened intently as each brief message came through the earpiece, they all said the same. Shell shocked Mike reached for the remote control of the television pressing the on button and waited as the picture came vividly on the screen. It was total carnage! Bodies strewn across grass and tarmac with equal disregard, people desperately trying to help others trapped in the torn rubble that held them. A child's body lay contorted as if made of rag, a man knelt wailing beside him his face skywards. Mike could see not only the sorrow but the question in his dark eyes. Why? No one was immune, White man, Black man, Chinese, Japanese, Arab, Christian, Muslim, Jew, Roman Catholic. There were no exceptions. They all bore loss, they had all suffered and for what? Because one man somewhere had greed, and it was greed, it was greed to be recognised, greed to be powerful, greed to be worshipped as some sort of hero, whichever way it is disguised it still comes down to that.... GREED! Yet worst still was the fact that the greed was laced with cowardice, no face to face, man to man here no just a coward hiding behind the ignorance of his minions and all that innocence destroyed by some faceless greedy coward. Mike wept, he wept for the dead, he wept for the injured, he wept for the grief that would follow for those with loved ones that were there, he wept for the world that allowed such atrocities, he even wept for those that supported it and he wept for racing, he wept for the stupidity and pointlessness of it all! He put the phone down on its cradle and it immediately rang, he looked at the caller display, John, wearily he picked up the phone again.

Peter Stokes a powerfully built man, his frame, work hardened from his youth paced in front of the television his anger at boiling point, Geoff spoke. "Calm down dad."

"Calm down! Look at what those bastards have done!"

"Grand dad! That's not a very nice word." Peter's anger subsided a little, he walked over to where Becky was sitting, picked her up and hugged her. He didn't aim his comment at anybody in particular as he now paced with less purpose hugging Becky as though he would never put her down.

"Sorry sweetheart but the people who did this are very bad and it's going to make everybody extremely angry."

"I know granddad but calling them names won't help a bit!" A child's perspective is often far more sensible and logical than an adult, there is no pre-conception involved. "Maybe we should ring someone and see if we can do anything to help. I could make soup or something!" The simplicity of Becky's comment stopped her grandfather's pacing and he smiled warmly at her, grateful that they were not a part of such a tragedy. The sight of the man's image taken as he suffered a grief greater than words would haunt not only him but the thousands that saw the news that day for a long time to come.

"You're right Beck's we should do something. We all have to pull together in a situation like this, we can't allow such actions to go without showing our determination that they will not defeat or intimidate us....! Geoff get the car, we're going to see what we can do to help." Becky made to speak but was stopped by the continuation of her grandfather. "And as for you young lady, I have the most important job of all!" Becky looked suitably pleased. "I want you to go and fetch your mother from the kitchen and then you and her will have to get busy. I need you to help mum to phone the.... You go and get your mother first then I'll explain what I need you to do."

"Hi John...... yes I've seen it, though I still don't believe it.... How can people do such a thing? I don't know if we can do anything but of course I'd sure as hell like to help.... You have?.... right I'll ring everybody and see what I can arrange, call you back in fifteen minutes... okay!" Mike's disgusted form channelled itself into a hive of activity, frantically phoning everyone that worked for him. He was stunned when he discovered that they had without exception already left and were all on their way to the yard. He was a tad disappointed in himself for being so tied up with his own problems and so appalled at the catastrophe he had witnessed on the news yet had sat in his chair not thinking to go and offer help. John on the other hand had been galvanised into immediate action. Phoning the authorities and finding out in what way they could offer assistance. He had already organised half a dozen diggers that were now being loaded to make their way to the disaster site as soon as was humanly possible. The yard staff members had taken it on themselves to make their way to Mike's they would have friends that had become unwilling parties to the terrorist attack on Newbury racecourse and they wanted to help. The same scenario would be happening all over the south, in fact the country but those in the south would be close enough to help. Racing the world over mourned this pointless and utterly despicable act of violence. If there is a God he would too, whatever name you chose to give him.

At Geoff's house Peter was explaining to Kate what he would like her to do, she and Becky got to work immediately. Peter owned a plant hire company and Kate called the manager at home instructing him to put every available piece of equipment that may prove useful on lorries and send them straight to the racecourse at Newbury. There was no exasperation at being disturbed at home just total willingness from all concerned. Peter and Geoff left Kate busy on the phone talking to officials and gaining agreement for the help that was on offer. The news of the bombing of Newbury racecourse still rolled on the television screen, one hundred and fifty dead, three hundred and twenty-five injured. "Oh my God," Kate exclaimed aloud, "please don't let there be any more." But as she looked at the piles of rubble that was once the main stand she knew her plea would go unheeded. She sat hunched by the telephone unable to talk as the tears coursed down her face, Becky placed her arms around her mother. "There, there mummy." As if she were the adult and her mother the child. "We have to keep ourselves together you know, we have to if we are to be any help at all!" and with those words Kate straightened her shoulders and resumed her phone calls.

John sat beside Mike in the M15 his hands gripping tightly to the edge of the seat as Mike pressed the accelerator to the floor the car gliding around the corners they negotiated as if on rails, by the time they had reached the A303 and Mike hurtled onto the dual carriageway John was twitching nervously with every car they passed. The road was surprisingly empty for that time of the evening and as they were on a piece of road with no traffic in sight Mike started to drive the car with serious intent, John took a worried sideways glance at the needle on the speedometer which had passed one hundred and fifty and was still climbing rapidly. "Mike for Christ's sake slow down, you'll get us killed, or at the very least locked up and what good will we be then?" Mike realising that John was quite right immediately back off on the accelerator bringing the car back to about ninety miles an hour. "I'm in as much of a hurry to get there and help as you are but I would like to get there!" Mike briefly looked over at John with an apologetic grin. The rest of their journey was made at a slightly more sedate pace though John had to occasionally make a coughing 'harrumph' when Mike started to forget himself and allow his right foot to wander deeper towards the floor. As they were pulling into the racecourse the full impact of the devastation that had been caused became aware to them. There were ambulances, police, fire crews, bomb disposal teams, dust, rubble but the thing that struck them both was the appalling look of horror on everyone's faces as they viewed the carnage. They spoke to the police officers holding sub machine guns that were guarding the entrance and after a brief radio call to a superior waved Mike and John through the gates. Mike parked his car in the saddling area and both he and John hurried to the normal entrance where a temporary command post had been situated. They explained that there were more hands on their way from the yard and that John had organised half a dozen diggers that were on their way. The police sergeant and army Captain that were in control voiced their appreciation telling John and Mike there were still people trapped in the rubble and it would be helpful if they would go and help in trying to clear as much as possible. The police sergeant, who appeared quite young, seemed far more effected by the disaster than the army officer, he turned towards both men saying in an emotion filled voice that was close to breaking point. "My God how could anybody do such a thing... there are women children... they were here to have a fun day..." the older army officer put a reassuring arm around his shoulder. "Steady now! Stay strong, we can't let the bastards that did this win, stay strong." Mike could see the pain in his eyes of this and past memories, he had seen atrocities before and was as much as anyone ever can be more able to deal with the situation than a young man that had probably road traffic accidents of horrendous magnitude but nothing that could compare to chaos such as this. They made their way to what was once a stand full of joy, laughter and colour. It was now just a massive pile of rubble. There were black body bags lying in rows spreading from the centre of the parade ring, people wailing, crying, hurting. Voices that sounded almost ethereal came from with the rubble and Mike looking at the full devastation knew there would be many more that were not still crying out. He tore off his shirt and ran towards the pile moving as quickly as he could the broken masonry that led before him. John worked stoically beside him both stopping occasionally to mop their brow and call out listening intently for any sound or sign of life. So intent were they on the immense task they failed to notice Peter and Geoff working with the same fervour only yards away until Geoff's voice reached them. "Someone here.... There's someone here... I think they're alive." Mike and John joined them no one speaking, there was no need a bond in their efforts was more than words could say. "It's a little girl." There was an enormous concrete lintel wedged across the small figure of a child, her pretty dress ragged and torn, her frail body blood soaked. Peter grabbed the end of the lintel lifting with a super human strength found from God knows where. Geoff immediately dove beneath it pushing his back against the underside and lifting it higher. "Bastards!" he screamed as he found the strength to help his father. Mike and John reached gently in the gap that Geoff and Peter had made, carefully lifting the mercifully unconscious form to safety. Paramedics rushed to their aid, stretchering the little girl off for emergency treatment.

Everyone worked tirelessly, not sleeping, hardly stopping to eat or drink, the urgency that grasp them was almost unbearable. Seamus arrived with the rest of the yard staff and after finding Mike and the other three worked as a team. They saw things that no man whatever religion, creed or belief should never see and for what purpose? The maiming and killing of the young, the old, the innocent could only promote hatred and determination. Mike was talking with the army officer he had met earlier and asked, "How can anyone believe this to be right?" the officer looked through sad experienced eyes as he replied.

"I've seen atrocities throughout the world. I've seen the bodies of mothers, their children, they're always the ones to suffer and do you know what does nothing less than disgust me is that the perpetrators want something... never specific.... But they always do want something and they're never going to get it with a bomb or violence... they'll never be listened too you see…. Would you listen to them now? No, you wouldn't! Nor would anyone else you see they haven't really the honesty, the strength, or the courage to stand in front of their fellow man and talk because they are all cowards! They are I can assure you all the same and I'm sorry that I think it will always be the same. They'll probably catch the people that did this and they'll scream at the top of their voices about human rights… theirs mind you not the rest of the world's population…. They shout about their God and how they did this for their cause…. What God would condone this yet they still think they have the right to be protected and treated humanely themselves?" He swept his arm across the scene of devastation that led before them. "The really sick thing is that some wishy-washy liberal that has never done more than mow his lawn on a Sunday will stand with them and they'll end up getting a couple of years in prison where they'll be looked after get parole and come out and do it all again, and what makes me really sick is that they'll still be treated with humanity!" His cheek muscles clenched with emotion and the memories of conflicts and sights seen were almost tangible in his eyes. "My unit was in the Middle East during the Gulf war, three of my men were helping a boy that they had found lying abandoned on the street, he appeared to be very ill. He wasn't he was a sniper trap. He was put there as a lure knowing that a patrol was due. Two were killed one was seriously injured. When the sniper had done his work, the boy jumped up and ran off. How can you deal with someone who is prepared to use a child in that manner? How can you deal with someone who is prepared to do this…? There is only one way my friend for we are well past the talking stage. We have to get tough or they will not be stopped and trust me we will get tough one way or another. I've seen it in the eyes of my men. We will find those behind this, they think they can hide from us forever but they can't we get closer to them everyday and when we find them justice will be done. We'll see what their God has to offer them then!"

It was a weary, saddened, group that left the racecourse to

return to the yard and their homes respectively. The consequences of the devastation they had witnessed first-hand would be with them forever. The body count had reached three hundred and seventy dead, there were over five hundred injured some seriously. To see broken lifeless bodies lying before you is so different than watching from the comfort of your armchair as it flicks across the television screen. To feel the lifeless bodies as you lift them from the rubble. To see the pain in the eyes of the injured. To hear the screams of the children. To feel the blood of the dead and injured mixing with the sweat, the dust. To know that this is, was a testament to man and that somewhere someone cried for the loss of a loved one and always would.

Mike felt completely insignificant and he and John drove in silence for the first part of the journey, then John much to Mike's surprised asked. "Mike can Rocket really win the race!"

"How the hell can you be worried about winning a fucking race after what we've just seen… I'm disgusted …! John looked hurt, assumption can be a dangerous thing.

"Do you really think I'm that shallow!" He almost shouted back at Mike. "I thought we knew each other better than that… sometimes I just don't believe you…. I was thinking that if Rocket could win we could ask all the big boys to put a few more quid in the pot and put all the prize money to helping sort out this awful tragedy. Maybe set up some sort of fund to aid victims and their families. I'm lost for words that you should think me that selfish!"

Mike looked ashamed John was right he tried to explain himself. "I am sorry John. Christ, I should know better and I can't apologise enough. I don't know maybe I'm too tired or maybe all that we saw has got to me, it's no excuse I know but perhaps you can forgive me. I know in my heart what a selfless man you are…. I'm sorry I just don't know what else to say!" John reached out his hand and Mike taking one hand from the steering wheel shook it with genuine warmth. Both suffered mentally in what they had seen and maybe that along with the tiredness made for errors of judgement. Both men knew that they had lost faith in each other at times in their friendship and both men hoped that the friendship was strong enough to withstand the odd error of judgement. They drove the rest of the way back in virtual silence but there seemed to be an understanding that neither would make assumptions of the other again.

CHAPTER FOURTEEN

Becky and Kate were ecstatic to see Peter and Geoff return. Both men were on the point of exhaustion but Kate and Becky insisted they sit and eat something before retiring, she had made up the spare bedroom for Peter even though his own house was only half a mile away. Becky jumped up and down with excitement as they entered the kitchen. On the middle of the kitchen table sat a cake iced with the words 'My Heroes'. Becky couldn't contain herself anymore. "I made the cake," she said proudly. She grabbed both men's hands half dragging, half leading them to the table, sitting next to the cake was a pile of newspapers the front cover showing a picture of Geoff and his father straining to hold up the lintel whilst Mike and John pulled the inert form of the little girl from the wreckage the headline read, 'YOU WILL NEVER BEAT US WHILST WE HAVE STRENGTH AND COURAGE'. The front-page article continued throughout the papers hailing the superhuman efforts of Geoff and Peter along with the gentleness of John and Mike's lifting of the little girl from the rubble. Terrorists would not win as long as there were men such as these. They should be recognised as true heroes. It told of their tireless efforts in helping with the aftermath, it showed more pictures of them the pain, the anger, the weariness plain to see on their faces. Unwittingly they had become England's unsung heroes. Becky waited for her mother to sit at the table beside them. "Can I give it to daddy and granddad now…. please mummy?" Kate passed a small sealed envelope with telegram in bold letters written across the front. Geoff studied it for a moment then broke the seal reading the contents, he silently passed it to his father. Becky jumped up and down. "What does it say daddy…. I know it's from the Queen it says so, on the envelope." It was Peter that spoke.

"It's an invite my darling, an invite to Buckingham Palace! We've been offered a medal for our bravery, an OBE but we're not the brave one's sweetheart we did nothing more than any other person would do and did. They should give the medal to someone who deserves it like that little girl…. She was brave." Kate interrupted her father in law.

"Peter the medal is more than that, it's about backbone and the willingness to help when the chips are down, you two did. Did you sit watching the television and say how despicable this act was? No! You got on the phone and in the car and went to help. That's what the medal is about. It's about showing the world that we care and will not be intimidated, it's about not being afraid to stand up and be counted, it's not really about you two, oh it recognises that you did something extraordinary but although it's given to you it's for everybody that was there. If you feel strongly about it have them put in a glass case when they rebuild the racecourse donating them to all those that suffered and all those that helped!" Kate had become quite animated and both Peter and Geoff rose from the table moving to her side, each in turn bent down and kissed her cheek lovingly. Peter turned to Geoff. "You look after this young lady son she's got more sense than the lot of us put together. She's special!" Kate burst into tears and no one knew why except for her.

Mike slept like he had never slept before slipping into a blackness that cocooned him from the atrocities of man. He was so tired on his return that he didn't even check his horses apart from a short visit to Rockets barn. Even though his sleep was long and deep he awoke feeling drained and sorrowful, he made tea checked the post and walked across the yard. Everybody was quietly sorrowful as they worked, they had been there and seen the trauma, felt the trauma. They had seen things, things that were indescribable, things that would haunt them forever. Nick had done a marvellous job keeping the yard together for the two days they had been away. There was not a wisp of straw or a speck of dust to be seen. Anita approached Mike and ask him if they could have a short meeting with him and Mike agreed they should all come up to the house as normal for breakfast and they would talk then. He wandered off towards Rockets barn. Rocket whickered as he entered and Mike smiled. "Hello my son. You won't be racing for a while after what's happened. Oh Rock's you can't believe what one man can do to another…. If only man could be more like you guys and be happy. Look how amazingly powerful you are but you don't take that out on something else! You don't look to batter a sheep or a cow if you're all in the same field, you just live your own life, live in harmony, see there's no greed with you guys you don't try to stop something just because they're different from you." Rocket nuzzled Mike and Mike longed to hear his voice but it didn't come, he stroked Rockets sleek muscular neck turned and walked off towards the kitchen where he was certain that Vi would already be fussing around everybody like an old mother hen. It was an unusually sombre atmosphere that greeted Mike as he entered the kitchen. The atrocity of Newbury still fresh in the mind of all present. As soon as he was seated Anita spoke. "We know there are numerous charities that help when things like this happen but there were some lads in the stands, none of us knew them well but, well I don't have to tell you you've been in racing longer than any of us! Anyway, we thought if it's all right with you we'd like to donate whatever there is in the racing pool to the stable lads association. At least that way it might ease the burden for those left behind." Mike knew what such a gesture meant. Stable lads (lasses) work hard to prepared the horses in their charge, rain sun or whatever and every time a horse wins or is placed the 'yard' have a percentage of the winnings put aside for them. Some yards distribute it every six months some every year, normally at Christmas. The yard had, had quite a good season, Mike knew there would be a few thousand in the pool not hundreds and that the staff would have planned their spending sprees, so for them to give it up was magnanimous. He agreed saying that he personally would match whatever was in the pool to add before they donated it and that they should take the credit for the whole donation, his name was not to be mentioned.

It made for a less sorrowful breakfast and within a few minutes the ribaldry came back to the fore. Vi clipped Seamus round the ear for cursing 'at her breakfast table' which brought much merriment to everybody including Seamus, and Nicky received a severe telling off when she said what she would like to do with Steven if she ever manages to drag him from his precious cars and get him alone. In all it was a far happier bunch that left the kitchen than went in.

Mike retired to his office, spoke to John, and asked him to come over. He asked Seamus to come to the office when John arrived. As he waited he sat studying the Racing Calendar, which arrives regularly every Thursday. His motives were two sided he desperately wanted to find a race for Sunrise because of his fondness for Becky but more so he desperately wanted to find a way in which he could see Kate again even if it was from a proverbial distance. His eyes scanned the pages until he found exactly what he was looking for, class 5 six furlong at Salisbury. Albeit the finish is stiff at Salisbury but he thought on the fillies work at home she would cope well with the extra effort that would be required, she had certainly come on for the run. When Seamus arrived with John, Mike told them of his idea. Asking Seamus opinion of the fillies chances in the race. Seamus believed she'd take all the beating, adding that he would certainly be having more than a few quid each way on her! Mike laughed. "You'll have to leave that with us I'm afraid Seamus, you know the rules about a jockey betting on a race, it's you I intend should ride her!" Seamus did another Irish jig. Mike was in good form, "After all we've a lot to do now to organise a new venue for Rocket's race and I thought after seeing you ride this morning you could do with the practice!"

"Bollocks!" Seamus replied with a huge grin.

"Look. Being serious we could start to cover our asses a bit here, if we do it right." He directed this at John. "With a bit of luck we might just get decent odds on Sunrise. You must have plenty of runners available, especially now you own more bookmakers. If we put one or two around the bigger towns and a few at the racecourse…." John and Seamus started to see where Mike was going. "If we can lay enough money on Sunrise to at least star to recoup any potential loss we might suffer on Rocket." John interrupted.

"That should be me not we guys. I'm the one that got in this mess!"

"I said we and meant we…" Mike said with a half smile. "One for all and all that, we agreed we'd stand together and that's just what we're going to do. Look I've worked it out if we can get say 7-1, which we ought too, think about it she was a rank outsider on her first run and I know she ran a real good one but she's improved for the run this race is hotter than her first and we have matey boy determined to make me look like a fool, so I'm sure he'll write another scathing article, which will be exactly what we need. We'll have to put a hellavu lot on the rails or we'll never get enough on to even make a dent in any potential loss. What do you think Seamus, do you think she can win?"

"I think she'll take all the beating Mike, she's working like a train and if you're serious about me riding her … well she knows me and I know her so that gives us a bit of an advantage. I think we could do it, though I have to say I can't see how the hell you're expecting to win two hundred million. I'm up for helping …. Whatever… don't get me wrong but I just don't see how you hope to make that sort of money."

"Look a long time ago I remember my old 'guvnor' asking me how much money I wanted, and I said enough to be comfortable. Ahh but how comfortable, it's not how much you wanted or need it's how much satisfies you. I'm not saying that we need or want this money at the moment what I am saying is that should and I know it looks a strong possibility that I've bitten off more than Rocket can chew! You see John if I hadn't gone along with the idea in the first place you wouldn't have taken the bet and we wouldn't be worrying. So I'm as responsible as you! What I'm suggesting is that we all now have a lifestyle we don't wish to lose so if we can have a decent result on Sunrise we'll stick it in a separate account overseas in a different name, so that if we lose at least we still have a fall back and can retain our lifestyle. If by any chance we don't, we have a slush fund that we can afford to do whatever we want with! If each of us put up £500,000 at seven to one that's £10,500,000!"

John looked across at Seamus, it was Seamus that spoke first. "Well I'm in I've nothing to lose! I didn't have that sort of money until you decided I should be a millionaire! So even if we lose I'm still half a millionaire… and that my friends is more than I wanted needed or expected! I'm still going to be a happy man whatever the result!"

John smiled. "I'm in, I can always pick up a paint brush if it goes tits up!" three hands reached out and grabbed each other. "All for one!"

John excused himself and went off in search of Alice and Mike who he hadn't spent a great deal of time with lately with all that was happening. Seamus and Mike continued sitting at the kitchen table pouring over the Racing Calendar.

"You know Michael." Seamus looked up from their studies to speak. "We should be looking for a race for that little bay gelding, the one little one's called Dusk. He'd be ready for a run and he's well enough in himself, we should be looking to get him a handicap mark so that we can win a little race with him."

"Alright I'll leave that up to you. I've a feeling I'm going to be really busy with the Jockey Club. We've got to sort out what's happening about Rockets race, I've not bothered following things up after Newbury but we still need to sort it out, hiding won't help. How did the boy do this morning?" Mike asked rather tongue in cheek believing he would already know Seamus reply.

"Oh he really enjoyed himself this morning." Seamus said sarcastically, "Jumped off at the start about ten lengths behind that nice four-year-old, went at a nice strong canter for a furlong, stopped and I swear he did a little dance, he was spinning round and pissing about, not being bad just pissing about making me look like a fool, then he takes off. Jesus, I forgot how quick he is! Catches that four-year-old like he was stood still and as soon as he's got about five lengths on him stops dead again. Dropped me a treat the bastard. Stood there he did just watching me then wanders off to find a dandelion! You know I think the world of him Mike but I'm beginning to have serious doubts, at least he started to work half properly before the Derby but he's gone back to his old self with no interest in doing anything on the gallops but make a fool of everyone, especially me. The weird thing is though that even when he does show his ability and I know it's for a short time he never seems to blow at all. I still don't see how the hell we can get him fit enough for the race, even if we get another six months!" Mike felt dejection wash over him and there was a long pause before he replied to Seamus. "Well Seamus they say where there's life there's hope and at the moment the only thing we have is hope. Maybe he'll give us a surprise and start getting down to his work." Mike continued trying to sound confident. "I know he's a quirky old bugger but he's done it to us before, give him an hour on the walker in the afternoon, then turn him out in the paddock with Storm, maybe the little fella will get him to run 'round a bit."

Mike leaned on the top rail of Rocket's paddock with Seamus alongside him. "Well Michael me boy it looks as though there keen as mustard!" the Irish accent seemed always to be stronger when Seamus was near a horse Mike thought as he surveyed the father and son duo casually stretched out in the sun. It seemed that running was the last thing on either of the horse's minds. Mike threw his hands in the air. "What the fuck are we going to do Seamus?" and as answer Seamus too threw his hands in the air.

Mike returned to his office where Vi immediately showered him with tea and cake, after sitting for half an hour considering the situation Mike picked up the phone and dialled the Jockey Club.

Major Alfred Mapperton was still reeling from the horror of the Newbury atrocity and was vociferous in its condemnation for a full five minutes ending in hearty congratulations for the efforts of Mike, the staff and friends for their efforts in helping as much as they did. Mike glossed over the thanks and concentrated on discussing how they would bring about the re-scheduling of the race. Newmarket was suggested as a replacement venue but Mike objected on the same grounds that he had before saying that he thought the home of racing gained enough and that somehow he thought one of the smaller tracks should be given a chance. Salisbury racecourse was prepared he said to give any gate profits from the meeting to charity, specifically on an even split between the Newbury victim's charity that was set up immediately after the bombing and half again in equal shares to the injured jockey fund, the stable lads association and one of the rehabilitation of racehorse charities selected by the Jockey Club. Major Alfred Mapperton laughed down the phone it was the first time since that dreadful day at Newbury. "Michael you are a breath of fresh air! You're also a clever young bugger to boot! It would be more than churlish for me not to support such a generous offer from the committee of Salisbury, especially as it is pretty local to you! However, I do have reservations as to whether the racecourse is of sufficient area to cater for the crowds?" Mike interjected.

"I had a feeling you would say that!"

"Now why doesn't that surprise me I wonder!"

"We've worked it out and both the racecourse staff and myself believe that if we open up the end of the course enclosure do the same with the stand side and I think if we lined the whole racecourse we might just get them all in. it'll be difficult but with modern technology we can set up enough screens for everyone to see. It's going to be hard wherever we go, room is going to be at a premium but I personally think that a lot of the people that attend won't be the normal racegoers, of course there will be thousands that attend that are but there will be thousands that attend solely because it's been given such a build up. Would you miss the opportunity to tell your grandchildren you were there when the race of all time was held, even if you normally had no interest in racing whatsoever? I wouldn't! I appreciate your point of holding this race at one of the bigger courses but we've given one place for a wild card which is coming from one of the smallest trainers in the country, Salisbury might not be the biggest but it's a cracking course, bloody good test of stamina for the horses, well run and I think they can do it. If you get your heads together with the Salisbury management I reckon we'd not only do the punters proud but racing as well. What do you say?"

"Well…!" the major was a bit taken aback by the emotive deliverance of Mike's speech.

"Well….as I said Michael you're a bit of a clever young bugger. Mmm…maybe you are right perhaps we shouldn't be so dyed in the wool about things…. Yes, what the heck, let's as you say go for it. It's about time we showed everybody that we're not just a load of pompous old farts drinking pink gin in a private club… "The major went into battle mode. "Let's show the blighters we can put on a bloody good show even in the midst of adversity and at the same time give credit to one of our highly respected but smaller courses at the same time. Bring them on I say, we'll jolly well kick their asses I believe that's the saying…? I'll speak to Salisbury this afternoon and start the ball rolling." Mike replaced the receiver pleased that he had achieved his aim. Salisbury racecourse it would be…. all he had to do now was get Rocket fit enough to race!!! He was just about to leave when the phone rang. His heart missed a beat as he heard Kate's voice. "Mike I'm sorry to bother you but I was wondering if you would do me a real favour?"

"Of course, what can I do to help? Oh by the way I've entered Sunrise in a six-furlong maiden at Salisbury and if it's okay with you I'd like to put Seamus on board?"

"That sounds great, though you'd better run it by madam first or I'll never hear the last of it!" Mike chuckled. "My favour…. I wanted to take Geoff and Peter out for dinner not to celebrate because one could never do that after such an appalling…. Well I suppose I'm really proud of them both and even more so that they are going to give their OBE's to Newbury racecourse when it's rebuilt in honour of all those that suffered and all those that helped. I'd just like to show them my appreciation, it's not a lot I'll grant you but I thought if I took them out to a surprise dinner it would be my way of saying thank you on behalf of everybody. Anyway I know how well you and Beck's get on and she suggested," 'nice move' thought Mike, "that I ask you if you would mind coming over to baby sit so to speak…." Mike was thinking how he and John, selfish though it may have been had also been there in the thick of things. He even felt a bit truculent at Kate asking him yet not recognising that fact but he felt that his might just have something to do with the fact that he had fallen in love with Kate and here she was talking of her hero. "Well!" He thought to himself before answering, "I suppose it's only fair John and I didn't lift that bloody great lintel… we only did the easy bit."

"Love too. What time would you like me there…… okay look forward to it…see you at seven thirty…. bye." In truth Mike was looking forward to it since sitting by Becky's bed and telling her a bedtime story he realised how much difference his life would be with a child in it. He didn't regret that he never had children but he did regret not having that special magic that a child brings into one's life, he looked in the long mirror by the door of his office. "You'd have made a good dad you know! Even if I do say so myself."

Mikes Noble purred up the drive of Kate's house the exhaust sound reverberating under the elegant copper beech trees. He pulled to a stop and before he got one foot out of the car door there was a little face close to his. "Oohh we're going to have such fun I've planned everything. We can play on the play station dad bought me today. There's a really good jockey game and I'm absolutely brilliant at it... you'll never manage to beat me! Mummy and I have done loads of nibbly things for us and I haven't got to go to bed until ten! Isn't it exciting!" Mike wondered how such a little thing could produce so much air and talk for so long without drawing breath.

"Okay kiddo." He said. "Just let's see just how good you are on this new jockey game." And he stepped out of the car. Becky ran excitedly back to the house shouting frantically to her mother that Mike had arrived. By the time Mike walked to the front door Kate appeared. She took Mike's breath away. "God she's beautiful." He thought and said, "Wow you look incredible!" Mike was sure Kate knew the effect she had on him and she smiled that devastating smile before inviting him in and walking Mike was certain more seductively than normal towards the lounge. He watched her hips swing and her firm pert bottom as he followed her, her dress accentuating her movement, the light green blue material swishing with every step she took Geoff and Peter were already sitting watching Becky who was in the process of resetting her game. Both men rose to their feet and greeted Mike warmly. The conversation stemmed around the extra bond they had formed through the act of violence at Newbury then on to the inevitable, the horses. Mike explained his intention to run Sunrise at Salisbury and to look for a race for Dusk. Becky forgot her game and went into raptures, even more so when Mike explained that Seamus would be the jockey. Becky was thrilled telling her mum dad and grandfather they should go. Much to every ones amusement, surplus to present requirements was how Mike explained it,

Becky's horses having taken over the front row. Kate turned to Mike kissed his cheek and told him that Becky's bed time was nine thirty, which caused Becky to blush and receive a sideways glance from Mike. "Okay kiddo, if you don't tell mum or dad we'll make it ten for your cheek!" Which awarded him a hug. The two hours until ten o'clock flew by true to her word Becky had mastered the jockey game and thrashed Mike in every game, they pigged out on the mountain of nibbles that Kate had prepared and Mike then told Becky it was time for her to hit the hay. "When I'm a famous trainer like you I'll have to go to bed even earlier, won't I or I'll never get up in the morning!" Mike felt as proud at that moment as he ever felt in his life, here was, an albeit small person, but nonetheless intelligent one, who wanted to follow in his footsteps. No one had in his memory ever wanted to be like him before.

"Do you remember that you said you would tell me that other story?"

"Which one was that?" Mike asked.

"I think it was called The Stallion!"

"Okay but only the one story then you are straight off to sleep young lady." Mike said impressed at her memory and amused that she should want to hear the story.

With Becky tucked in, Mike sat on the edge of the bed looking at the two small eyes that stared intently at his face from just above the top of the duvet. "Are you comfy?" He asked and received a nodded reply. "Then I shall begin." He said rather dramatically. "The Stallion...... I watched with baited breath as dawn broke, and the silhouette of the horse appeared on the horizon, rearing high as though greeting the warmth of the new-born sun. Every morning I had crept silently to the hill. Always keeping downwind of the herd, watching, waiting, my plan formulating. He was magnificent, rearing on his hind legs and striking the air in a challenge to the elements, the muscles rippling beneath his chestnut hide. I watched entranced by his perfection, his beauty. Suddenly his demeanour changed, no longer the carefree spirit, alert to his surroundings, something had disturbed him. His eyes searching, ears forward, his nostrils flared seeking to place the unfamiliar scent. He had seen something that was causing him great concern, he pawed the ground stamping his feet... causing small plumes of dust to rise above the purple heather. He had lived on the moor all of his life wild and free, had he sensed I was there, perhaps he had read my thoughts? My mind drifted as I once again dreamed of sitting on his back feeling the strong back and muscle rippling as we sped across the soft turf. His warning snort brought me back from my daydream, he was telling his mares to beware. His fine head turned in my direction, ears forward, straining to hear any tell-tale sound. Eyes alight, reflecting the morning sun. Was it me? No surely not. He had seen me before even though I had been careful in my observations, never startling him, always keeping downwind and quiet until he saw I meant him no harm. The low guttural rumble made my hair stand on end. Almost afraid to move, I turned. I blinked unable to believe my eyes. I looked again and found myself staring at what appeared to be a very large black cat its cold yellow eyes fixed on me. I could not move, I could not shout, just stare. Fear froze my very being. One minute I was considering how to take my stallions freedom. Now my freedom was to be taken by the cruel form that stalked me, its sharp fangs bared, its long-curved claws ready to dig into my flesh so that the fangs could do their work.

The cat crouched readying itself for the spring. It's funny what you think, even through the fear, but I remember thinking how sinuous and sleek it looked. Somehow cruelly beautiful. The thunder of hooves deafened my thoughts as the stallion galloped at the cat. So quickly had all this taken place that even the cat could not prepare for the onslaught as the enraged stallion struck him. The cat tried to turn its attack on the stallion, but he had already turned, lashing out with his hind legs bowling the cat over on to his back. Lunging again at the cat with hoof and teeth, furious at this predator's intrusion into his domain. The cat managed to slash at the stallion with his front paw, raking his shoulder with its claws. I shall never forget the scream in my head as I saw his blood well from the lacerations. Anger possessed me totally, I grabbed a fallen branch and rushed at the cat cudgelling the creature until my breath and strength had gone. I looked briefly at the broken body of the cat as I gasped for breath. Then fearfully I looked toward the stallion. He stood some ten feet from me, blood oozing down his side. Frothy white sweat beaded his neck and flanks, his sides heaving as he struggled to keep his feet. Slowly I moved towards him holding out my hand in the hope he would accept my approach. My whole body shook maybe it was fear maybe it was excitement, I was unsure. Deep down I knew I owed my life to him and he had accepted me as a friend. I was overcome with the conviction that I could no longer seek to capture his wild heart.... He would be made well and then given his birthright............FREEDOM. Something I had no right to take. Memories linger on, many times since I have walked the moors seeing him prance round his mares, tail held high. He has never allowed me to touch him since that time to mend his wounds. But our minds touch always."

"Oohh, Becky said that was a bit scary but it's a wonderful story…. Did that really happen?" She asked desperately trying to stifle a yawn as sleepiness at being up so late tried to overtake her. "I'm glad you smashed that horrible old cat thing!" and before Mike could say another word she was sound asleep.

By the time Kate and Geoff returned Mike was sound asleep on the couch, Kate smiled fondly and as Geoff made his way to the bedroom she took a blanket and carefully covered him in it. She looked down at him leaning forward to kiss his forehead. "Another time another place is what they say. Maybe in another life ehh?" and she made her own way to the bedroom.

Mike nearly had an apoplexy when the tiny hands grabbed him shaking him awake. "Come on sleepy head!" the hands voice cried, "it's time for breakfast!"

"What… what?" Mike stuttered. "What time is it?"

"You're really funny when you've just woken up!" She giggled. "It's six o'clock. Mummy said that we could all go to see the horses today and I thought I'd get everybody up so we could get an early start." Mike was trying to get his bearing and to shake the sleep from his eyes. He suddenly became wide awake as Kate walk into the lounge wearing nothing but a short open shirt hiding nothing of her naked body. "Oh! I'm sorry I forget you were here!" and she ran from the room to change with Mike's eyes glue to her lithe form. "Wow!" Mike thought. "What I'd give for an alarm clock like that!"

"You really like my mummy, don't you?" Becky's head was held to one side in a questioning gesture, her face screwed up tight in concentration waiting for an answer. "Why don't you move in with us then we could have fun all the time, you and mummy get on really well and daddy likes you and you live alone in that big house of yours and I like you and we could play the jockey game on my play station and you could teach me more about horses and…"

"Whoa there kiddo!" Mike interrupted, thinking how wonderfully simple life is being a child.

"It's a bit more complicated than that, oh God how do I explain this? Right, mum and dad love each other, just like they love you and they're married, it's really different for friends, which is what I am to mum and dad, and anyway who would look after the horses. You'd soon get very bored with me around 'cause I'm a grumpy old guvnor!" Mike jumped up from the couch grabbed Becky and swung her round she chuckled gleefully, he thanked the innocence and simplicity of a child's mind for such a task to remove all thoughts of the conversation. "I thought you said we were going to have some breakfast?" He said

"We'll have to wait for mummy to come back down. She won't let me use the cooker in case I burn myself… that was funny though!" Mike looked puzzled Becky looked exasperated. "When mummy came in…. she went so red… and you saw her bottom." Becky burst into laughter running 'round the couch singing.

"Mike saw mummy's bottom… Mike saw mummy's

bottom!" Mike nearly laughed himself though he wasn't sure if it was from actually seeing 'mummy's bottom' or at Becky's impromptu performance he knew however that the subject should be changed not only to save Kate's blushes but also to save an explanation to Geoff. Things like that have a habit of leading down roads that should be avoided. "Come on you." Mike grabbed Becky by the hand as she continued her singing and dancing act around the couch. "Take me to the kitchen and I'll cook the breakfast!" By the time Kate came back down Mike was well into Jamie Oliver mode and there was a sizeable heap of delicious looking bacon, sausage and eggs piling up. Kate was a bit sheepish and she put it down to too much drink the night before when questioned by Geoff, Mike thought Becky might say something and quickly changed the subject back to horses. Mike thought to himself that it was paranoia setting in, telling himself not to be so stupid. It was only an innocent mistake after all!

Mike gunned the M15 back to the yard hoping to catch last lot but as he pulled into the drive Seamus and the lads were just coming back in from the gallops. Seamus didn't look overjoyed.

"You don't look too happy?" Mike leaned out of the window of the Noble to aim his question at Seamus. Seamus was sitting astride a prancing Rocket and Mike grumbled at him telling him to stop pratting about. Rocket obediently stood still.

"It's a fucking shame you can't get him to listen and do some work!" Seamus spat in his broadest accent. "Went half way up the gallops like a missile, stopped turned 'round and shot back down the way he'd just come. Fucking frightened me half to death he did. It's a good job these girls have more sense than him and got off the gallops when they saw him tanking back towards them or it might have been bumper cars and not fucking dodgems!" Seamus became more serious.

"Shit he's good this horse Michael but for sure as eggs he's more cantankerous than he's ever been. I've never been so pleased as when you told me I was riding him in the race but I'm worried the daft old sods going to hurt himself if he doesn't get on with his work and get fit!" Rocket reared nearly catching Seamus unawares and took off towards the stables. "Bastard....!" Was all the others and Mike heard as Seamus disappeared around the corner of the yard.

Mike fell into despair. It was nothing to do with the way Rocket was behaving, he was worried about his level of fitness but deep down inside he still had that unbreakable optimism that all trainers hold about their horses, it was nothing to do with the huge sums of money involved in the race, it was the vision of Kate walking in front of his sleep laden eyes that morning and his knowing that there might be a corner in her heart for someone else but it would only ever be a corner. Geoff held the majority shareholding it was plain when she looked and spoke to him. He wondered in his despair if a corner would be enough and knew that however he cloaked it, it never would be. Mike decided he would shut Kate from his mind other than as a friend. Mikes despair deepened, the words of his old guvnor rang in his memory, 'a taste of somethin' is better than a taste of nothing boy' the trouble was Mike wanted the full three courses not just a taste. He made his way to the house and opened a bottle of Jameson's staring at the liquid as he poured the first.

"Oh well." He said aloud. "I haven't been pissed for a long time it'll do me good to let go." It never does.

Seamus called at the house late that afternoon to find Mike slumped drunkenly in a chair.

"Jesus Michael you're not starting with all that nonsense again now are you?" Mike replied with a drunken grin. "You'll not be smilin' in the mornin' me lad. Now if you can talk any sense at all in that state perhaps you'd like to tell me what's brought it all on?" Seamus sat and listened as Mike told him how he could not stop thinking of Kate, of how he worried over Rocket, of how tired he was of not having any love in his life. "At least when I thought Rocket was talking to me I thought someone cared." He told of Becky's innocent request of him that morning, Seamus sat without a word as Mike poured his heart out. "Well you missed your chance this morning Michael lad, them two fillies came to see you and I didn't have a clue where you were and it's just as well by the look of you. Now don't you start going all self-sympathetic on me because I know you better than that. You've a lot of people that care for you including them two, I know that's not what you're hoping for but you of all people wouldn't want to try to split up a family now I know, for sure it's against everything you believe. There's someone there… Christ it took me long enough to find someone after my problems with the first wife, well you know but there is always someone, you know, for everyone. I can see how much you think of the girl a blind man could see it but unless there's something I don't know. It looks to me like you're trying to climb up a greasy pole and that my friend can't be done!" Seamus threw a blanket over Mike saying he would come back in a couple of hours to make sure he was all right and left to make his way home. Seamus good for his word wandered back up to the house at eleven to find the downstairs lights ablaze, knowing the state Mike was in when he left he entered the house cautiously creeping on tip toe through the door. The huge shape that suddenly appeared from the side of the door knocked the wind clean out of him. "Got ya! Yuh shit, try to break in ehh!" Seamus tried to speak but couldn't he gasped for air.

"Get off 'im you bug lummock, it's Seamus." Vi's voice drifted across the kitchen and the weight was immediately gone from Seamus wiry but small body.

"Sorry!" Nick apologised as he helped Seamus to his feet patting him on the back in an effort to help him breathe. "I thought you was a burglar!" Seamus managed to breathe properly again.

"I'm bloody glad I'm not!" and they all laughed Nick looking down on Seamus with concern.

"I ain't 'urt you 'ave I?"

"It's all right Nick I was just a bit winded. Christ Vi I can see now why you never worry about locking your cottage," he pocked a finger into Nicks bicep, "he's better than a Rottweiler and a damn sight bigger!" and they all laughed again. "How's Mike? He wasn't looking too good when I left him. More than a few too many I think?"

"I got Nick to carry him upstairs." Then as if in explanation, "I brought some flowers up to brighten the place up, Nick wantin' to go and see that little 'orse of 'is. Well he was sprawled on the couch wiv just an old blanket over 'im. 'e needs a good woman, needs some love in 'is life 'e does. Jus' sittin' 'ere every night on 'is own. It's no good you know!"

Seamus spoke before thinking. "I think that's half his trouble Vi but I think it's more he wants what he can't have!" Seamus could have kicked himself. "For God's sake don't say I said that Vi!"

"Don't you worry. I ain't daft! I see what 'e's like when that Kate's about. Why a blind man could see it, hook line an' sinker is what. Why if she clicked 'er fingers 'e'd go running like a little love-sick puppy an' that ain't no good either! You need's love on both sides. We got to try an' 'elp 'im poor mite, 'e's the nicest chap I ever met an' 'e's been dead good to my Nick. Don't know 'ow though it'll want some thinkin' about but for now let's just all try to forgive 'is going off the rails a bit." Seamus agreed with Vi though he was thinking that the last time Mike went off the rails it was big time and no one could afford him to do that with the race and all that was connected to it.

Mike was woken by the incessant ringing of the phone. He open bleary eyes and closed them again quickly as the searing pain in his head raced across his forehead. He tried again adjusting slightly to the light. "Hello?" the soft voice of Kate came floating down the line and for a moment Mike thought he must still be asleep and dreaming. "Mike?" Mike made a half-hearted response.

"God you sound dreadful, are you ill?"

"Bit of a cold coming on I think." Mike lied.

"Would you like Beck's and I to come over I make very good soup and Beck's is very good at playing the nursemaid?" Mike didn't know whether Kate was being facetious or not, sure that she saw through his cold story but declined all the same. "Look I'm sorry to bother you when you're not feeling well but Beck's has taken it into her head to ask her school mates to Sunrise's next race, I do hope that's all right? She's rather proud that she knows you, you're quite famous you know." Mike said it was fine agreeing that he would organise their entrance to the racecourse, put the phone down and went back under the duvet. He didn't reappear until midday.

It was only two days away from Sunrises second run and the excitement was already building in the yard. Seamus pleased with her progress and nervous of his first race ride for many a year was the brunt of much leg pulling, especially as he had set up a barrel in the barn where he practiced riding a finish, he was so determined that his comeback would be a good one. When he read the article written in *The Racegoer* his nervousness turned to anger. Whilst *The Racing Post* article had not exactly been complimentary, even unfair it did not appear to be written with malice. *The Racegoer* was inflammatory to say the least. To the members of the yard it was obvious *The Racegoer* had tried hard to discredit Mike and the yard during the period when Rocket first came to see the racetrack and during the Malek incident. It was back with a vengeance. Not only had they been scathing in their condemnation of Mike but the horses and moreover Seamus. They had even gone to visit Malek's son in prison and glorified the interview with him in no uncertain terms. Seamus anger was however brought to boiling point by the last sentence of the article. He strode up to the house and burst into Mike's office throwing the offending paper on Mike's desk, his Irish accent becoming so broad he was difficult to follow. "Have you been reading this fucking rubbish they call a racing paper?" He asked Mike without even bothering to say hello. Mike smiled despite himself, he was still feeling low over his plutonic arrangement with Kate and still dreaming of her in that shirt.

"Seamus, why do you buy that crap?"

"They always put the form of the horses from the start of

their career!"

"Then read just the form the rest of it isn't fit to wipe your…" Vi entered.

"'ello Seamus would you boy's like a cup of tea. I've just made a fruit cake I'll bring you some in." Without waiting for an answer Vi disappeared.

"They've printed that I did time! Said I'm an ex jailbird that isn't to be trusted! I'll fucking show them trusted when I get my hands on them I'll… I'll fucking trust them up like chickens… I'll show them jailbird I'll geld 'em so I will!"

Mike burst out laughing and it was several minutes before he was able to speak.

"You sound just like I do when I lose the plot. You should get out more and it's truss not trust."

"Whatever it is I'll fucking do it!" Seamus was red faced with anger.

"Seamus the way to show them is on the racecourse and that's exactly what you're going to do. As you have said to me in the past it's only words and actions speak louder than words. So let your actions do the talking! You've only to wait less than forty-eight hours and you'll wipe the smile right off the face of them all. Let them say what they want you'll be the one with the smile in the end." Seamus gained back some control and Vi entered with two mugs of tea and a mountain of cake.

"I can't eat all that Vi! I'll be about two stone overweight!" Seamus exclaimed.

"Rubbish there's nothing of you and you need to build up your strength. My Nick reckons you weigh no more than a feather."

"I'll be a bloody heavy feather if I eat all of this." Seamus mumbled.

"I heard that." Vi said coming back to Seamus side and looking fierce. "are you sayin' my cake's is 'eavy?"

Seamus gulped. "No just that there's rather a lot of it!" he muttered sheepishly.

"Well there better not be any when I come back or they'll be trouble," she turned to Mike, "Yes?" she said shortly.

"I wasn't going to say a word." Mike said in his best boyish tone.

"Good!" Vi flounced out of the room, both men pulled a childish face.

"And you can stop pulling faces, the pair of you!" The two men spoke in harmony.

"How do they do that?" Each with a huge mouth full of cake.

CHAPTER FIFTEEN

Becky was standing in the lounge unaware that her mother, father and grandfather were watching her from the kitchen. She had an army of friends standing neatly in a line in front of her all standing to attention and taking each word spoken by General Beck's very seriously. "Now when Sunrise comes to the furlong marker." They all looked at each other confused. "Don't worry when we get to the racecourse I'll show you what it is. Anyway when Sunrise gets to the furlong marker that's when we all have to cheer... we have to get this perfect or she won't hear us... they'll be a lot of other people shouting so we have to be the loudest and do it all together. Let's have another practice. One two three 'Come on Sunrise you're the best we know you can beat the rest'! That was really good."

"Oh my God! I think I might just stay in the bar when the horse is racing." Geoff said to Kate and Peter, who were both in hysterics. "It's not funny it's bloody embarrassing, they've even got the actions. God, they look like miniature cheerleaders imported from America! They can't do it! I'm going to have a word!"

"Don't you dare Geoffrey Stokes!" Kate said with a steely look. "They are her friends and it's her horse and it's up to her how she wants to cheer her on. We agreed not to interfere where the horse was concerned and I think it's really sweet." Geoff made to object. "If you do!" Kate warned before Geoff had even opened his mouth. "I might join them in a very very short skirt… I quite fancy being a cheerleader!" Peter laughed and Geoff spluttered a begrudging agreement.

"We'd better start getting this lot loaded!" Peter declared. "I reckon it'll take us as long to get this lot in the limo as it will to get to the races! Come on girls let's get going." He shouted to the ensemble.

Becky and her friend's eyes lit up when they saw the limo. "You'd better go and give your gramps a big kiss young lady. It's not everyday you get to ride to the races in a limo." Becky's smile was worth every cent as she looked from her mum to the car, she ran over and embraced her grandfather. "Thank you granddad!" and she ran excitedly back to her friends who were all trying to get in at the same time. There were a multitude of buttons and switches that needed attending to and the girls were made for the job. The first five minutes of the journey consisted of windows, sunroof, screens, cocktail cabinets and anything else that could possibly be operated opening and closing at lightning speed and great amusement. Someone then suggested that people might think they were famous, even a pop group so all went still apart from the windows which were opened ever so slightly, just enough so as the girls could produce an arm and wave at an unsuspecting public. Salisbury racecourse came in sight and the girls forgot their games and started to concentrate on the job in hand.

Salisbury racecourse is a lovely course both for the public and the horses and the party trooped through the owner's entrance to the smiles of officials, Becky telling each and every one as she went that her horse Sunrise was in a race today, and of course that she was the 'bestest' horse in the whole world. Peter Geoff and Kate steered the miniature army towards the owner's bar where they had arranged to meet Mike. After the girls had been seated at a table and left chattering excitedly over copious amounts of Coca Cola purchased from the bar and a pile of sandwiches and crisps that are always supplied free of charge by the racecourse for owners, though it didn't look like the owners were going to see too many sandwiches today after Becky's army and their rapacious appetites had finished. Kate Geoff and Peter settled themselves at a table close by to await the arrival of Mike.

Mike stood in the weighing room chatting to Seamus who had objected strongly to not being in the stables with his horse but was told in no uncertain terms by the girls that he was the jockey today and not the assistant trainer and should therefore have a bit more trust and be the jockey, leaving the preparation of the horse up to them. Anita was there to supervise whilst Nicky and Hannah would get the horse ready. They were Anita assured everybody more than capable, it was after all not the first time they had been to the races. Seamus and Mike thought discretion the better part of valour and exited the stables before the girls closed ranks on them completely. There was quite a lot of light hearted sarcasm over Seamus getting his licence back, which came from the younger jocks who had never seen him ride, there were one or two journeymen there that could remember Seamus from their era, they kept quiet remembering his ability as a lad. Judgement on his riding in the present would be better left until after the race.

Seamus was worried the stewards had 'called' Mike to the weighing room and Seamus had a suspicion that it was to do with him riding the horse. Mike was trying to allay Seamus fears.

"Don't be daft Seamus the stewards can't call me in about your riding before you've even sat on the horse!"

"But what if they're going to take my licence back."

"Ahh, Michael could you spare me a couple of minutes?" It was Major Alfred Mapperton voice. He gestured towards the door of the steward's room.

"Well we'll soon find out." Mike threw at Seamus as he made his way towards the open door.

He entered the room and the door was closed behind him.

Major Mapperton held out his hand.

"Good to actually meet you in person old chap." Mike took his hand shaking it firmly.

"My pleasure Major." He said.

"Alfred please, I think we've got to know each other well enough on the telephone to dispense with the formalities, from what I have learnt about you, formality is not a word you relish anyway!" He laughed and Mike relaxed.

"What can I do for you? It's a little unusual to be called to the stewards before the horse is even out of the stable!" Mike said with an air of mild concern. The Major laughed again and gestured for Mike to take a seat as he did so himself.

"Nothing to do with your runner old chap. I thought it would be wise for us to meet at last and I've always like Salisbury plus it gets me out of that infernal office. Not really an office, you know, even after all these years, much prefer to be out in the open air! No I just wanted to meet with you and being here is ideal you can if you can make the time available run through your idea for the big race on site so to speak." Mike agreed that after the filly had run he would spend some time with 'Alfred' and show him how he thought it would be possible to accommodate the expected crowds for Rockets race. He made his way back to the weighing room where Seamus had very nearly worn a groove in the floor as he paced up and down. Mike explained what the meeting was about left Seamus to his own devices and went in search of his owners. He saw Kate standing by the winning post leaning against the rails her long tanned legs and trim figure standing out among the crowd that had begun to arrive. He noticed how many men received a sharp dig in the ribs from a wife or girlfriend as their eyes strayed towards the beautiful woman clad in a filmy blue summer frock cut about eight inches above her knee. One man actually tripped over when a light breeze lifted the back of the dress revealing a pert tanned and naked bottom. Mike stood for a few moments admiring Kate before venturing forth to say hello, he would have probably stayed there all day had the breeze not dropped sufficiently to allow Kate's dress to return to its normal position. The smile he received was the same dazzling knee weakener that he remembered from his stay in the Spanish hospital and it wilted his resolve not to try to expand their friendship. "Has anyone told you today how incredibly beautiful you are?" He said to Kate's back.

She turned to face him a look crossed between chastisement and longing on her face. "Mike behave yourself! Please!"

"Sorry it's just you look so bloody fantastic."

"Enough." She said sternly "We agreed... I'm a happily married woman."

Mike reined in. "I know but that doesn't mean I can't appreciate your beauty and compliment you does it. I don't think observation counts as infidelity?"

"No I suppose not but just remember that's as far as it goes from now on.... It's hard for me as well you know but we just can't be any more than friends. I can't put my marriage and my little girl in jeopardy."

"Speaking of shortcake... where is she. I'd have thought she'd have been plaguing everyone to death trying to get to see Sunrise." Kate chuckled.

"Are you in for a surprise Mike Willett." Mike raised his eyebrows and Kate laughed despite the hidden innuendo. "Behave! I'm afraid you might find the plan a little on the embarrassing side!"

"Plan what plan?"

"Becky had brought along a few of her friends. They've been practicing all morning, they're very good"! Kate was enjoying herself, Mike was looking more and more confused.

"Practicing what?"

"Why their cheerleading chant of course. Ready for when Sunrise races!"

"Oh my God!"

"Mike!" Becky appeared from the owner's bar with her friends, Geoff and Peter in tow. These are my friends Becky said swamping Mike in a fairly good impression of a bear hug and at the same time depositing a crumb laden kiss to his cheek. Becky introduced her friends one by one lining them up as she did so. "We'll show you what we've rehearsed for Sunrises race." She said with huge enthusiasm and it was all the adults could do to persuade her to leave it as a surprise for the race. Mike wasn't sure whether he was looking forward to seeing the 'chant' or not. He loved to see kids enjoying themselves but wondered what the racecourse officials would make of it. There was obviously no way Becky and her army were going to be talked out of it because they were already ensuring they had the rail by the winning post and looked as though they were going to be immovable. They had enough 'supplies' in the form of soft drinks and crisps to stick it out for a week. Mike excused himself and wandered off to saddle the horse. Kate looking radiant strode into the parade ring on Geoff's arm, Peter following close behind. Mike noticed that she attracted more interest than the horses and could understand why, his heart felt empty as he watched her arm in arm with Geoff.

Hannah had been given the job of leading up Sunrise as Kate asked if Anita and Nicky could keep an eye on Becky's army. The horses shone in the sunlight and Sunrise groomed to perfection lived up to her name as Hannah proudly walked her round the walkway in the parade ring. The jockeys filed out a colourful line of brave miniatures. Seamus looked as though he had never been away from the racetrack and as is customary tipped his cap to Kate, Geoff, and Peter. Mike had spent his life racing but the colours and the thrill remained ever sharp he breathed in the atmosphere as he always did, his stomach doing butterflies with excitement. "Guvnor." Seamus said tipping his hat out of respect. Mike gave him a look, talking in hushed tones he said. "Alright enough of the guvnor."

"Just doing things right." Was Seamus hushed reply.

"You know her better than anyone so just ride how you think. Just give it your best. You'll be fine." Mike said and it was obvious his pride in Seamus regaining his licence and in his first ride being Sunrise. Seamus was legged up into the saddle and led out on to the course, as she passed the stands a cry of SUNRISE rose above the buildings Becky's army was already in battle mode.

Sunrise went down to the start and loaded in the stalls perfectly and as they were waiting for the rest of the field to load Mike's mobile rang, it was John. John informed him that the bets had all gone on as planned and he would ring him after the race, which he was watching at home.

"And there off.... And its Excel that takes the early lead Baronita takes a strong hold in second Enchantress lies third then comes Sunrise and then a gap to the rest of four lengths. Excel going at a cracking pace Baronita dropping back Enchantress moves into third tracked by Sunrise Stronghold is starting to make headway on the inside they've hit the two-furlong mark and are kicking for home, it's still Excel that holds the lead with Enchantress and Stronghold both looking for a run on the inside, Sunrise starts to make progress on the outside coming with a really strong run, a furlong from home and it's Stronghold and Sunrise battling it out. "COME ON SUNRISE YOU'RE THE BEST WE KNOW YOU CAN BEAT THE REST!" Rose above the roar of the crowd as the tiny army with the help of Anita and Nicky jumped up and down punching the air as they chanted. Seamus didn't hear the chant but he felt the surge as Sunrise inched forward in front of Stronghold, "Come on my girl you can do it, go on!" he screamed in Sunrises ear and the post flashed by. "Photo, photo." The tannoy announced and Mike ran to the top of the parade ring to meet with Seamus and Sunrise. Hannah had the lead rein already on Sunrise by the time he got there and was manoeuvring her in front of the winner's enclosure much to the disgruntlement of the lad leading up Stronghold. "I think we got it." He said.

"In your dreams," was the curt reply from Hannah. No one ever believed their horse was beat.

The tannoy announced, winner by a short head number seven second number four third number eight. That's first number seven, second number four and third number eight.

Mike Seamus and Hannah looked at each other with practical disbelief. "You old Irish bugger!" Mike shouted. "You bloody well did it." They all slapped each other's backs. "Jesus Seamus, try not to make it so close next time…. My hearts not as young as it used to be!" Seamus couldn't speak he was grinning too much. He grabbed the saddle and rushed off to the weighing room to be weighed back in. Mike made sure Hannah was okay and rushed off to find Kate and the rest of the gang. He turned the corner to see 'Becky's army', which now included Anita and Nicky being frantically photographed by the press and television. He received a hearty slap on the back and turned to see who was congratulating him. "Bloody marvellous idea old boy, bloody marvellous. The originator of the Rocket race and her associates!" he waved an arm in the general direction of the army. "Doing a chant for their horse, couldn't get better advertising. Bloody good idea!"

"But," Mike interrupted, "It wasn't my idea it was Becky's!"

"Don't be modest Michael my boy it doesn't suit you!"

"No but it really was Becky's idea! I didn't know anything about it until I arrived and if I'm honest I wasn't too keen… thought it might be a bit over the top."

"Then bloody good show on her. I'll buy the lot of them as much ice cream as they want! Over the top indeed! Need more young blood with that sort of enthusiasm don't you know!" Major Alfred Mapperton announced and walked forward to congratulate the stars.

When it had quietened down a bit the racecourse kindly agreed that Becky should be allowed to receive the trophy presentation, which she did with all her friends much to the pleasure of the press the crowd and her parents. Becky even said a few words which brought oohs and ahhs from the crowd. Mike thought to himself that in a few years she would be a force no one with any sense would stand in the way of, especially when she started her short speech with "I shall remember this day for the rest of my life." The press, the crowd in fact, everyone was hers! There was a new chant that evening as the party made their way back home. Becky's army never drew breath as they chanted *we are the champions* all the way home. Mike and Seamus declined an offer from Geoff and his father to return with them and celebrate making the excuse that by the time they had returned to the yard and sorted everything out it would be too late. They did agree to give them a ring the following day and arrange something, Kate suggesting that John and Alice should be invited also.

John stood in the drive of his house awaiting the arrival of Mike and Seamus, greeting them with a huge smile when they pulled up at the top of the drive.

"Shit Mike I know we've had a few touches but I really did think your plan was a bit too ambitious to say the least…. Fucking hell, do you know what we've managed? We managed to get 25-1 on the rails on at least two twenty grand win bets, I haven't had all the odds back yet but at a conservative estimate I reckon we've returned closer to fifteen million! … I can't believe it!"

Mike appreciated John's enthusiasm but seeing Kate had depressed him slightly and he poured cold water on the other two's obvious delight without even meaning too.

"It still leaves us about a hundred and eighty-five million short! We've got to be a bit more realistic I'm afraid… there's no way we can cover the bet in the time we've got so we need to get this money hidden and quickly. I spoke to the bank I used when I was in Spain and they've put me on to bank in Andorra where he knows the manager and he's going to arrange for them to open an account for us. I thought just to keep things straight we should be joint signatories. We can fly out to the Aeropeurto de la Sue and hire a car, it's only half an hour or so from there. I suggest we go the day after tomorrow if that's okay with you guys… perhaps you can organise a flight for us John? You'll also have to organise getting the money into an account here so that we can transfer it. I don't think we should use our normal account… bit fishy and traceable." This was readily agreed and the three made their way to John's kitchen. It was Seamus who explained the offer of a night out with Geoff, Kate and Peter and John suggested that they should go to his restaurant which he hadn't visited for some weeks. John shrugged smiling resignedly. "On me. After all a few more quid isn't going to make a lot of difference if we lose. One hundred and eighty million makes the bill for a night out pale into insignificance!"

"We haven't lost yet!" Seamus said. "Let's leave the losing till we actually do ehh. Fat lady hasn't sung yet and all that jazz?"

They sunk a bottle of Jameson's between them and John rang for a taxi to take Mike and Seamus back to the yard. It was with a feeling of true camaraderie that the three parted that night. It was Seamus that stuck his hand out to the other two. "One for all and all for ne!" and they all felt they had a friendship that could not be broken.

Mike rang Kate first thing in the morning telling her of the plan to go to John's restaurant, and they made arrangements to meet at there at around eight. Alice was going to bring Michael junior and Mike suggested it would be nice as it was Becky's horse if she were to come along as well. Mike felt as though he was riding a double edge sword. He was desperate to see Kate but didn't want that awful feeling of dejection when he saw her with Geoff. "You've got to sort yourself out boy!" he said out loud to himself as he came off the telephone. *The Racing Post* came rocketing through the door and Mike wandered to the front door to collect it. He unfolded the paper and looked at the front page, he nearly fell through the floor. There was Becky's army photographed in full cry with Anita and Nicky in unison. The headline read: *The Sunrises For Becky's Army.* The article covered two pages extolling the virtues of the enthusiasm of youth and praising Salisbury racecourse for having the sense to allow a minor to collect the prize even though she could not be registered as the owner because of her age. Becky's short speech was quoted word perfect. There was not a dry eye in the place the reporter wrote and he would be amazed if there was one person that had not fallen for the charms of such a delightful and intelligent child. The phone rang. "Did you know I'm delightful and intelligent?" A small smug voice asked down the phone before giggling hysterically. "Isn't it fun! They want me to go on the television for an interview thing and I've been asked if I would go on Channel Four... The Morning Line and I always watch that every Saturday. I'm going to tell them what a super trainer you are and what great stories you tell."

"I think you had better have a word with mum and dad first sweetie." Mike was thinking Becky's imagination had run riot.

"Oh, it's okay mummy took the phone calls... She's so proud of me... anyway she's going to be there on the telly too. See you tonight." And the tiny voice was gone.

Mike walked out into the yard to be confronted by the staff who were just as excited as Becky, Anita and Hannah had the offers too and from the look of joy on their faces they were certainly not going to turn the opportunity down. Mike decided to go for a drive. He jumped in the Navara just as Seamus came 'round the corner. "Mike." He shouted. "Hang on I'm just about to saddle Rocket are you going to watch him?" Mike wasn't going too but decided it wouldn't be so bad after all. He had left the horses to Seamus for the last few days and it would do him good to get back on the gallops and see what was happening. He nodded ascent and drove off towards the top of the gallops. It was a gorgeous day, sun shining with a light gentle breeze that took the sting off the suns heat. Everything looked amazingly crisp and clean from the morning dew. Flowers seemed to have thrown out every petal they processed in an effort to benefit themselves from the sun's rays and in reply the sun had cast its light upon them to enhance the brilliant colours they displayed. Mike absorbed the blues, yellows and red that the flowers proudly declared along the edge of the gallops. Reaching the top he looked back down the hill. "I may not be lucky in love." He exclaimed. "But for sure as eggs I'm bloody lucky to have all this! It makes you think why we all strive for so much when we already have so much if we just open our eyes." Seamus appeared at the bottom of the gallops and Mike's thoughts went back to the horses, Anita, Hannah and Nicky jumped off going at a strong clip. Seamus still circled on Rocket at the start of the gallops, Mike could see that Seamus was trying to get Rocket to follow but he seemed to be getting even more cantankerous with every day that passed. The others were a good furlong up the gallop before Rocket turned and took after them. Mike watched as he ate up the ground, thinking to himself that even Rocket couldn't get on terms with the other such was there lead but with every stride he pegged them back. By the time they had reached the four-furlong marker Rocket had passed them and raced to the end of the gallops without stopping. Mike felt the exhilaration that comes from watching a horse with such an amazing ability put it too use. At the end of the gallops Rocket did a small rear and what looked to Mike suspiciously like a bow and trotted over to where he stood nuzzling his neck affectionately. "I told you when he was in the Derby he can't be beat." Seamus had renewed his membership of the 'I Love Rocket' fan club. "Fuck I swear Mike he's faster now than he's ever been, and did you see him that rear and he took a bow like he was telling the others to appreciate real class!" Mike looked first at Rocket then at Seamus as he spoke he gently stroked Rockets neck. "He's one helluva horse Seamus there's no doubting that. He's faster than anything I've ever seen but the trouble is he's only doing seven furlongs he's got to perform over a mile and a half in the race. I love the old sod to bits but I'm still not sure that he's going to be fit enough to take on the world, which is exactly what he's going to be doing. I'm afraid he'll not get the trip."

"Don't you go worrying yourself now Michael me boy by the time them other horses has reached the finish we'll be in the lorry and on our way home. Look at him now…couldn't blow a candle out and after a performance like that. I'm tellin' you Michael he does not get beat!"

"Oh my God!" thought Mike "Too much deja vous!" Rocket snorted in Mike's ear did another small rear and took off down the gallops at a steady canter tail held high in the air.

After breakfast Mike asked Seamus to run him over to Johns to collect his car. They caught John just as he was sitting down to a large plate of bacon and eggs and it was all they could do to convince Alice that they really didn't need feeding as they had just eaten, they settled on tea and playing with Michael junior whilst John and Alice ate. Seamus, used to having children, rolled the little one along the floor, then pulling him back by his leg when he tried to make his escape. Michael junior had just started to crawl and it was the best game he had ever played chuckling loudly every time Seamus grabbed him and dragged him back. "Careful Seamus." Mike protested. "He's only little!" for the first time in months Alice spoke to him with affection in her voice. Since his split with Ann they had spoken but it was only really when necessary, most of the time Alice seemed to avoid contact with Mike. It appeared that now Ann was settling with someone else the pressure was released. "He's okay Mike, you forget Seamus has brought up one or two himself. There as tough as old boots at that age. You don't want your namesake growing up a softy, do you?" Mike laughed but kept a guarded eye on the playtime. Alice said she had things to do and walked over to pick up Michael jnr. Mike reached down to pick him up so that he could pass him to Alice. The little bundle chuckled and blew raspberries. Mike was fascinated at how tiny he was, Michael junior flailed his arms around trying to grab Mike's hair catching Mike a corker just under his eye.

"Plucky little chap aren't you." Mike said bouncing him up and down and making him chuckle louder. Alice took him from Mike with a broad grin. "And you've got a fair whack on you!"

"I wonder who he takes after for that!" Alice said still smiling and it broke the ice between her and Mike properly, they could be friends again. Alice left and John told of the plan he made for the day. "I couldn't find a flight to Aeropuerto de la Seu, so I've hired a small jet to take us. It is a bit expensive I'm afraid but as we did rather better than we expected I thought we just as well go in style! They'll be a car waiting for us at the airport, so all you need to do Mike is confirm with your friendly bank manager the time of our arrival. Oh I arranged to collect a couple of the wins on our way so that we have a decent amount to open the account with, we can explain to the bank there will be large sums to be deposited over the next few days by credit transfer as I'm afraid I didn't manage to collect in all the bets. Those I did I have deposited at the bank Jeremy has been told that it is to go under a pseudonym and although he wasn't very happy about it after I suggested that his neighbours were itching to meet me I think its covered. I still haven't worked out what the final figure will be but I expect it to be better than I believed it would be last night!"

"Brilliant, well done John that sounds perfect. We couldn't have planned it better and we do have to do the trip as quickly as we can and not make it a holiday!" Mike said.

"You'll need to be here by ten." John looked at his watch, "which only gives you three quarters of an hour before the cars here to collect us!.. look you guys get back and get changed and I'll pick you up from the yard, it's only a small detour so it shouldn't affect our timetable." Mike and Seamus hurried out of the kitchen and jumped in Mike's car. By the time they had travelled back to the yard Seamus was looking pale.

"Why did we hire a plane… you should have driven… we'd have got there quicker. Jesus Christ Michael you've got to slow down or put wings on this thing!" Mike patted Seamus on the back.

"Well we don't have much time to get ready so I thought…"

"Next time I'm in that beast… please don't think just keep it in first gear! Or I'll be doing more than playing with a baby I'll be having one!" Both men cracked up at Seamus last comment.

John arrived and the three men set off for Bournemouth airport where John had hired the charter jet. It was only forty-five minutes away and so there was not a lot of time to discuss things in detail so the conversation centred on small talk apart from John saying that he had still not reached a final tally but could report that they had managed to get all the money 'on' and not one bet was less than 8-1. The flight was uneventful and they reached the bank in good time. Mike decided they should pick up some duty free whilst they were there, Andorra being one of the cheapest places to buy. The manager came as a surprise she was an attractive woman somewhere in her mid-forties she was very efficient having tea and coffee ready as they entered her office and all the paperwork ready to sign. She questioned all three men to reassure herself that she was not getting her bank involved in some international fraud or crime ring and on hearing that they were looking to invest funds from their horse racing, which tallied with her friends request from Spain pushed the papers forward to be signed. Within two hours the three happy musketeers were back at the airport waiting to take off for home. They landed at Bournemouth airport shortly before five in the afternoon. Mike did a double take as they passed out of customs and wandered towards the exit. The news stand displayed a picture of '*Becky's Army*' below the headline *Becky Stokes Hits Stardom*. Mike went into the shop and purchased the paper.

It was a rushed entrance into the car by all three and the moment they had settled into the back seat, Seamus and John started to badger Mike to read the article. The driver who had become their regular since John and Mike became friends spoke up. "Sorry to comment gents but I couldn't help overhearing and I'll tell you what. That little girl has hit the big time! She's better known than most of these so-called movie stars. She's the talk of the town. If what that article says is true by the time the weekend is over she'll be famous worldwide and you along with her Mike!"

John and Seamus started badgering Mike again to read the article out loud. "If you two comedians shut up for a minute I might be able to." The car became automatically silent.

"Are you sitting comfortably?"

"Just get on with it!" John said impatiently.

Mike couldn't resist it. "Then I shall begin!"

"Bollocks." In unison from John and Seamus.

At two-thirty on Tuesday a star was born! No astronomer to

discover this brighter than bright light but the race enthusiasts at Salisbury racecourse. Becky Stokes, a seven-year-old, astonished race goers when her friends and members of Mike Willett's yard cheer led her horse to victory. Not satisfied with winning the hearts of all that were privileged to view the spectacle she stepped up to receive the trophy, giving an impromptu speech on collection. I can tell you first hand there was not a dry eye in the place, and those whose hearts had not yet been won were followers from the moment the tiny creature opened her mouth. The eloquence from someone of such tender years was astounding, her enthusiasm unbounded, her gratitude humbling. Her annunciation perfect. What a fantastic model for the children of today.

It goes further, such is the publicity that this small child has received already ours and it would appear many other newspapers are flooded with letters from children of Becky's age group wanting to 'join the army'. In one small voice this child has hushed the screams of a racecourse and given racing an avenue it has so desperately strived for over the past few years. She has given racing a child's enthusiasm, not just one but from our post box alone, a nations. If I were younger I would be applying to the army myself! I can't wait to see Becky Stokes when she takes her seat on The Morning Line on Saturday morning and I look forward even more to her sitting opposite Michael Parkinson on Saturday night. The master of the interview will have his hands full I can tell you.

"Jesus Christ. The little girls a good 'un, Michael Parkinson an' all!" Seamus declared.

"What a fantastic article, bit flowery but bloody good all the same!" John joined in.

"I just hope it doesn't back fire on us!" Mike followed.

CHAPTER SIXTEEN

Seamus and Mary joined the table where John, Alice, Geoff, Kate, Peter and Mike were sitting, they apologised for being slightly late but their babysitter's car had broken down, which meant they had to collect her. Mike suggested that they leave their car in the car park and travel back with him to which they gratefully agreed. Becky was playing the role of babysitter to Michael junior with both Alice and Kate supervising, Mike overheard Alice say, "You should have another you're such a fantastic mum Kate."

"I would but Geoff doesn't want anymore." Kate replied regretfully. She was in her element excusing herself from the table to alternate her affection between her daughter and the tiny mite.

Mike didn't say too much during the meal, he listened to the others discussing Becky's new found fame, it was the only time Kate paid her full attention rather than watching the little ones. Mike felt a bit like a gooseberry, everybody was a couple apart from Peter and himself and Peter was obviously not only happy in his role as grandfather but also very proud. Mike looked around at these people, his friends who he was proud of and yet he had never felt as lonely in his life.

"Well Mike? What do you think? Kate reckons that Becky's too young to have all this attention but I say she's enough sense to get herself there in the first place she should take the praise and enjoy it. After all how often do you get a chance for fame such as this and at seven!" Geoff asked Mike across the table, his voice oozing the pride he felt for his daughter.

"It must be a dilemma for you. I see where Kate's coming from but then I can also see your point of view. Maybe if you keep control of the situation and by that I mean don't allow the media to sweep you to one side, sort of make sure that you're not put in the wings so to speak. From my own experience I know how the media can turn on you without notice, maybe you need to make sure they don't convince you that they are doing everything for you and not themselves. They'll only sail along with a story because they're making money. Always be there… I know you would but what I mean is if Becky's on the morning line for instance make sure that you are sitting next to her rather than as I've already said kept in the wings that way you stay in control and they know it. If things start to go off track just get up and take Becky with you. As for the actual press… you know as well as I do they're a bit harder to control, personally I'd sell the exclusive to one of the dailies, signed and sealed mind you, then at least you have recourse if they print anything you don't like and you always have someone who is contracted to print the right thing if one of the others start to print a load of nonsense." It was more than Mike had said all evening and everybody listened raptly to his emotive oratory. "She's a great kid Geoff I don't need to tell you that, this could be a fantastic start for her who knows. If it's done right who knows where it may take her in the future."

"I'm really not that interested." A small voice piped up from its ministrations of the tiny bundle now sound asleep in its pushchair. "I'm enjoying it but I don't want to be a film star. I want to be a trainer. I think that lots of people will know me now and when I get my licence they will all want to bring me their horses. I'm going to win the Derby just like Mike." The table was totally stunned even though they were used to the extraordinary conversational skills of Beck's this last comment was so well thought out and so grown up they were astounded.

"I really don't think either of you should worry!" Mike exclaimed. "I think the media just might have met their match!" laughter rang throughout the restaurant. It was well past midnight before the party dispersed and Kate's gentle kiss to Mike's cheek brought his first real smile of the evening and when the car dropped him off at home he went straight to bed dreaming of holding her in his arms.

Saturday morning came and it looked as though The Morning Line was set to have record viewers everybody who read a paper couldn't help but know who the guest was as every headline read Becky's army to be screened on The Morning Line for starters…. And the main course Parkinson!

Everyone from the yard sat in Mike's lounge waiting for the well-known theme tune to start and signal the beginning of the programme on Mikes 48-inch-wide screen television. The moment it began everyone went silent. Becky sat in a chair next to her mother. "Kate looks stunning, doesn't she?" Anita said. "She looks like she belongs there like some film star!" and they all agreed except for Mike who sat entranced as he looked at the stunning woman on the screen before him. Becky was grinning broadly at something off screen. The interview began. John Francome asked the first question. "Well what do you think of all the attention you're getting?" Mike noticed that not only John but the other three men had not yet taken their eyes off of Kate's tanned legs which stretched out from the cream summer dress decorated with butterflies.

"It's really good but it's more about the horses you know!" Her reply jolted everybody, so adult and unexpected, Becky continued without pause. "Mummy's very pretty isn't she" the camera wobbled as the cameraman burst into laughter. "Mike… he's my bestest friend in the whole world and the most famous and bestest trainer thinks so! He saw her bottom the other morning." Kate was desperately trying to attract Becky's attention. Becky didn't notice she was in full flow, everybody sat open mouthed as the little girl took over the complete programme in one foul swoop without even trying. "It was so funny, Mike's eyes nearly popped out of his head because I think he loves mummy, boys do that sort of thing you know! Anyway," John Francome was trying hard to remain in his chair he was doubled over with laughter. "Mike looked after me when mummy and daddy went out and, oohh! He told me this brilliant story I'll ask him if he'll tell you if you like, it's really scary though. Well he fell asleep after I had gone to bed and mummy, that's my mummy there." She said as if to reassure herself that Kate was still there, Kate was red faced and stammering still in an effort to gain control of Becky's tongue, Becky was oblivious. "Anyway mummy went so red because in the morning she forgot Mike was there and came down in just daddy's shirt and that's when Mike saw her bottom! Shall I call in my friends so that we can show you what we do at the races. We've got a new one we're practicing but you're not allowed to see that yet because it's for Rockets big race. Have you met Rocket? He's lovely he blows on my head and it tickles me." Becky jumped up and signalled to her friends to join her organising them efficiently in a line before taking centre stage herself. 'COME ON SUNRISE YOU'RE THE BEST WE KNOW YOU CAN BEAT THE REST' no one was quite expecting such small bodies to be so quick off the mark nor to have the capacity for such great levels of volume. The sound man tore the headphones from his ears in pain the cameraman lost control of the camera which panned unfortunately to give the nation a view of Kate's beautiful legs and an expanse of inner thigh. John Francome could contain himself no longer and fell from his chair Derek Thompson managed to salvage the programme to a degree shouting between gasps for breath "I think we'll take a break there." And the adverts rolled.

Kate was horrified, the monitor that showed the filming was holding an image that made Sharon Stone look ordinary, beautiful smooth tanned legs disappearing under a light summer frock with a hint of white underwear. Kate jumped up quickly.

"I'm doing really well aren't I mummy. Everybody including the crew was writhing around in hysterics holding their sides for fear they would split. Kate looked lovingly at her daughter and her friends. "You're doing just fine sweetheart, you're just being you!"

The Morning Line returned after the break with tear stained faces. "We'll be talking to our guest Becky Stokes and her friends again shortly…. That's if we can keep enough control in the studio…. If you've only just switched on you've just missed the greatest moment in Morning Line history… what a delightful girl!" John Francome managed before the Morning Line was off on location to discuss the days racing.

Mike was beside himself, Seamus and the others were ribbing him terribly. "So it's come to that has it?" Seamus directed at Mike.

"Come to what?" Mike asked, his face red after Becky's admission.

"Boy's and girls!" Seamus announced dramatically. "I would like to introduce you to our most famous trainer with a bottomless talent." Everybody cracked up leaving Mike with an even more red face.

By six o'clock Becky had hit the sports news and the commentator was urging the nation to watch 'this spectacular little girl' on the Parkinson Show. The nation waited with baited breath.

Becky sat listening to her mother as the make-up artist applied the finishing touches to her. Becky loved it, the pampering, being made to feel special, it took her about two seconds to realise that if she hinted at fancying something it appeared almost as quickly and she was revelling in the attention. Kate had made her have a snooze in the afternoon knowing that it was going to be a late night.

"Now please don't go mentioning things that aren't connected to the horses." Kate requested of her daughter hoping that she would stay away from embarrassing subjects, the young make-up artist overheard. "God, you must have wished there was a hole to swallow you up!" she said, "talk about embarrassing. Mind you I saw a picture of that Mike and he could look at mine any time he liked!" Kate smiled the embarrassment of Becky's statement to the nation having waned. "He is quite handsome I'll admit but you can't believe how embarrassing it was and I'm a happily married woman!" Kate added the last few words almost as an afterthought, she continued. "Mind you not half as embarrassing as having a certain person tell half the nation."

"Well married or not I'd saddle up for him!" The make up girl cheekily replied laughing. Kate laughed too though she felt her emotion rising with the urge to slap this young girl as unwanted jealousy coursed through her veins. The dressing room door opened and a young man's head popped into sight. "Five minutes!" and he was gone. Kate and Becky were shown to the green room ready to be called out on set, they were to be the third and final guests.

The theme tune played and Michael Parkinson sat in his famous chair smiling broadly. "Good evening on tonight's show we have three guests who have made their mark on our nation in one way or another. Please welcome my first guest, an example to the young people of this country Amir Khan. The audience clapped vigorously as Amir Khan came down the famous steps and the show began proper. Michael Parkinson as always was skilful in his technique and Amir Khan witty and modest in answering the interview showed him as a young man of great determination and dedication. It left the audience in no doubt that the United Kingdom had a future world champion. Michael introduced his second guest, one of his favourites. "My second guest has become a regular and I always look forward to talking with him, ladies and gentleman Mr.. Billy Connelly." The audience again clapped loudly as Billy Connelly came skipping down the steps causing the watchers to break into spontaneous laughter. As always Billy had the audience, Amir and Michael chuckling throughout the interview. Michael thanked him saying there would be more after the break when his final guest Miss Becky Stokes would join them. The adverts started.

The national grid dimmed as households everywhere rushed to the kitchen to make tea, viewing figures had never been so great.

Michael Parkinson swivelled in his chair. "My last but certainly not least guest is a young lady that in the last few days has become the talk of the nation, her antics at the racecourse brought a new meaning to shouting one home. Let's hope I retain my seat and don't lose it to this amazing young lady. Ladies and gentlemen Miss Becky Stokes." The audience went wild and for the first time in history gave a standing ovation to one of Michael's guests. Becky walked down the steps with an air of confidence that belied her years closely followed by her mother looking every inch a film star in a tight blue dress with lace sides. Becky walked straight up to Billy Connelly with a quizzical look on her face and he automatically bent to her level. She gently reached up and tugged his beard. "Ooh it is real, why is it such a funny colour?" Billy couldn't answer he along with everybody else was already chuckling uncontrollably. Without pause she wandered across to Amir Khan. "I bet it hurts a lot when you get hit! Is that why you wear those big mittens? Mummy makes me wear ones like that in the winter, you must get awfully hot!" She then turned to Michael Parkinson tears of laughter streaming down his face. "Mummy says you have lots of wrinkles because you laugh a lot! Are you crying to wash them away? I think it's very good to laugh you know, it makes my tummy feel really funny." And she took her place next to where her mother had sat. She never gave anyone a chance to recover before starting again.

"Would you like to see our cheer? I can get everybody else to come in if you like! Anita and Hannah have come too. They were at the races with me you know! Mummy gave me a real telling off this morning." You could see the signs of worry spread across Kate's face. "But Mike did see her bottom and he looked very happy!" The show continued in total, wonderful chaos and Becky's fame spread. Michael Parkinson finally gained enough control to ask Becky a question just before they went off air. Was she planning anything for Rockets big race. "Oh yes we have a really big surprise planned. I can't tell you what it is because it's a secret but it's going to be fantastic. Mummy's helping us aren't you mummy?" A red faced Kate nodded her agreement. "Mummy says it's going to be really gizzy, though she said we couldn't do one thing because it would be too dangerous and would upset the horses. Anyway I'm very tired now!" Becky climbed up onto her mum's lap, gave a gaping yawn and promptly fell asleep to the delight of the audience and the nation.

Mike rose the following morning to a persistent banging on his door, he looked at his watch it was six thirty. He pulled on a pair of jeans and hurried downstairs. It was Nick. "Nick! It's six thirty on a Sunday bloody morning, what the hells the matter." Nicks face looked pale and he was shaking. He appeared totally lost nervously shifting from one foot to the other.

"I don't know what to do, its Vi...?" Mike jumped past Nick running bare foot towards the other side of the yard to reach the cottage. He burst through the front door with Nick on his heels.

"Where is she." He shouted towards Nick, he pointed towards the kitchen. Vi was leaning heavily against the sink. Mike could see blood splashed everywhere in the vicinity. Vi had a towel against her stomach which had soaked up what seemed an impossible amount of blood. Mike rushed to her side. "Nick bring me a chair and call an ambulance!"

"Now don't you start fussing, I'm all right!" Vi said weakly and slumped to the floor dropping the towel as she did so. Nick came rushing back into the kitchen with an armchair from their lounge, and the two of them gently picked Vi up and manoeuvred her into it. Blood was pulsing from Vi's stomach region. "I tried to get 'er to sit down but she wouldn't." Nick said he was almost in tears. "Said she'd make a mess on the nice new furniture you bought us!"

"Nick go and find Seamus tell him to bring the pick up here as quick as he can, give me your mobile phone," Nick grabbed the phone from his pocket and passed it to Mike, he stood there looking completely dazed. "Nick!" Mike shouted. "Pull yourself together, come on, go and get Seamus. Mike was desperately trying to find the wound and had torn open the bottom of Vi's shirt. He wiped the blood away from the area as best he could, there was a small cut about half an inch across that was pouring blood, he held the towel firmly against the cut in an effort to stem the flow with one hand whilst dialling 999 with the other. He was put through to the ambulance service and explained he had a woman that was bleeding badly from a stomach wound and had collapsed. He was going to make towards the hospital in a metallic red pickup he would have the lights and hazards on. It would save time. Seamus appeared concern showing on his face and between the three of them they carried Vi to the pickup and Mike sped off down the road. Seamus took a traumatised Nick with him, fetched his own car, and raced after the pickup.

Mike had travelled about ten miles before he heard the sirens and stopped. With Mike flashing his lights, the ambulance screeched to a stop in front of him. A paramedic jumped from the passenger seat medical bag in hand and ran towards the pickup, the driver of the ambulance pulled away looking for somewhere to turn around. After examining the wound the paramedic from the ambulance which was now alongside Mikes pickup jumped out and Vi was stretchered into the ambulance with urgency, the paramedics went to work immediately to stem the blood flow and set up a saline drip. "Is she going to be okay!" Mike was now shaking. One of the paramedics looked up.

"She's lost a hellavu lot of blood we need to get her to the hospital. I'm afraid it's going to be touch and go, there may be more internal damage. Christ how the hell did this happen? This looks like a stab wound!"

Vi had not regained consciousness. The ambulance went

haring off lights flashing and sirens screaming. Mike stood by the pick up looking totally lost. It was another five minutes before Seamus and Nick appeared. Seamus offered for Mike to get in his car but Mike said he would take Nick to the hospital and Seamus should take the pickup back to the yard. Mike and Nick sped off in the direction the ambulance had taken.

On the journey to the emergency department the ambulance men had radioed in to warn of their arrival with a suspect stab wound. By the time Mike and Nick raced into the hospital the police were already there to greet them.

The morning papers heralded the arrival of a new chat show star. Becky and Kate's face were plastered all over the nationals. Becky held the nations hearts in her hand. Geoff was not in the best of tempers the phone had not stopped ringing all morning with requests from just about every men's magazine there was asking if Kate would pose for them. One well known international glamour magazine had offered half a million and a three-week break in Mustique or a location of Kate's choice, where they said the shoot would take place and 'they' the family would be placed in the best hotel all expenses paid. Geoff was complimented and was also happy for Becky who was loving every minute of the attention she received he just hadn't realised just how invasive his daughter's antics were going to become. He was a very private man, not one to boast of his wealth or be pretentious and he suddenly found his personal space invaded and he didn't like that one bit. Kate secretly found it all rather exciting, the thought of posing naked in front of loads of people and cameras was quite enthralling and the thought of half a million pounds just to take her clothes of was enticing to say the least. Geoff's anger became greater when Kate announce that if the magazine up their offer to 750,000 she would seriously consider it. Geoff forgot his daughter was the main star and blew his top. "You're prepared to pose naked so that every bloke with three quid in his pocket can ogle you! I don't fucking believe you! Where the hell are you coming from? What's your daughter going to think her mother spread legged across the middle of a magazine! There's no way it's going to happen! Do you hear me!" Kate heard Geoff only too well. She didn't answer but stormed tearfully from the room and the tirade that Geoff had aimed at her. The tears came because Geoff had slipped back into his, 'I'm the boss mode and you'll be the obedient wife and do as I say not as I do' and it made Kate angrier than she had been for a long, long time. "Why is daddy shouting at you mummy? I thought he said you weren't going to shout at each other anymore!" Kate as always stuck up for Geoff. "Oh it's nothing darling." She said quickly wiping her face so that her daughter did not see her tears. "Daddy's just having a bad morning that's all, you know what he's like in the morning!" and Becky nodded knowledgably. Unbeknown to any but herself Kate's resolve strengthened.

Mike saw there was a police presence at the foyer of the hospital but assumed they were there for some drunken fight that had ended up with one or more of the participants needing hospital treatment, he was stunned when the two officers walked towards Nick and himself and asked them to go off to a side room. Mike and Nick went and as soon as they had entered the room Mike asked the officers what was going on. "Before you say anything else sir, I must caution you both that anything you say……." Mike and Nick looked at each other stunned, Mike saw the look in Nick's eyes as he started to move forward and quickly grabbed his arm. "Steady Nick! Let's find out what this is about, is it okay if Nick goes to see how his wife is?" he asked the officers who looked rather confusedly at each other, the older officer spoke. "Well sir it's a little awkward at the moment, umm, she's with the doctors at the moment and I'm afraid I'm going to have to question you both first. I'm waiting for my superior to come and subject to your answers and what he has to say on the matter we may have to take you to the station for further investigations. They are sending a team from forensics over to your house at the moment… hopefully that should shed some more light on this situation." The officers were looking nervously at each other and then at Nick and

Mike, Nick was clutching the side of the chair he sat in his cheek muscles doing overtime, Mike's eyes looked like ice. Mike took a deep breath and tried to control his emotions.

"This man's wife has been brought here seriously injured.... And you have detained us without explanation. Now gentlemen I don't wish to cause a problem but Nick here is going to see his wife... and if you try to stop him... which I have to tell you would be a bad mistake... not because of Nick here, who I wouldn't want to try to stop anyway ...but because of me." And without further ado Mike turned to Nick. "Go and find out how Vi is, I'll deal with this." Nick rose and made for the door without argument, all he was concerned for was his wife. The policeman reluctantly went to move after him and Mike barred their way. "I must warn you sir that obstructing a police officer is an offence."

"So in my book is this shit!" Mike retorted his anger starting to get the better of him, "and if someone doesn't tell me what the fuck this is all about I'm off too, and trust me you won't stop me!" Surprisingly it was the younger policeman who tried to calm the situation.

"Could we just calm things down a bit sir? Let's sit down and I'll try to explain.... You don't remember me do you sir....? I'm one of the officers that investigated your horses kidnap." Mike started to relax a little, taking the chair that was proffered him. "Please understand sir, this is routine and I hate to say that both you and your friend are shall we say known to be a little quick tempered....! We have to investigate any report of a stabbing or the like and the ambulance service is required to report such injuries to us immediately." Mike didn't know whether to feel relieved or angry. "Perhaps you wouldn't mind telling us what happened?"

"Well Nick," Mike began, "came rushing over to my house in a hell of a state, worried to death and said he didn't know what to do, it was Vi, she's my housekeeper and I think a great deal of her, so I ran straight over to the cottage and she was slumped in a chair holding a towel to her stomach. I told Nick to go and get Seamus,"

"Seamus?"

"He's my assistant trainer, get the pickup whilst I phoned for an ambulance, Vi was saying not to make a fuss then she fainted and the three of us carried her to the pickup and Seamus and Nick followed in Seamus car."

"Let me get this clear, Nick came to your house so you didn't see what happened?"

It began to dawn on Mike the direction in which the officers were going. "Whoa! Hold on a minute you don't honestly believe that Nick would do anything to hurt Vi do you? Why the man dotes on her!"

"You have to see how it looks sir!" The young officer said. "We have a stab victim, a man with a known temper and at the moment no witness's. We're bound to have questions." Nick came bursting back through the door. "She's going to be okay!" he said tears running down his face.

"She's got to stay in for a few days but she's okay. I've told 'er about doing that so many times but will she listen."

"Doing what sir?" the younger policeman asked.

"Filletin' fish. I don't like fish wiv bones in an' she always goes an' takes 'em out. I says get the fishmonger to do it but she reckons they don't do it right so she does it on the side."

"I'm sorry sir you've lost me a little!"

Nick strode towards the policemen purposefully and both took a step backwards, he stopped at the table standing in the centre room. "She does this." He said holding a pretend fish in one hand and a knife in the other. "I keeps tellin' 'er she's gonna cut 'erslef but did she listen. Well she's 'urrying see, wants to make the boss 'ere a cake, you likes my Vi's cakes don't you Mike." Nick asked proudly, Mike smiled and nodded his assent. "She uses this real sharp pointy little knife an' she goes too fast an' sticks it right in 'erself. Gawd I was frit to death so I ran an' got Mike."

When the superintendent arrived, the story was explained and Vi visited on the ward to confirm the story Mike and Nick were given an apology and allowed to go on their way. Mike secretly deciding that he would get Vi some help, even though he knew she would object but if he told her that as housekeeper her duties were far too important to be washing and cleaning. Anyway he would tell her she was far too important in the kitchen and with her experience she would have her 'apprentice' doing precisely as she wanted in a very short space of time, he thought he might just get away with it.

CHAPTER SEVENTEEN

Kate walked into the office her stomach doing somersaults, her palms sticky. She almost turned and walked back through the door but was determined that she would at least listen to what was to be said. She was stunned to find three people in the office. "I'm sorry!" she exclaimed rather formally, "I thought this was to be a private meeting between us?"

A trim man of about thirty rose from behind his desk and offered Kate a gentile handshake. His voice soft and effeminate. "Mrs. Stokes or may I call you Kate….? Fine. Kate my magazine is prepared to pay a staggering amount of money for your exclusive so to speak and in doing so we have to protect our own interests as editor I have the final say, this…" He pointed towards the two women that were sitting in the room, "Is our art director… she has to be satisfied that you are aware of what we require of you and that you are photogenic, though I feel that the latter is proved by the recent photographs of you in the newspapers and seeing your if I may say beautiful face on the television." The art director nodded in agreement.

"And this is our legal eagle who will if we agree draw up the contract. I'll get you a coffee and we can then get down to business!" Kate settled herself with the coffee brought in by a secretary. "You say you would consider posing for our magazine if the price was right? I have to be honest we already realise that you are a woman of high intelligence so we are not going to insult you by saying that it wouldn't be a coup for us, it would. I and Sheena," he indicated his art director, "agree that our circulation would go through the roof but we would have to have exclusivity so let's get down to the nitty gritty, give me some idea of what you're looking for." Kate hesitated for a moment before speaking.

"What are your circulation figures at the moment?" she was told one and a half million worldwide. "What do you think they would reach if we say connected this to the races considering that that's where it all started." Kate could see the cogs whirring in Sheena's head and Alex after a short pause smiled and said he thought it would probably quadruple. "If I give you exclusivity as you say and the pictures are used once and once only I think you may even do better than that!" Kate held her breath for a moment stealing herself for her coup de gras. "I want one million pounds and you can do the shoot at one of the racecourses if they'll let you, if not a stable yard but where ever the shoot is it must be done privately with just whoever is normally present at a shoot. I'm not taking my clothes off in front of an audience. I would also expect the poses to remain tasteful." There was frantic whispering between the three, it was a huge sum of money more than had ever been paid before but the rewards for the magazine could well be enormous too. The three looked up and Alex spoke. "You're one heck of a business woman Kate, but I think you knew before you even walked through the door you've got yourself a deal. You know I think our circulation will go through the roof. Looking at you I'm even thinking of going straight... And I've been gay since the day I was born!" Kate laughed. It didn't take too long for the paper work to be completed and Alex assured Kate the money would be in her account by the end of the week. The shoot would take place the following Monday weather permitting. Kate left the office with a spring in her step, she felt completely at ease with herself, brimming with confidence and totally self-assured. With one stroke she had made herself financially independent for life and had she had done something for herself not for her husband, even if it was going to create a huge argument.

Mike stood at the top of the gallops watching the circling horses through his binoculars as they prepared to work. Rocket was on his toes this morning and Mike hoped they would see him get to work properly, it was only three weeks from the new race date and he was still concerned that the horse's fitness level was nowhere near what it should be for a race. Rocket jumped off smartly working alongside the other two horses with consummate ease, suddenly he bolted forward leaving the other two behind in a matter of two or three strides, as soon as he had a lead of around ten lengths he slowed to a trot and let them come past him. Head held high he trotted cockily past where Mike stood, Mike was nearly certain that Rocket was never going to able to cope with the race. He left the gallops dejected going back to the house alone and feeling empty. He had an appointment at Salisbury racecourse along with John and Alfred Mapperton, they were to view the work that had been carried out to cope with the anticipated crowds for Rockets race. He was looking forward to it prior to watching Rocket, several of the horses that were to compete against Rocket were stabled there and he heard they were seriously good, he wanted to see with his own eyes exactly what they were up against. They entered the racetrack to be greeted by Alfred Mapperton and the Clerk of the course. "Well done old chap, "Alfred enthused ignoring the normal greetings, "you've arrived just in time. The Italian chap got quite irate this morning saying he needed to work his horse on the course not take them to the gallops as we'd organise." He didn't wait for anyone else to speak.

"We thought we ought to try and keep all these visiting chaps happy so we've let them use the course this once. Good show on you, your timing is impeccable they're just about to go down, you'll get to see the opposition work!" Alfred was obviously very pleased with how things had worked out. Four horses wandered out on to the track their work riders ignoring each other totally, something alien Mike thought but then perhaps there was a language barrier. Mike admired the horses the Australian horse looked a picture, strong and on his toes, the two American horses look marvellous but the Italian horse looked like a million dollars. Mike's fears over Rocket deepened. By the time the horses had completed their work out Mike was verging on depression. He really didn't know why he was surprised they were some of the best horses in the world after all! Had he expected them to work like sellers? Perhaps deep in his heart he had hoped against hope they weren't quite as good as everyone thought. He spent the rest of the morning in virtual silence letting John do most of the talking. Salisbury racecourse had worked wonders opening up the end of the enclosure so that punters would be able to literally line the course. Even Mike from his depression thought it amazing that one horse, which is what it boiled down to in the end, should command such support. It would regardless be a day that would make history.

Mike pointed the Noble towards home staring intently out of the windscreen his progress steady rather than at the speed he normally drove. "Come on Mike, what's wrong? You're far too quiet!"

Mike looked pensively in John's direction. "I can't say I'm not a bit concerned John. Shit, those horses are far better than I thought they'd be, and that Italian horse looks like it's going to take some beating, I liked that better than the others! I know the Aussie and American horses are the favourites but if an outsider like the Italian horse can perform like that what the hell else are we going up against, and for sure those boys had orders not to show too much. Christ I'm seriously beginning to think I've made a dreadful error!"

John looked at Mike patiently. "Seamus told me about Rocket's work the other morning. I think we're going to kick their ass! We've done it before and our boy can do it again.

Apart from which if you think that Italian horse is the good one we can have a little side bet to help things along, he's sixty-six to one at the moment. We could go each way on him and when he's second to our boy we'll clean up!"

Mike looked horrified. "Oh fuck!" he thought, "The I Love Rocket fan club is back in full flow, what the hell am I going to do now!"

The week went by quickly for Kate, her stomach churning every time she thought of the impending shoot. She received a call from her bank manager, which she actually found quite amusing seeing as how she normally heard from nothing other than a machine. The name of Stokes through her husband's millions would have commanded respect but to her credit she never used it and had always banked in her maiden name of Preston. The manager offered her in to discuss the investment of her money but she gracefully declined, Geoff had often said to her "bloody bank managers think they're so clever! So why are they working for a salary and not making fortunes for themselves?" Kate telephoned Alex and asked what she should bring and was told to bring herself, they would supply the wardrobe. Kate found herself quite amused by this, as an afterthought this was a glamour shoot she did not see the prospect of a wardrobe being paramount.

Mike had agreed that she could have the use of his lower yard where the young stock and horses out of training were kept and regardless of how he pressed her she would not give any hint of why she wanted it. All she would say was that he would be doing her a huge favour and that no one must be allowed anywhere near the yard for the day. Mike gave her his word. She arrived and met the crew from the magazine who were sitting in a large American type white camper and a Range Rover waiting at the gate. Kate quickly produced the key Mike had given her and with shaking hand unlocked and hurried the van through the entrance. The lower yard was secluded from the main yard, quiet and bordered by high hedges that obscured any vision from the road. There was then a long drive to the actual stables which nestled in a natural hollow giving perfect privacy. The cameras were set up Kate was taken to the camper for make-up and to discuss the shoot with Alex and Sheena and another chap who was introduced as Buck, the make-up artist was already working on Kate's face dabbing make up here and there to make sure there was no reflection. Buck would be doing the photography, he smiled at Kate, "Darling when Alex said you could turn him straight I was seriously jealous but I see what he means… you're gorgeous." Kate began to feel her confidence rising, being treated like a superstar was more than a little enjoyable. The make-up artist looked up, "she has lovely skin Buck, I really don't need to do much more, I'll work on the body when you guys have finished talking." And she wandered off in search of coffee from the back of the Range Rover. "Okay darling here's what I thought we'd do, we'll start with you on a horse sort of pouting with just a hint of boob showing the we'll do a sequence of you with less and less on and we'll finish with you completely starkers in the stable or something like that. We'll take a shot of you sitting astride a saddle that sort of thing, lying seductively across bales of hay." He looked Kate up and down. "You are going to be fantastic! What say we use the horse your daughter owns!" Kate explained that there was no one that could hold the horse and that it was in another yard, neither had she permission from Mike to use any of the horses. "Then let's ring him and ask him. We might even get him involved in the shoot, now that would be something, he's the chap that's training that really famous horse, isn't he?" Kate nodded, nervously picking up the phone.

"Mike… it's Kate… look this is a bit embarrassing really, I'm down the lower yard…. Yes, I'm there now… no there isn't anyone around thank you… yes, I appreciate you're good for your word… Mike shut up and listen please, do you think you could spare an hour or two and come down… thanks I don't want to tell you on the phone…. All right see you in ten minutes." Kate put the phone down. Mike arrived on cue, looking totally bemused. "Whatever is going on?" he asked

Kate. "What are all the lights for?" There were half a dozen people working frantically under the control of Buck, tipping a light this way another that, running cables from the back of the enormous camper van. "Come into the camper and I'll explain." Kate looked ill at ease, they walked across to the camper and went inside, everybody was out 'on site'. "I'm doing a photographic shoot."

"Fantastic, well done you, whose it for?"

"*Fantasy International.*"

"What the... in the ...I mean... like without...?" Mike stuttered away and in a funny sort of way it amused Kate and relaxed her, he was like a little boy.

"Yes, Mike in the nude!" Mike couldn't speak he just stood gawping at Kate his mouth opening and closing like a goldfish. Kate continued. "Oh come on Mike it's not that shocking loads of women do it and I'm being paid fortunes but I need someone to supply and hold a horse for me, it has to be you! It'll be embarrassing enough as it is without having some complete stranger that close to me when I'm naked." Mike was still goldfishing. "You can't tell a soul about this mind because Geoff has forbidden me to do it, silly man, he doesn't own me and the money I'm getting makes me very rich in my own right. I can't have anyone else around me please say you'll do it for me!"

Mike regained some composure. "Do it! Of course I'll do it, in fact I'd pay to do it!" Kate laughed at this and leaned out the door to call Alex over. She explained that Mike was happy to help with the horses, Mike was nervous when Alex began eyeing him up and down and even more so when he called Buck over. Buck started to walk around Mike with a critical look on his face. "*Mmm* follow your thought! He would look rather dishy in the photos and it would add a certain something and if I might be so bold a certain realism to the set, make it a sort of 'look we've caught you out' theme! Do we have anything in the wardrobe to spice him up a bit." He tugged effeminately at Mike's shirt and Mike nearly jumped to the far side of the trailer. Buck leant close to Mike.

"Don't be so afraid sweetheart I won't bite well not hurtfully. Anyway, you'd be a bit too butch for my tastes." Kate was in hysterics Mike was blatantly petrified even though to Alex and herself it was patently obvious that Buck was winding Mike up.

"Hang on Kate no one said anything about me being in the photos!" Kate was really beginning to enjoy herself. She put a hand on Mike's arm.

"You're not going to back out on me now Mike Willett. Are you...? Why, I do believe you're afraid!"

Before Mike put his brain in gear he fell well and truly into the trap. "I am not!" He said emphatically denying the innuendo of fear.

"Good that's settled then." Kate smiled very pleased with her sub diffuse.

Alex was searching through the built-in wardrobes at the end of the camper. "I think this might just do, it should fit okay." He looked at Mike with expert eye.

"It's the tiger tee shirt." He held up a white tee shirt that looked as if it had been mauled by a tiger's claws. "Here try this on." He continued throwing the tee shirt towards Mike. Mike stood not knowing what to do, reluctant to try anything on in front of the present company.

"For God's sake Mike stop being pathetic, they're not going to ravish you! You're not exactly instilling confidence in me. You're only taking your shirt off to put on another, in a minute I'll be taking everything off." Mike removed his shirt and pulled on the tee shirt, it was a bit tight across his chest but it had the desired effect of 'spicing him up a bit'. "He's bigger than he looks!" Alex said with a half-smile and one eyebrow raised. "If we wet him down a little he'll look like he's running around after our lady Kate. What do you think? The trusty old stable lad and mistress theme?" Buck smiled positively and wandered back outside to help Sheena oversee the set and to ensure the lights and cameras were in the right place. "Right butch!" Alex directed at Mike "You go and get a nice quiet horse for our

Kate here to sit on and we'll get changed! Go on shoo…"

Mike wandered over to the stables and chose a handsome five-year-old black gelding that he knew would rather stand still all day than put one foot on the gallops, he was a great horse if you wanted to go on a quiet hack but hated racing. Mike was going to sell him as a hack so it made sense to use him, as he would never be recognised on the racetrack because he would never have to go there.

Alex laid out the clothes Kate was to wear for the shoot, an Argentinean style riding skirt, very high cut white briefs and a white cotton riding shirt. "Time to get dressed darling." Alex said and the nerves started to churn Kate's stomach once again. She stood half expecting Alex to leave but he stayed firmly planted on the built-in couch in front of her. "Sweetheart you are about to bare more than your soul if you can't get undressed in front of me with my inclinations what hope is there. I'm almost as much female as you are! Look think of the money and if you want how many dreary lives you are going to cheer up. Your pictures may just put some spark into those that thought they had gone out, you may even save a few marriages. Think of yourself as an aid worker. One of life's missionaries!" Kate nervously removed her clothes standing naked with her back before Alex, she turned to pick up the clothes that were laid out beside him. "Why are you so nervous darling? You are absolutely stunning with or without clothes, my God if I wasn't with Buck I think I'd change and come after you myself!" Kate's ego soared and so did her confidence and resolve. She pulled on the clothes and stepped from the trailer. "By the way darling, you know your trainer chap is head over heels for you don't you. He seems like a really nice guy, don't be too hard on him." They walked onto the set. Mike didn't take much wetting down, it was hot and the thought of standing so close to Kate with no clothes on not only made his hands shake but he was sweating so hard that the crew had to mop his face and re-apply make-up before the shoot could start. It all became quiet and very serious as Buck took up his camera. "Okay darling you jump up on the horse and we'll start, Butch you look up at her submissively as though you're in awe of her." Mike winced a bit at being called Butch but carried on as he was bid. "Okay sweetie undo the buttons of your blouse and arch your back so that we just get I hint of nipple... fabulous now throw your head back ... great... now let the shirt fall open... great... great." Buck stopped shooting for a moment and walked over to where Kate sat on the horse. "That's fantastic you're an absolute natural." Kate felt exhilarated, her shyness had evaporated completely. "Now I'd like you to slide off the horse bit my bit because I want to get lots of frames. Butch you are going to help her getting off but you'll have to also help her to stay in place until I get off enough shots, every time I say you'll have to let her down a little, you need to sort of hold her from the side so that I get her in full focus and I need you to try to pin her skirt to the horses side so that as she slides down more of her is exposed to the camera. Okay let's go." The camera started to whirr as Mike held Kate in his arms. At Buck's instruction, he let her slide a bit further down the horse until she was about level with the gelding's ribs when her skirt had ridden up to her waist her back was slightly arched naturally and the small white high cut cotton briefs accentuated the shape of her body. Mike couldn't help himself his eyes wandering from Kate's face to her beautifully shaped womanhood that seemed to stretch the fabric of the briefs. "Oh, that's great... brilliant hold her there.... Super throw the head back... brilliant... toss your hair... great. Okay butch you can let her go now." Mike reluctantly released his grip on Kate's slim waist after he gently let her to the ground. "Okay let's have you over here sweetheart." Buck pointed to a stack of hay bales that had been placed in the centre of the yard. He paused and turned to Mike as Kate reached the stack. "I don't suppose you'd have a saddle lying around here anywhere would you?" he asked Mike hopefully.

"I can get one out of the tack room, there only GP's mind." Buck looked lost.

"We normally use exercise saddles on racehorses but because

these are either babies just learning the job or horses out of training we use ordinary saddles on them because they don't do proper work." Buck looked even more lost.

"Do you mean a saddle like I'd use when I go to riding lessons?" Buck asked.

"Yes."

"That's perfect, just what I want, do you think I could borrow one?" Mike nodded and went to the tack room returning with a saddle under his arm.

"Excellent. Now darling do you think you could wedge it on top of those bales so that it stays in place?" Mike hesitated for a moment not realising that his name had been changed from Butch to 'darling'. Buck stood camera in one hand and hand on hip. Mike realised, nodded and moved over to the bales sitting the saddle on the top of the stack and wedging handfuls of hay beneath it to help stabilise it. Buck walked over and gave the saddle a prod and it stayed in situ. "Brill, thanks darling. Right let's get on." He turned to Kate. "Right sweetie, take the skirt and blouse off and pop up on the saddle. I'd like you to make out you're riding across the range, the wind in your hair, throw your head around so your hair flicks up pout lick your lips, just whatever comes into your pretty head to do." Kate still felt exhilarated her ego flying at all the praise she had so far received, she slipped the blouse from her shoulders and allowed the skirt to fall to the floor, Buck frantically catching the moment on film as she did so. She swung a leg gracefully over the saddle and just as Buck asked, she rode the imaginary horse. Mike was mesmerised he couldn't take his eyes off of her and Kate knew it enjoying every second. Buck stopped shooting to reload his camera. "You know poppet." He turned to Alex. "I think this is the best shoot I've ever done; the end result is going to be wonderful!" Kate was buzzing, she thought that if this was how drugs made you feel she had more understanding of why people used them. Her whole body felt alive both physically and mentally, she felt so incredibly sexy both to the on looking crew and in her own body, her whole being tingled with excitement. "Darling we need to get what we call the money shot. It's time to remove the last vestige of cloth." Buck said rather theatrically. There was no hesitation any more, Kate stood proud sliding her briefs down her long slim legs to reveal her perfectly formed naked body. Even Buck gasped and Kate revelled in it. "Wow! You are spectacular! And the clean-shaven look is stupendous! Mike." Mike noticed the Butch had gone but looking at Kate he didn't care all he wanted to do was to absorb her beauty once more. "Do you think we could have your horse again." Mike acknowledged dumbly.

Once Mike returned with the horse Buck asked him to put the saddle on him. Mike with shaking hand threw the saddle on the horse and pulled the girth up.

"Okay could you bring him over so that he's about five-feet away from the hay….? Brill….. right Kate could you get on the horse and put your feet in the stirrups so that I can get a few shots of you standing… excellent… put one hand over your eyes as though you're looking for someone… super." Kate stood her naked body arched as she held the reins in one hand with the other over her eyes scanning the horizon. This time there was no white cotton to hide her nakedness and her clean body proud and uninhibited gloried to the camera. "Okay sweetie sit back in the saddle and Mike can you climb up behind her and put your arms around her waist like she's found you….? Yes, that's it… lean back into him Kate…. Yes brill…push your hips forward… fantastic." Kate could feel herself becoming wet, Mike's strong arms encircling her waist the hardness that she felt pressing against her as she leaned back and the open-mouthed stares of the crew brought her near the point of orgasm. She was so incredibly turned on she found it hard to believe. The shoot ended with huge praise and thanks from all involved. The camper and Range Rover left everyone overjoyed at the success, so much so that no one except Mike had noticed that Kate had not bothered to dress. She had gathered her clothes from the camper thrown them in the back of her car and remained naked. She felt totally liberated, free and carried along by the shoot hardly noticed her lack of clothing herself. Mike walked up to where she stood.

"Not only are you incredibly beautiful but you ensnare every one you meet. You're a bloody wonderful person." Mike leaned forward and kissed the top of her head and she slid her arm around his neck. "And you my little stable boy!" she laughed, "if my lower back is any judge at all are as horny as hell and so am I." She pulled him towards her, sliding her tongue into his willing mouth, her hand reaching down to pull at his zipper, she expertly flicked the button of his jeans opening the front completely and slipped her hand inside to grab his hardness. Mike explored Kate's body, stroking her hard nipples and sliding his hand over her smooth stomach before pushing her legs apart. They made love on the hay bales, against the wall of the stable, in the tack room, giggling uncontrollably until both lay shaking exhausted in each other's arms.

It was Mike who spoke first. "You are so beautiful I could lay here with you forever, the world could rush by and I wouldn't even notice!"

Kate's elation sunk like a stone in deep water, Alex's words ringing in her ears. What had she done again! "Oh Mike!" She said looking directly into his eyes, "I think a lot of you, you're very sweet but you know that won't happen! I'm married and always will be. I don't know what's happening to me. Every time I'm near you I seem to lose all self-control, I really don't know why for some reason I've become sort of rebellious and wild in your company. I find myself longing to have sex with you, you just seem to have the knack of either finding me in the right situation or just turning me on by being close but I'm married to Geoff and I love him. I think the photo shoot has gone to my head a little. I'm sorry!" Mike moved his arm from around Kate and sat up. Kate could see the hurt in his eyes.

"So I'm just the stable lad after all!" he almost spat. "Come here boy I have a need and you shall be the lucky servant to fulfil me!" Mike's temper had begun to rise. "You're such a tosser!" Kate suddenly screamed jumping up.

"That is not what I meant and you know it...! Fuck you Mike Willett!"

"You do whenever you feel like it!" Mike shouted sarcastically. And Kate stormed off to her car quickly dressed, threw the gate keys back in Mike's direction and roared off in the car.

CHAPTER SEVENTEEN

Kate and Geoff had an enormous row. It started over nothing as it usually does. It was a simple enough question, probably spoken a little acidly but a simple question. Where had Kate been? Kate had retorted with venom saying when did Geoff ever tell her where he had been, she had a life as well. Geoff became suspicious, it was the first time Kate had refused to give him an explanation of her whereabouts. He pushed the issue. She became more venomous and ended up telling him with a certain smugness that she had just earned a million pounds for doing a photographic shoot with *Fantasy International* adding that unlike Geoff who only she spat ever criticised her she had received so many compliments on her body and face she was thinking of doing it again, even though she wasn't! Geoff went into a rage like Kate never saw before, she became frightened, which only made her more vociferous, Geoff became worse until unable to control his anger any further he purposefully and with malice walked into the lounge picked up the crystal horse that Kate had been left by her grandmother and was her most treasured possession, spitefully he threw the horse with such force into the fireplace it shattered into a thousand pieces. Becky ran into the room tears streaming down her face. "*STOP*

IT! STOP IT!" she cried, Geoff gave Kate a look of despise and stormed from the house. Kate fell onto the couch sobbing loudly. Becky ran to her and tried to console her. "What's happening mummy?" the worried face of Becky stared at Kate and Kate couldn't answer because she really did not know. Geoff did not return until late that evening, Kate was already in bed and Geoff slid in beside her without a word. Silence had gathered over the Stokes house and looked to be well settled.

Mike watched Rocket work on the gallops or rather misbehave but his mind was elsewhere. He was about to go with his horse to the most auspicious race there had ever been and all he could think of was Kate. It had been nearly two weeks since the photo shoot and he had not heard one word from her. When he telephoned it was answered by either the cleaner, who though he asked for Kate always put Becky on the line, or Becky herself. Mike was in inner turmoil. He had broken every principal he lived by, he was not putting his all into his horse's, he went through the motions then hid himself away in the house. Seamus and John were worried he was slipping away again but he left the bottle to its own devices and eventually they understood he needed time on his own to sort things out for himself.

The day of the race came and Mike for a moment forgot his woes. He marched round the yard making sure that the girls hadn't forgotten anything, which they never did but they were so used to Mike they carried on allowing him to interfere with their tasks. Rocket came out of his box with Seamus proudly holding his lead rein. He looked marvellous, every inch a racehorse skittering around and neighing at everything he saw. Mike still wasn't happy with his fitness level and even less about his recent work attitude. He walked over to meet Seamus and Rocket before he was loaded onto the lorry. "Hi old fella!" He said to Rocket, he felt so emotional at seeing his boy for some reason he had a catch in his throat. "You just do the best you can and don't you go hurting yourself. If you're stone wall last you'll do fine by me!" He finished gently stroking the sleek neck of Rocket. Rocket gently nuzzled Mike's neck. "Don't you be worrying about the old fella." Seamus piped. "I'll look after him. He'll be fine he's a grand lad!" Seamus winked. "And I still think the only thing them others will see is his heels." Mike wasn't convinced Seamus believed his own statement whole heartedly. Rocket turned his head back towards the barn and whickered and a shrill whinny replied from the direction of Storms box.

Even though the yard had set out at six to reach the race course they found themselves grid locked in traffic. Mike always edgy on race days was even more so today. "What the bloody hell is going on? What the hell is all this traffic doing on the road?"

"Going to the greatest race in history I expect!" Seamus laughed.

"Shit, at this rate it'll take us hours and I don't want the boy standing in the lorry for half a day before his biggest race yet!" Mike was becoming more agitated. Seamus remaining totally calm and logical reasoned that if they had the most important horse in history on board it might seem possible that they could get a little help. "I know we'll get there with plenty of time to spare anyway but if you're that worried why don't you ring the police and see if they can clear the way a bit?"

Mike smiled Seamus was very good at staying calm when things were going wrong then finding the simplest of solutions. Mike called the local police and within a short period of time they heard a siren. They were soon being escorted by the patrol car passing waving occupants of the jammed traffic who realised that it was The Rocket queue jumping. They reached the racecourse which was already bursting with people. Mike looked at the scene and was staggered. "Christ look at the people here already. How the hell is John going to get here on time with all the traffic? What's it going to be like by mid-day? I never dreamed we'd end up with crowds like this!"

Seamus laughed. "We've not all been mooning around for the past few weeks Michael my lad! John is coming in style...."

He's hired himself a helicopter for the day! So I don't think the traffic will pose any problem to him whatsoever!"

Rocket came off the lorry head held high screaming like only a stallion can.

"Steady old lad." Mike said with a grin at Rocket he turned to Seamus. "Well he knows where he is Seamus."

"I told you Michael he'll be just fine whatever he does I'll look after him!"

Rocket was still prancing around and Seamus was nearly dragged off his feet as a lad walked by leading another horse it was All Aglow on of the American horses, Rocket lunged at him aggressively. "You wanna keep that old hack under control mister, this here's the horse that's gonna win!"

"I don't believe he thinks so!" Seamus was highly amused as he patted Rocket even though his heart and nearly jumped out onto the tarmac! The lad moved on muttering curses and saying how his lad was going to "beat the crap outta that old donkey they called a racehorse."

Seamus installed Rocket into one of the racecourse stables leaving the girls to look after him, he had brought one of the lads along and was now glad he had.

"I think you'd better help Hannah lead up Bruce he might just be a bit of a handful today." Both looked worried, "Mike will be in the parade ring so if he does get a bit too much he'll jump in and sort him out." Seamus went off to the weighing room to give his gear to the valet.

The air of excitement was already building and it was still only ten-thirty, the race didn't start until two-thirty but already the place was crowded, queues formed in front of the bookies and Mike watched the betting exchange on the television in the owner's bar. Rocket was drifting big time going out to 5-1, All Aglow was favourite at 2-1, followed by Orange County Blues at 3's then came the Australian horse Boomerue at 4's the Italian horse that had impressed Mike was 7's and much to Mike surprise the wild card High Spec had come in from 100-1 to 16's. If Rocket did win they would be laughing, if he didn't then they may just scrape through as long as All Aglow or Orange County Blues didn't take first. Mike began to feel that familiar tingle in his stomach that proceeded the race and he walked back to the bar to await John's arrival. The clerk of the course was there and Mike went over to speak with him. "Hi, you've done a marvellous job though I think we may well struggle to get everyone in."

"Oh I think we'll be okay, there's still a lot of room on the enclosure side towards the start itself. I expected a huge crowd, though I suppose in truth I hadn't realised just how big it would be but we worked it out that we could at a push get just over a hundred thousand people in if we line the whole course and most people just want to say they were here on the day. It'll be one helluva story to tell the grandchildren. Anyway, we've large screens all the way along the course both sides so everyone should get a good view!"

"But what are the three fenced off areas just outside by the winning post?" the clerk chuckled.

"One for you and the Jockey club officials, one for visiting trainers and owners and the other for Becky's Army!"

"Oh fuck." Mike said as John arrived.

"You're not moaning I hope Mike." John said grinning from ear to ear obviously in fine spirit.

"No, I've just been told that Becky's Army has a reserved place by the winning post!"

"I know! Great, isn't it?" John said still grinning broadly. The clerk of the course excused himself and went off to ensure the machine was still running smoothly.

"You know! How do you know?"

John swallowed before answering.

"Now don't go getting all prickly but Kate phoned me, said you and her were not really on speaking terms at the moment, wouldn't say why but then what the heck it's between you two. If you want to behave like children and not speak who am I to say you shouldn't."

"What do you mean Kate phoned you?" Mike's voice held an

edge of belligerence. John put an arm on his shoulder. "I said don't get prickly it's not me is it, you and I are speaking." Mike apologised. "Anyway, she asked if I could let her have Alfred's number at the Jockey Club so I did, she told me you weren't speaking when I asked her why she hadn't called you. She said she wanted the number because Becky was organising something to do with the race. I think Becky wants it to be a surprise for you so don't go spoiling it, she thinks the world of you that little girl!"

Mike agreed but now he knew there was a possibility Kate would be there he searched every group that passed by the door hoping to catch a glimpse of her. It was Becky he saw with her army trailing faithfully behind her, they were obviously resolute in their leader's ability. "Mike!" She cried throwing her arms around his neck forcing him to pick her up. "Isn't it exciting! You just wait until you see our plan. It's amazing, it's going to be the gizziest thing ever in the whole world!" Kate walked in the bar and there was an awkward silence for several seconds.

"Hi Kate." Mike said as noncommittally as he could. Kate returned his greeting and Mike asked if she would like a drink. "Scotch and dry with ice please." Mike placed Becky back on the floor and went to the bar ordering drinks for the whole party. "All drinks are on the house for you and your party sir." The girl who was serving him said. Mike thanked her and returned with a tray full of drinks.

"Let's go see our spot." Becky said to her adoring army and they trooped off sandwich in one hand coke in the other. John excused himself and Mike and Kate were left alone. Kate stared at Mike with her big blue eyes. "Can't we be friends again?"

"Oh Kate, I don't know, I want to be of course I do but I just don't think it's enough. Being around you is great but it's also painful. I can probably cope with occasionally seeing you in the yard but I can't be alone with you. If that's good enough for you then fine but it has to be that for me. I've broken every principal I believe in and I'm at the stage where if I'm going to have a friendship like we had I would want more and I don't think it's fair for either of us to be in that position!"

"Okay." Was all Kate said taking a sip of her scotch, Mike noticed her eyes looked as though tears were building and he thought his heart would break right there.

Geoff and Peter duly arrived and although Pete was his normal self-Mike noticed that the atmosphere between Kate and Geoff was more than a little strained. He had no time for more thoughts on the matter as Kate announced she had to go and sort the kids out and he realised that it was time he went and made sure all was well with Rocket. Rocket was immaculate but the girls were looking worried.

"What's wrong?" Mike asked and the crash from inside the stable answered his question. "What the hell," Mike dived in the stable, Rocket was kicking the side wall. "Pack it up you old bugger, you're scaring the girls." Rocket aimed another kick at the side wall before standing still much as a child would try once more when being told to stop. "Stop I said you'll bloody well hurt yourself." And Mike went up to Rocket and inspected his back legs until he was satisfied there was no harm done. "You guys go and enjoy yourself until after the race I'll lead him up. He's a bit on his toes and he'll probably settle with me." Hannah and Bruce looked relieved Hannah turning as they went to leave. "I can lead him in after the race guv can't I!" Mike had to smile the love and dedication of most stable staff never ceased to amaze him. The rest of the horses were being led out and Mike tucked in behind them leaving a gap of twenty feet between him and the horse in front. Rocket lunged forward again nearly catching Mike unaware.

"What the hell's got into you!" He complained to the horse. "This is not like you at all, now come on and be good, show them you're still the best!" He whispered to the horse as they continued towards the parade ring. Rocket began to settle but still looked extremely bad tempered compared to his normal laid-back self. Mike could hear loud clapping and an occasional horse's name being shouted as each horse entered the parade ring. "Come on son it's our turn let's show them what a real racehorse looks like." Mike said to Rocket as they entered the parade ring. For a second the crowd hushed then a tumultuous roar came from the crowd it travelled down the race course right down to the starting stalls. 'Rocket, Rocket, Rocket!' It was several minutes before the roar stopped, even those that bet they're hard earned cash on the opposition had cheered. Rocket stood stock still looked around the crowd did a small rear and casually walked on with his tail in the air. "That's my boy!" Mike said proudly as the crowd applauded Rocket once more. Rocket behaved impeccably whilst being paraded and when Seamus was legged up he stood like a statue. "You know him Seamus so I'm not going to insult you by telling you what to do, just enjoy the moment whatever he does and bring him home safe."

"On my life, I will Michael." Seamus said reaching down to touch Mike's shoulder. "I love the old sod nearly as much as you do!"

"Good luck!" Seamus turned the horse and cantered him down to the starting stalls.

"Welcome to Salisbury racecourse ladies and gentlemen on this most auspicious of occasions. As you know we are privilege to have the greatest horses of the era here today to race against each other and all of them bar none to race against The Rocket." The crowd applauded. "We would like on behalf of British racing to welcome our friends from overseas and wish them well…The horses are being loaded, three to go, two, it just remains for The Rocket who seems to be more interested in grazing than racing at the moment." Mike felt deflated. "He's going in." Mike's heart leapt with excitement. "and they're off," the crowd let go a huge roar, "and its Gondola that takes the early lead then comes All Aglow. Orange County Blues, Boomerrue, High Spec, The Rocket and the rest of the field are left tailed off behind." Seamus sat on Rocket knowing there was no effort being made beneath him at all.

"Come on son I know you're not trying and you've a lot to prove here today." He shouted in the horse's ear. "Now come on let's show them what we're made of!" and he shook up the reins. The effect was instantaneous, Seamus had expected to have to work at Rocket but he didn't. Rocket pulled himself off the rail to the outside and literally flew past the others. Becky's army rose to their cheer jumping up and down in their Rocket costumes, sparklers in each hand waving furiously.

"And The Rocket has taken it up five out going at a blistering pace, he can't keep this up surely. I've never seen anything like it he leads by ten lengths, twelve, fifteen, twenty and still the gap widens." Rocket reached the winning post and stopped abruptly, just the wrong side, looking back behind him as the others raced towards where he stood. Seamus pleaded with him to go forward but he would not. "The Rocket has refused to continue over the line it looks like it's going to be High Spec... no The Rockets crossed the line it's the Rocket that gets it High Spec takes second, Gondola third followed by All Aglow, Boomerue, Orange County Blues......."

"Rocket you're a piss taker!" Seamus said hugging the horse's neck. "I Love yuh!"

The crowd gave a thunderous roar as Rocket casually walked back to where Mike stood with John slumped on the rail, both men looking totally drained. The voice in Mike's head rang clear. *"From Rocket with Love!"* and Rocket bowed. The crowd went crazy everyone wanting to touch this incredible horse. Mike had a spur of the moment idea, he grabbed Becky picking her up and handed her up to Seamus. The crowd were heard in Cornwall as Seamus with Becky sitting in full Rocket costume trotted to the winner's enclosure her sparklers still going and waving frantically in the air. Becky was the proudest person in the world as the crowd roared their approval and millions of people all over the world watched an historic image of a horse an Irishman and a little girl in full fancy dress trot into the winner's enclosure. Kate stood at the rail of the winner's enclosure tears of pride and joy streaming down her cheeks as she watched Becky's beaming face. She turned and threw her arms instinctively around Geoff's neck and kissed him lovingly just as Mike turned to look at her. He had hoped to gain something he didn't know what, a look of approval maybe even pride in what he had done or rather Rocket had done. He didn't know he just wanted, needed to see Kate smile at him, see in her face that there was something, instead he saw the kiss.

Mike really couldn't remember much more of the day his back was sore from being patted, his eyes hurt from flashing cameras and holding back the tears, his throat sore from calling Rocket home and from choking back the tears, but he was still carried along with the elation even though he thought his heart would break.

Mike wasn't sure why he cried as he turned the M15 into the drive, he didn't know if it was sorrow or happiness. He was buzzing over the race but it was very nearly grief that gripped him as he remembered Kate and Geoff taking Becky from the winner's enclosure, Becky looking back tearfully wishing to stay. He saw in his mind's eye the back of Kate, no glance over the shoulder, no parting smile just her back her arm tightly around Geoff's waist. His beautiful Kate he thought but then realised she wasn't, she was someone else's beautiful Kate and probably always would be. He opened the door to the kitchen went to the cupboard and poured himself a Jamesons, pulled out a chair and sat at the kitchen table. There was an enormous chocolate cake in the centre. He read the note that laid next to it. 'Thought you might find room for a slice seeing as how I've been away for a few days. See you in the morning love Vi. Silly lot of fuss over a tiny little cut'. Mike laughed despite his sorrow. "I think I might retire!" he said out loud as the phone rang constantly, he knew it would be John, Seamus and the guys trying to contact him to join them for the celebrations, he knew in his present frame of mind they would be better off without him. The voice in his head piped up. "I don't think so! It might be the easy life for me but you've got a Storm brewing and I think it might just be even cloudier than I've been!"

"Oh SHIT!" Mike sighed.

"See you in the morning!" the voice came back.

Mike closed his eyes drifting into that indeterminate state

that leaves you half asleep yet half-awake he dreamed of races to be won, of Kate, of Ann, of Storm, of Rocket, his friends, of Becky, he saw Kate naked and wanting as they joined together in a stable, he dreamed of Spain and of the time he first laid eyes upon her, his half sleep deepened with every mouthful of whisky. Slowly sleep overcame him and he drifted further into unconsciousness and in his sleep his heart cried for that it could not have. The voice returned. "Live with hope… and see what you've achieved. There is always something new around the corner.!" Laughter echoed in Mike's head, the glass slipped from his hand, falling with a thud onto the carpet and sleep over took him.

ABOUT THE AUTHOR

Chris Dyer has spent most of his life around horses. Described by one of his friends as "the man that doesn't fit in" he is never afraid to voice an opinion regardless of the consequences. Disparaging of bureaucracy and unpredictable – the probable cause of "not fitting in!" He has without credit worked on many horses from unknown ponies to well-known racehorses without bothering to attention seek. He has trained Arabian racehorses and pre-trained thoroughbreds. His knowledge and occasionally his opinions are evident as he weaves his tale around the books characters.

A man of extremes Chris is either irritatingly happy or manically depressed (though more often than not the former). To describe Chris is almost impossible - he is a bit like pulling a Christmas Cracker… you never quite know what you will find on the inside!

A close friend.

For more information about Chris and a list of his other books, visit www.chrisdyerauthor.com

The Rocket Series
Sting in the Tail: Book 1
From Rocket with Love: Book 2
Storm Brewing: Book 3

www.ingramcontent.com/pod-product-compliance
Lightning Source LLC
Chambersburg PA
CBHW070926180626
46817CB00003B/1205